Lucia on Holiday

Guy Fraser-Sampson

First published 2012 by Elliott and Thompson Limited
27 John Street, London WC1N 2BX
www.eandtbooks.com

Published in both print and electronic formats
978-1-907642-51-7 (printed edition)
978-1-907642-52-4 (epub edition)
978-1-907642-91-3 (mobi edition)
978-1-907642-99-9 (PDF edition)

9 8 7 6 5 4 3 2 1

A CIP catalogue record for this book is
available from the British Library.

Typeset by PDQ Media

This edition is not for sale in the United States of America.
Printed and bound by CPI Group (UK) Ltd, Croydon, CR0 4YY

Author's Note

Those readers with even a passing knowledge of history will notice that *Lucia on Holiday* makes use of certain real-life events, the timing of which may not appear to sit easily within whatever chronology can be discerned from Benson's own novels. By way of mitigation, it can however be safely submitted that Benson himself was obviously not much concerned with the time and space continuum of the physical world. Anyone who can change the spelling of people's names (a proud tradition occasionally also practised by the writer), allow characters to disappear without explanation, move an entire town at will from one county to another, and completely ignore any mention of the First World War is most unlikely to have been troubled by such trifles as international conflicts, the fall of thrones, and the gyrations of financial markets. Thus it is to be hoped that any readers who exhibit a tiresome attachment to reality may be prevailed upon to treat any such aberrations as occasions when Homer has nodded.

The Bugatti Royale, known more prosaically as the Type 41, was indeed intended by Ettore Bugatti to be owned only by royalty. However, in the event just seven were ever built, partly because the Great Depression affected even royalty, and partly perhaps because Bugatti was rather too choosy about his customers. As well as rejecting requests from numerous millionaires, it is said that he refused to supply one crowned head because he disapproved of His Majesty's table manners.

Of the seven, four are now on permanent exhibition in museums, one is in private ownership (thought to be that of a Swiss millionaire), and one is owned by the relatively prosaic marque of Volkswagen, who now also own the rights to the Bugatti name itself. The seventh went missing in mysterious circumstances which this narrative may perhaps seek to explain.

While the cars themselves proved an expensive flop (Bugatti had planned on selling at least twenty) the overall project became a great commercial success as it was discovered that the cars' great engines could be used to power railway locomotives, and nearly two hundred were bought for this purpose by the French railways, the locomotives remaining in service until the late 1950s. Since one of these was officially clocked at an *average* speed of 122 miles an hour *while pulling a train*, the effect of driving a car similarly powered, but with 1920s brakes and steering, and without a train to encumber it, is perhaps better imagined than experienced. Surely Major Flint cannot have been alone in finding it a challenging task.

Throughout the book there are passing references to certain other artistic works. Each is intended by way of what is now in America called an 'homage' (pronounced, naturally, in an affected French manner), in other words an affectionate and respectful nod, carrying comforting overtones of nostalgia and massive intellectual superiority. In the hope that the writer may be reckoned to be just as affected and superior as the next pretentious intellectual, astute readers may spot such nods to the likes of Frank Richards, Sapper, E.M. Forster, Clive James, Dorothy L. Sayers, and Daphne du Maurier. However, no prize is offered for correctly identifying these, other than the natural comfort of knowing that, compared with you, your family and friends are irredeemably ill-read.

Certain liberties have been taken with the plot and locations of Manzoni's classic *I promessi sposi*, which are in truth much more complex ('tarsome'?) than would have been convenient, but the truth is fundamentally as stated.

While on the subject of other works, habitués of the internet will hopefully have come across the Mapp and Lucia Glossary, tirelessly maintained by Deryck Solomon and an invaluable ready-reference tool, which the writer has plundered shamelessly.

Bellagio is a real place, and quite as delightful in the flesh as it is here described. The hotel is similarly painted from life, though disguised with a different name. The writer has stayed there, yes, and danced an Argentinian tango to its piano trio too.

Turkish cigarettes were once in common use, at least outside the United States, where the good old no-nonsense domestic Virginia tobacco always enjoyed a near-monopoly, but though polite society would indeed have had their cigarettes handmade to their own specifications, few would have been as exotic as those used by Francesco. Devotees of period fiction will know that it was considered good form to have both in one's cigarette case when offering it to a third party ('Fancy a gasper? Turkish on the right, Virginia on the left.'). However, by the time our story takes place (whenever that may be) Turkish cigarettes have been almost completely supplanted by Virginia, partly on grounds of cost, and have come to have a very louche image indeed, the word 'gasper' now being employed to mean specifically a Virginia cigarette as opposed to one of those nasty, effete, foreign jobbies, which are chiefly reserved for Armenian art dealers, Russian emigré ballet dancers, and the more culturally pretentious residents of Hampstead and Bloomsbury.

Those unversed in the history of horticulture may be mystified by Lucia's reference to John Transcendent. Come to that, so might horticultural experts. It is likely that she actually had in mind John Tradescant, who designed the gardens at Hatfield House.

Mapp's grasp of the French language is of course either legendary or infamous, depending on your viewpoint. Even having made allowances for her not knowing that '*cracher*' is 'to spit' rather than 'to crash', and that '*rognons*' are kidneys rather than onions, what are we to make of '*tout égout*'? It is likely that what the dear lady really meant was '*tout égal*, as in '*c'est tout égal à moi*' (it's all the same to me), whereas '*égout*' is of course a sewer. Her unfortunate substitution for '*carte blanche*' (full discretion) is explained in the text. There again, it is possible that Mapp is deliberately avoiding being heard to speak French well for fear of being accused of having had a grammar-school education.

For the financially curious, Lucia's description of fractional reserve banking is perfectly accurate (as indeed is her grasp of a control premium). Nor were she and Brabazon Lodge alone in assuming that a situation could never arise in which all the depositors of a bank would ask for their money back at the same time. Readers will be happy to know that fractional reserve banking is alive and well, having survived the Wall Street Crash and been practised subsequently by every bank in the world, including Lehman Brothers and Northern Rock.

Incidentally, Brabazon, apart from being the name of one of many ill-fated projects launched by the British aircraft industry in heroic defiance of commercial logic, was one of the various names, both real and assumed, used by the British writer James Hadley Chase, best known for *The Postman Always Rings Twice* and *No Orchids For Miss Blandish*.

Finally, there really is a vintage Bugatti at the bottom of Lake Como. It was dumped there by an irate Italian businessman as a protest when it was about to be confiscated and auctioned for unpaid taxes, thus proving the old proverb that you can do what you like to an Italian's wife, provided both of you exercise all proper discretion, but that if you wish your various body parts to remain properly connected to each other then you should keep your hands off his daughter, his mistress, and his car.

Chapter 1

Emmeline Pillson, known universally as 'Lucia' in honour of her late Italophile husband, Philip ('Pepino') Lucas, was staring at the financial pages of her newspaper so intently that she entirely failed to notice when her current husband entered the room and sat down opposite her at the breakfast table. It was only when he greeted her with a diffident 'Good morning, Lucia' that she looked up and acknowledged his presence with something of a start.

'Oh, good morning, Georgie,' she replied. 'I'm so sorry, my dear, I didn't hear you come in.'

She seemed in two minds whether to continue with her newspaper or lay it down. After a few seconds' wavering she chose the latter course – in consequence, she would doubtless have pointed out had anybody enquired, of her marital responsibility to engage her husband in conversation. Had anybody asked Georgie, he would have suggested that it may have had rather more to do with the smell of the fresh toast which Grosvenor had just placed before them. It was as well, therefore, that no third party was in fact present to raise any such issue, since Georgie's explanation would have caused Lucia to stare at him coldly and silently over her reading glasses before saying in a voice of stone, 'Whatever the case, Georgie, I *did* put it down.'

The sort of tone, in fact, which she had used on so many occasions in the old days back in Riseholme, to quell the occasional dissident element in her kingdom (not for nothing was she known as 'Queen Lucia') or to ensure the smooth running of the many Elizabethan pageants which only she could possibly organise, despite her well-worn protest of 'How you all work me so'. Naturally for such events there could be no other conceivable candidate to play the role of the great Elizabeth herself. Indeed there had been one celebrated occasion when she had scathingly told the local fishmonger, masquerading as a sixteenth-century royal adviser, '*Must* is not a word to be used to princes, little man,' with such majestic menace that a halberdier had dropped his weapon with a dreadful crash, and two turnspits had fallen clean off the stern of the *Golden Hind*. Georgie, though he was standing fully ten feet away, had felt a cold hand clutch at his vitals, and poor Daisy Quantock had let out an involuntary screech of terror which she had tried to camouflage by pointing at the luckless turnspits, by now splashing disconsolately in the village pond.

It was a tone of voice which had already seen her through one term of office as mayor of Tilling and, it was rumoured, would shortly secure her a second. It had been used to good effect on those Tillingites who had dared to doubt her claim to have entertained a Duchess to dinner, and on many occasions on recalcitrant workmen when their plans for a tea break had clashed with her own idea of a proper working schedule. It was one of many weapons in Lucia's considerable armoury, all designed and kept properly oiled and sharpened for one purpose only: to get her own way no matter how difficult the circumstances might seem, and no matter how insuperable the obstacles that might be placed in her way. Truly, Lucia was the irresistible force for which no immovable object seemed to exist.

Only once had the irresistible force met its match, during the celebrated Tilling mayoral lectures, which she had inaugurated. Mr Noel Coward had been sufficiently ill-bred as to refuse five separate invitations addressed to him in her own fair hand to come and lecture the intellectual cream of Tilling on the technique of the modern stage. 'Really!' Lucia had finally commented in exasperation. 'You would think the man would jump at an opportunity to become better known.'

However, the irresistible force had simply eddied and flowed around the immovable object, as irresistible forces are wont to do, and had substituted members of the Tilling Society as lecturers. Lucia herself had naturally spoken on Shakespeare, on which subject she was a self-proclaimed expert, culminating in a performance of Lady Macbeth's sleepwalking scene of a dramatic intensity that would surely have been instantly acclaimed by John Gielgud or Herbert Marshall, had either gentleman been able to accept her invitation to attend.

Major Benjamin Flint, now officially Mapp-Flint since his marriage to the redoubtable Elizabeth Mapp but known widely as Major Benjy, had equally naturally spoken on tiger-shooting, and in a finale no less gripping then Lucia's sleepwalking scene had demonstrated how he had once hit a tiger smartly across the nose with his riding crop before seizing his trusty Mauser to despatch the beast with a single shot. Actually firing the Mauser had perhaps been taking verisimilitude too far, but a collection was taken up for the broken window, and everyone agreed afterwards that in all the several dozen times they had heard the Major's tiger stories, never had they been rendered better.

Irene Coles had been enlisted to talk about modern painting, while Mr Bartlett the vicar (known as 'Padre') was asked to speak on the Power of Free Will and the Origins of Evil, but he got rather mixed up and talked about the Power of Evil instead. Diva Plaistow spoke on cake-making, Mr Wyse on social etiquette, and Georgie on the techniques of needlepoint. Only Elizabeth Mapp-Flint had not been called upon since, as Lucia innocently explained, she was unable to think of a single subject on which dear Elizabeth might possibly have anything of interest to say.

For the moment, the irresistible force was spreading marmalade on a piece of toast with a slightly distracted air.

'Do you know, Georgie,' she purred contentedly, 'moving my money into shares from those boring old bonds was the best decision I ever took.'

'Really?' asked Georgie, not because he was truly interested but rather because some sort of response was clearly expected of him. Georgie's mother had held very firm views about speculation, claiming it to be a short cut to the workhouse, and he had never really approved of Lucia's forays into South African goldfields and American motor manufacturers. His own money was held, as it had always been, in British government bonds.

'Georgie!' Lucia said more sharply, as though aware that he was not really paying attention. 'Do you have any idea how much profit I have made so far this year? I was just totting it up in my head when you came in.'

'I'm sure I haven't the slightest idea,' he replied vaguely, reaching for the teapot.

'Eight thousand pounds!' cried Lucia triumphantly.

Gratifyingly, this had the intended effect. Georgie's hand remained suspended in mid-air and his jaw dropped a good inch. After a few seconds his mouth started to open and close and he formed the words 'eight thousand pounds' soundlessly a few times as though he was working them around on his tongue to see if he enjoyed their taste. Lucia arched her eyebrows and waited for him to recover the power of speech.

'But that is a simply enormous amount of money,' he gasped at last. He remembered from the days of Lucia and Elizabeth Mapp (as she then was) being presumed lost at sea that it was exactly the amount that Major Flint had been told to expect as the value of Miss Mapp's entire estate. So in the space of a mere six months the gains on Lucia's share portfolio had been equivalent to Mapp's total worldly worth, grimly husbanded and, where possible, augmented over several generations.

'Yes, isn't it?' said Lucia delightedly. 'It's a gain of ten per cent, but as it's only over half a year then I suppose that really means twenty per cent. What do you think, Georgie? That must be right, mustn't it?'

Georgie's mind seemed to be elsewhere, however. He was performing some rapid mental arithmetic based on his recollection that at much the same time as Major Flint had been told to expect eight thousand pounds, he himself had been warned to expect ten times

4

that amount. He remembered the Major's involuntary ejaculation of 'Congratulations!' before he had realised that such sentiments may not be deemed in the best of taste.

'Hang on, do you mean to say that you have put *all* your money into shares?' he cried in horror. 'Oh really, Lucia, how could you? It's too bad of you. Very irresponsible, I must say. Tut, tut!'

'Oh, fie to your 'tut, tut', Georgie,' came the spirited response. 'Fie and pish and tush and ... whatever else you care to,' she finished, slightly lamely. 'Eight thousand pounds is eight thousand pounds.'

'Well, there's no arguing with that,' agreed Georgie, 'but suppose you were to lose eight thousand pounds instead – you could just as easily, you know.'

'Fiddlesticks!' snapped Lucia. 'Where is your sense of adventure, Georgie? Where is your *courage?*'

As she uttered the last word, Lucia's voice dropped an octave and gave off a dramatic vibrato. Georgie groaned inwardly as he saw a distinctly Elizabethan glint come into her eyes. He knew what was coming next: a quotation. He was not to be disappointed.

'Does Shakespeare not say ...' She paused for dramatic effect, squared her shoulders and drew a deep breath, as was only proper when quoting the immortal bard; it was perhaps the literary equivalent of her Beethoven face.

'Be strong and of a good courage; be not afraid. Neither be thou dismayed.'

Being quoted at by Lucia could be a disturbing experience, as the Riseholme fishmonger could well attest. She did so in the best dramatic tradition, albeit the dramatic tradition of a bygone age now happily departed. Her eyes flashed and her chest heaved, and she frequently crumpled slightly at the end as though to indicate the emotional effort which she had put into the phrase, leaving herself spiritually spent.

As she dropped her head to allow the unfathomably deep feelings which Shakespeare always aroused in her to drain away, she doubtless

5

felt that she had carried all before her, and that there would be no more carping from her hopelessly defeated consort. In this she was to be disappointed, as Georgie reached for the milk jug and said quietly, 'It's the Bible actually.'

'Oh, Georgie,' Lucia reproached him briskly, 'I think I can be trusted to know my Shakespeare. All those wonderful, wonderful hours in my Elizabethan garden in dear old Riseholme – how I miss it so.'

'And I know my Bible,' retorted Georgie, who was clearly not in a mood for surrender this early in the day. 'I think you'll find it's Joshua and I'm pretty sure it goes on 'for the Lord thy God is with thee', and it would hardly do that if it was Shakespeare now, would it?'

'Ah, but that exquisite Elizabethan prose,' Lucia said dreamily. 'What a natural mistake for me to make.'

'Jacobean, actually,' muttered Georgie, but Lucia chose not to hear that.

'And, of course, as Dante would have said …'

Lucia paused and gazed soulfully at the ceiling, but when she looked down again found that Georgie had fixed her with a stern stare. They both knew this was taking things a step too far.

'Don't for goodness sake start pretending to speak Italian again,' he said sharply. 'Remember what a mess you got into when Olga sat you next to *signor* Cortese at dinner and all you could do was to go on repeating the same two lines of Dante over and over again. Really, Lucia, I would have thought that your blood would run cold at the very thought.'

'Georgino,' Lucia said reprovingly and then pouted, a sure sign that she was about to lapse into the baby-talk which was her final resort when Georgie's defences remained unbreached.

'Is oo cwoss wiv ickle me?'

Major Benjamin Flint, now the husband of the said Elizabeth Mapp, had once involuntarily witnessed Lucia employing this mode of speech and had felt a strong impulse to be suddenly a long way away, and preferably in close proximity to a well-charged glass of something restorative. The hideous thought had flashed through his head that his own wife might one day choose to employ such gross tactics upon himself. This had however been closely followed by a strong feeling of sympathy for Pillson, who perhaps wasn't such a bad fellow after all. A trifle strange perhaps, with his wig and his embroidery and his effeminate ways, but when it came to matrimony it could not be overlooked that he was a fellow-sufferer.

Ickle me knew her man, however. Georgie was genuinely devoted to Lucia and was rarely able to resist this ultimate fatal appeal to his sentimental instincts. However, on this occasion he resolved to be firm.

'Yes, Lucia,' he said. 'If you must know, I'm very vexed with you. It's all very well this speculating of yours, and I own you've proved very good at it, just as you seem to be very good at everything you attempt, but please just stop and consider for a minute what could happen if anything went wrong.'

This sugar-coated flattery was the only way in which criticism could ever be countenanced (though not actually accepted – that would be going too far) by Lucia, and she paused for thought.

'Well, Georgie,' she replied, thankfully in her normal voice, 'if it really makes you unhappy then of course I will think about what you say, but I simply cannot see what you're so worried about.'

'Oh honestly, Lucia, surely you've got enough money already? Even after you've bought every piece of new equipment under the sun for the hospital, and a new roller for the cricket club, and a new cup for the golf club, and goodness knows what else, you know very well that you've got oodles of money. Now just think for a moment what would happen if you lost it. We couldn't afford to live here in Mallards on my money, you know. We'd have to sell up, and let Grosvenor and Cadman go, and move to a little cottage – and you wouldn't like that, would you?'

Lucia gave the matter a moment's reflection and realised that no, she would not like that one little bit.

'Isn't that just like you, Georgino,' she cooed, 'thinking of me all the time. Do not worry, *caro mio*. *Non dimenticare*.' She gave a declamatory ring to the Italian words.

'I don't think that's right, actually,' he said as he poured himself another cup of tea. '*Dimenticare* means "forget", I'm pretty sure.'

'Georgie,' said Lucia, ignoring his comment completely, 'I've had an idea.'

Lucia's ideas were not like those of other people – ordinary, normal, everyday people who walked the streets and did their shopping and came home to have tea in their carpet slippers. Lucia's ideas were grandiose affairs on a par with the building projects of a renaissance pope, or the conquest of a new province by a Roman emperor. The more brightly she smiled when unveiling the idea, the more magnificent and ambitious a conception it was likely to be, and she was smiling very brightly right now, as Georgie noticed to his alarm.

Lucia's ideas were rarely to his liking. They usually envisaged her being swept along in a chariot receiving the adulation of cheering crowds, but every triumph requires a supporting cast, and Georgie invariably featured prominently among these serried ranks of spear-carriers. When Lucia mounted her famous pageant in Riseholme, Georgie had to stand around dressed as Sir Francis Drake, waving his hat and shouting 'Hurrah' every so often while Lucia delivered page after page of Elizabethan oratory in between changing into three different outfits. When Lucia wanted to endow a new organ for the church, and play it at its introductory service, it was Georgie who had to sit beside her, play the pedals and then slip away discreetly into the background while she received the acclaim which she naturally felt to be her due. When Lucia decided to dig for Roman remains in the back garden, it was Georgie who actually had to spend hours down the hole giving himself blisters and backache while Lucia sat in state in the Garden Room reading her encyclopaedia, giving interviews to the press, and urging him on to greater efforts.

'Oh yes?' he said, warily.

'We shall take a holiday!' she enthused. 'A change of air, Georgie, a change of scene, why it will buck you up enormously. You were only saying yesterday how peaky you've been feeling lately.'

'Well, that's true, certainly,' mused Georgie, an enthusiastic hypochondriac who was cursed by robust good health. 'But, Lucia, surely you haven't forgotten that we *are* going on holiday in a few weeks' time? I've been looking forward to it.'

'Oh, that!' said Lucia dismissively.

'I don't call two weeks at the Grand in Brighton "that",' came Georgie's rejoinder. 'It's jolly expensive, as you well know, and worth every penny. I intend to pamper myself outrageously. I've ordered a new outfit specially – I do hope you like it.'

'No, *caro mio*,' cried Lucia, on fire with frustration that Georgie had not caught her drift. 'I mean a *real* holiday. The south of France, Salzburg, Vienna, wherever you like.'

'Italy?' breathed Georgie.

'Italy!' she repeated. 'Yes, of course, Georgie. That should have been at the top of my list.'

They both gazed at each other in rapt silence. Though they affected to speak Italian to each other, and Lucia gave somewhat laborious lessons on Dante to local ladies, they had actually been to Italy just once, on holiday a few years previously. In the case of Lucia's Dante lessons, this was not a practical drawback since she prepared them from an English translation which she kept tucked away in her bedroom. In any event, these academic labours occurred but rarely. In the first place it was difficult to gather together three or four ladies who had not already been forewarned by those who had attended previous such events. In the second, the class tended to dwindle away to nothing after the first lesson owing to sudden dental appointments, summer colds, domestic crises or even unexpected family bereavements. Thus Lucia's mental grasp of thirteenth-century Italian had never been seriously tested beyond the first eight lines or so of the *Inferno*. Her place as Tilling's foremost authority on The Supreme Poet was nonetheless unchallenged, though Mr Wyse had once so far forgotten himself as to raise his eyebrows when Lucia, asked why Dante's greatest work was called *The Divine Comedy*, had held forth at some length on the poet's use of humour.

Their love of Italy, and all things Italian, was quite genuine. Yet their 'Italy' was not the area which appears on maps of Europe stretching out into the Mediterranean like a big, bullying boot kicking poor little Sicily. Rather, theirs was an enchanted land of poets and artists and musicians which they could, and did, quite easily inhabit without leaving Tilling. Indeed, on the one occasion when they had actually visited Italy unwelcome reality had threatened to intrude on a number of occasions in the shape of primitive plumbing arrangements, chronic stomach upsets, food heavily laced with garlic, myriad beggars, and all sorts of disgraceful foreign behaviour. One day in Florence an Italian had even had the temerity to pinch Lucia's bottom on the Ponte Vecchio. This was naturally not an experience which she had shared with anyone else, but the memory of it haunted her still.

Though they may both have chosen to forget it, the trip had disclosed something else as well. While they shared a vision of Italy which was idealistic rather than grounded in solid, empirical observation, they had rather different views on how best to enjoy it. For Lucia, Italy meant getting up at first light, performing her calisthenics on the balcony, eating a frugal breakfast, and then heading off for the first museum of the day, notebook and pencil in hand. Georgie, in the neighbouring room, would be greatly disturbed by the sound of Lucia shouting '*uno*, *due*, *tre*' as she bounced up and down enthusiastically, and burrow under the bedclothes, dreading the knock on his door which would shortly summon him to join her on her first cultural mission of the day.

Georgie probably had a greater true feeling for art than his wife, and was certainly much better read, but he found the prospect of traipsing round interminable museums in the growing heat of the day for hours on end too much of a good thing. Before long his feet were hurting from the new shoes, of purest faun buckskin, which he had bought specially for the trip but which pinched his toes abominably, and he was several rooms ahead of his spouse, who was by now waving her lorgnette and talking in a loud voice to anyone who would listen about the patina, and Michelangelo's use of *chiaroscuro*. Italy for him conjured up visions of himself in an immaculately tailored summer suit sitting in a shady corner of an elegant terrace sipping a heavily watered gin and it, and occasionally standing up to raise his hat to any particularly interesting-looking people who might wander past. However, in the full flush of one of Lucia's ideas, such trifling practical matters were of little consequence.

Much as the Mapp-Flints' marriage had been saved, if truth be told, by their unexpected discovery of a box marked 'Monopoly' on the top of a wardrobe in their hotel bedroom, so the Pillsons' holiday had been dramatically improved by a prolonged attack of enteritis which claimed first Georgie and then Lucia in turn, confining one or both to their respective rooms for days on end. For Georgie, this had in fact been one of the highlights of the trip. Genuinely ill for once and visited daily by a doctor for a lengthy discussion of his symptoms, he had amassed a most satisfying collection of pills and potions on his bedroom table, and in the days of convalescence which followed would sit on the terrace and allow a nice young waiter to tuck a blanket around his legs, after which he would sit with a piece of embroidery in his lap, apologising to anyone who enquired that he was much too weak to rise to greet them.

'Well,' he said, 'where should we go?'

'Anywhere you like, Georgie,' replied Lucia, still entranced with having had the idea in the first place. 'You must choose everything and make all the arrangements. This shall be like a present from me to you. Like that time I sent you to stay in that gorgeous hotel in Folkestone with Cadman and Foljambe – do you remember?'

Georgie remembered all too well, and could not help thinking that this was not very good tactics on Lucia's part. He had not so much been going on holiday as scuttling away from Tilling with his tail between his legs after Lucia, once again, had got them both into a very

11

tiresome situation by being over-liberal with her supposed command of Italian. It had transpired that Mr Wyse's sister was an Italian countess, and he had let it be known that he was so looking forward to hearing her and Lucia prattle away fluently during the countess's forthcoming visit. So Georgie had been packed off to Folkestone, where he had spent a pleasant week wandering around in a blazer and yachting cap and watching the steamer come in and go out again, while Lucia had been attacked by a virulent strain of influenza and had confined herself to bed. It had been a clever scheme, spoiled only by Miss Mapp, as she then was, spying on Lucia from the top of the church tower and seeing her performing her exercises in rude health in the garden at Mallards. However, this was no time to be churlish, and he shook off the thought.

'Oh, how frightfully diffy!' he murmured, teetering on the brink of lapsing into baby-talk himself. 'I would so love to go to Venice, but then there's Rome, and Florence, and San Remo and all sorts of other places as well.'

'Why, Georgie, what a silly boy you are,' said Lucia at once, her eyes wide with astonishment that Georgie should not have grasped instantly the full grandeur of her plans. Yet the fact was not entirely unwelcome. This would surely teach him once and for all to show the proper level of enthusiasm for her occasional but regular flashes of genius. 'You can go anywhere and everywhere. Don't you see? That's my idea.'

'You don't mean …?' Georgie gasped.

'I most certainly do,' averred Lucia. 'Why, it's perfect, Georgie. You said yourself that I didn't really need the money, and as it's just come to me out of nowhere, so to speak, I shall cash in eight thousand pounds of shares and spend the lot on the holiday of a lifetime.'

Once again Georgie's mouth started opening and shutting. Rather like a goldfish, Lucia thought mischievously, and so she pressed on without waiting for a response.

'There, then, that's all settled. We shall leave at the beginning of

July, and you must choose exactly where you would like to go Georgie, and make all the arrangements of course. Perhaps you could go up to London and do some research in the library at the British Museum, and then go and see someone like Thomas Cook's? Stay the night if you like and go to a concert, or the opera or something.'

'The opera!' cried Georgie. 'Olga!'

Lucia frowned and gazed out of the window. This was hardly the response she had expected to her generous bombshell. Had Georgie possessed an ounce of sensitivity, appreciation or even common courtesy he would have spent at least the next ten minutes exclaiming at her uncommon altruism before seizing a shopping basket to venture forth and spread the tidings amongst Tilling's finest. Instead, his mind was already running in the direction of a meeting with that Bracely woman.

'But why don't you come too, Lucia?' asked Georgie, emerging (with a guilty start, doubtless, thought Lucia) from his little reverie. 'I'm sure Olga would be delighted to see you.'

'Too kind, Georgie,' replied Lucia in that wonderful distracted way she had when she wanted to express severe disappointment with her interlocutor, 'but of course I have far too much to attend to here.' She waved a hand vaguely in the direction of the piano, the desk and her embossed stationery while she waited for Georgie to press his case and overwhelm her understandable reluctance. Alas, she waited in vain.

'Oh well, that's settled then,' murmured Georgie contentedly as he went in search of the railway timetable.

By the time he had settled his travel arrangements and held what Lucia could only describe as a very loud, indeed raucous, telephone conversation with Olga, there was little time left for him to change into a much more splendid outfit and head off to the station at a discreet trot clutching a Gladstone bag hastily packed by Foljambe, and showing, if not a fine turn of speed, at least a fine flash of lavender spats.

By the time he had settled into his carriage and decided which of his magazines to read first, Lucia had swept grimly into action, despatching one telegram to her stockbroker, Mr Mammoncash, instructing him to liquidate eight thousand pounds' worth of shares and remit the same to her bankers, and a second to the Grand Hotel in Brighton informing them that they would not after all be experiencing the pleasure of her company as originally arranged.

By the time all this had transpired it was long past the time when Tilling society traditionally gathered in the cobbled streets of the old town and discussed the great issues of the day. Since Georgie had failed so completely in his duties to spread the news of their impending Grand Tour, Lucia had little choice but to send Cadman out with notes inviting both Diva Plaistow and Evie Bartlett to tea, during the course of which she was able to impart these momentous tidings, having first abjured them both to the strictest confidentiality.

As they left Mallards later that afternoon Lucia explained, with great delicacy, that she would be most unhappy if word of her Italian venture was to leak out, since she had no wish to embarrass or upset Elizabeth Mapp-Flint, who had been in the habit of going with her husband, Major Benjy, to stay with some obscure cousins in Worthing. However, on the last such occasion they had arrived only to find that the said cousins had quite inexplicably moved away leaving no forwarding address, and thus the Mapp-Flints now typically took no summer holiday at all. Each lady swore a solemn oath eternally to respect the secrecy of Lucia's holiday plans. The latter retired happily to her garden room for a small glass of medium sherry, content that the secret would be common knowledge in the living rooms of Tilling within the hour.

Chapter 2

The next morning found Georgie ensconced in the Palm Court at the Ritz Hotel with his great friend Olga Bracely. Since Olga was one of the great divas of the age, a gratifying number of heads had turned in their direction as they entered, and the pianist had spontaneously broken into '*La Vergine Degli Angeli*', since Olga had the previous night starred in *La Forza del Destino* at Covent Garden, with Georgie watching adoringly from a box and weeping buckets into his handkerchief.

They had both risen late in consequence. Georgie had just had time to effect a highly enjoyable promenade among the hatters, perfumers, shirt-makers and tailors of St James's before returning to the Ritz, where he was staying, dab himself with a newly purchased bottle of lavender water and take the lift downstairs to wait for Olga. He had been tempted to make a grand entrance down the very fine staircase, but the steps of the last two flights were of the finest marble, and he had learned to his cost that marble surfaces and leather-soled shoes (even those made to measure in St James's) could prove an unhappy combination.

'So there you are,' said Georgie as he sipped his gin and it, 'she's got this idea into her head that we should go off on a long holiday.'

'You don't sound very pleased, darling,' Olga replied, looking at him reproachfully.

'Yes, well, I was at first,' Georgie admitted, 'but then the more I thought about it, the more I went off the idea.'

'I would have thought you'd be positively thrilled at the prospect of all that lovely Italy. Just like Boswell on the Grand Tour – or is it Johnson? I never can remember.'

'Boswell,' Georgie confirmed automatically, his mind elsewhere. 'Yes, but that's it – don't you see? The Grand Tour. You know what Lucia's like. It'll be a different gallery or museum every day, with her holding forth on everything, and me getting a headache from the heat and her going on all the time. I won't even be able to relax in the evenings, because she'll make me test her from the guidebook on whatever we're going to see the next day, so she'll be ready to appear the great expert all over again. Oh, really. It's too bad.'

He pouted, looking very sorry for himself.

'Poor Georgie,' said Olga, reaching across and patting his hand.

'Poor Georgie indeed,' he echoed with feeling. 'Oh, if only I was going with you instead, Olga. Then everything would be so lovely.'

'Georgie!' she exclaimed, pretending to be deeply shocked. 'What sort of way is that for a happily married man to talk?'

'I suppose it is rather disloyal, particularly when she's proposing to spend so much money,' he replied lamely, 'but honestly, Olga, you know what she's like.'

'I do,' she admitted. 'I can just see her clutching her Vasari, and correcting the guide when he gets anything wrong, even if it's the name of a muscle in a sculpture.'

'She does!' he cried. 'She did it when we were in Rome! All I wanted to do was sit down and have a cool prosecco, and she spent twenty minutes lecturing someone about the Bernini fountains from under her parasol.'

'Hm, I see the difficulty,' Olga murmured sympathetically. Then she fell silent and gazed off into the distance, looking vacantly at the people wandering backwards and forwards past the palm court, her fingers drumming idly on the tablecloth. Georgie took another sip at his drink, and studied her.

'Olga,' he ventured, 'why, I do believe you've got an idea.'

'Georgie,' she replied with the beginnings of one of her special smiles, 'I do believe I have. Why don't you buy me lunch, and I'll tell you what it is. I'm starving!'

'You're always starving,' he chided her, at which she stuck her tongue out at him.

'But you are also very wonderful,' Georgie observed contentedly, as he looked up and beckoned the waiter in what he thought was a highly polished way, showing exactly the right amount of cuff.

'*Where*, Georgie dear?' Lucia enquired, laying down her lorgnette.

'Bellagio,' he repeated.

'Which is *where*, dear, exactly?' she asked distractedly, as if to emphasise that this exchange was keeping her from her morning correspondence. 'Do remind me.'

'It's near Milan, I think,' he said, remembering what Olga had told him to say. 'Milan has a wonderful *duomo* apparently, and you haven't seen it, you know. It's just a little railway journey away from there, but we can take Cadman, of course – and Foljambe, naturally.'

Lucia looked dubious.

'I hardly think, Georgie,' she intoned, 'that Milan is our sort of place. Certainly I've never heard Mr Wyse or the Contessa mention it. One must be very careful when visiting unknown locations on the Continent, you know. Why, it might be positively full of Italians.'

Georgie was taken aback.

'Well, it is in Italy, you know,' he said with some asperity. 'I understand most Italian towns have quite a high proportion of Italian inhabitants.'

Lucia looked at him severely.

'Don't be silly, Georgie,' she admonished him. 'I mean the *wrong sort* of Italians, naturally.'

'And just what is the wrong sort of Italian?'

'Oh, the northerners, you know,' she said, waving her hand grandly as if to consign most of the Renaissance city-states to the far corners of

17

historical reckoning, and with the memory of that humiliating incident on the Ponte Vecchio flooding back. 'All that Borgia blood – clearly most unsuitable.'

She sighed deeply.

'Well, there's no Borgia blood in Milan,' Georgie insisted. 'That was Florence. Milan had the Viscontis and the Sforzas.'

Lucia sighed deeply again and gave one of her little non-committal noises, which generally presaged her taking serious issue with her interlocutor.

'And anyway,' Georgie pressed on firmly, 'as for meeting the wrong sort of people, nothing could be further from the truth. Olga has been to Bellagio herself many times, and says it's one of the most stylish and exclusive resorts in Europe. Why, she met the Prince of Wales there the last time, I think.'

'That,' said Lucia with a distinct shudder, 'is hardly a recommendation.'

'Well, I've already made the arrangements,' he said recklessly. 'Anyway, I'm sure we can go somewhere else if you don't like it. We will have the Rolls, after all.'

'I see, Georgie,' Lucia said sharply. 'No thought of consulting me first, then?'

'But you *told* me to choose, and make the arrangements,' Georgie replied in exasperation, 'and that's exactly what I've done.'

'I see,' Lucia repeated distantly, looking away from him.

'Oh, but you will like it, Lucia, just you wait and see,' he said enthusiastically. 'Olga says it's ever so much fun. They have a lake, and beautiful gardens, and a wonderful restaurant.'

'I see,' she repeated, more distantly still, her head tilted slightly upwards and held motionless.

'And concerts outside in the evening,' he finished, triumphantly. 'There! You'll like that, won't you?'

'Mosquitoes, Georgie,' she breathed forlornly, gazing fixedly at the dado rail. 'Mosquitoes.'

*

'Any news?' Diva asked, rather breathlessly as usual, as Georgie and Lucia approached.

'Rather!' said Georgie. 'Guess where we have decided to take our holidays this summer.'

'Oh dear,' said Diva, looking rather flummoxed, since of course she already knew but had to pretend not to, 'no good at guessing things.'

'Riseholme, I'll be bound,' Elizabeth said as she joined the group, Major Benjy having been despatched to the golf links.

Elizabeth had previously been the proud owner of Mallards but had speculated less successfully than Lucia, and been forced, with much wailing and rending of garments, to accept Grebe in part-exchange for Mallards. Since Grebe stood on the marshes, well out of town, she was frequently now, to her chagrin, the last rather than the first to hear a piece of 'news'. This was one of those occasions.

'Pardon me,' she sang, 'but I couldn't help overhearing. So nice in the summer. Why, I remember my stay there with great affection.'

'Wrong,' came Georgie's instant rejoinder. 'Try again.'

'I really couldn't say then, I'm sure,' said Elizabeth, her smile growing wider despite a sour tone creeping in. 'Perhaps you're off to the North Pole or going to take tea with the King!'

She laughed shrilly while looking at the surrounding houses as if in search of further inspiration, and then was clearly struck by a most painful possibility.

'You haven't,' she asked, with a grimace which she attempted unsuccessfully to moderate, 'been invited to Capri with the Wyses by the Contessa?'

Elizabeth had been angling for an invitation herself for years without success, largely because the Contessa, Mr Wyse's sister, had an unfathomable aversion to spending any time in Mrs Mapp-Flint's company, usually referring to her simply as 'that woman', and with a scowl to boot, as she lit a new cheroot.

As if conjured up by the underlying venom of this demand, the Wyses' Rolls (or 'the Royce' as Susan referred to it) drew up smoothly alongside, the chauffeur walked round to open the door, and Susan alighted in a tidal wave of furs. Mr Wyse followed, less opulently but more colourfully clad in plum velvet plus fours.

'Dear Susan,' said Lucia, 'how opportune your arrival. Elizabeth was just conjecturing on our holiday destination, and Capri was mentioned, along with your dear Amelia.'

'And *are* you going to Capri, Lucia?' asked Susan.

'Why, that would be nice,' she continued, with an uncertain glance at her husband. 'It would be wonderful to see you there.'

'No,' Georgie burst out, unable to contain his news any longer. 'We're going to Bellagio.'

There was a bemused silence at this revelation, save only for Mr Wyse, who managed to look reflective, knowledgeable and approving in quick succession.

'Bellagio?' Mr Wyse mused, with a respectful bow in its general direction out across the salt flats. 'Indeed, I believe I have heard my sister speak of it.'

'It would not surprise me,' Lucia said airily. 'It is of course frequented by the very best sort of people. I positively *insisted* to Georgie that we should go there.'

Georgie gave a little 'oh' which got lost in the background as Lucia flowed majestically on.

'We will go by sea to Genoa, I think, and then take the Rolls on from there to Milan. Dear Milan, with its *duomo*! Why, I can hardly wait.'

She clapped her gloved hands lightly together to add emphasis to her impatience.

'Why Georgie, come to think of it, I'm sure Genoa must have a *duomo* too, *non* è *vero*?' she added.

'Indeed it must,' Elizabeth said acidly. 'Why, you'll be able to have a positive feast of *duomos*, Lucia dear. *Duomos* for breakfast, lunch and dinner, I shouldn't wonder.'

There was an embarrassed pause, as there often was after Elizabeth attempted to inject irony into a conversation, for hers was not of the lightest variety. Elizabeth, however, viewed reducing any conversation to silence as a significant achievement in itself, particularly if Lucia had been talking at the time, and allowed herself a brief smile. Then the knowledge of what she had to impart swelled within her already ample bosom, and the smile broadened.

'But how silly of me! I have news of my own.'

'No!' said Diva automatically, but somewhat half-heartedly.

'Yes!' countered Elizabeth equally automatically, but much more enthusiastically. 'We're entertaining a maharajah to lunch tomorrow. There! What do you think of that?'

This time the chorus of 'No!' was spontaneous and heartfelt.

'Would this be the maharajah whom dear Major Benjy saved from a tiger with a sword?' asked Lucia, recovering quickly.

'Oh, dear me.' She pressed her knuckles against her forehead with a puzzled expression. 'Or was it a rifle, or perhaps a revolver? I really should know, shouldn't I? After all, I've heard the story so many times.'

'His son, dear, I assume,' Elizabeth said curtly. 'I would imagine that Benjy's dear old maharajah would be pretty ancient by now, wouldn't you?'

'But no older than Major Benjy, surely?' Lucia enquired innocently, at which Elizabeth looked most disagreeable and clutched the handle of her shopping bag very tightly indeed.

'Well, we shall see, dear,' she said with some acerbity, 'and now I really must be off. So many things to be done for His Highness's visit, of course. *Au reservoir!*'

There was a dutiful chorus of '*Au reservoir*' in return, and a raising of hats from Georgie and Mr Wyse, as she rolled away with heavy dignity.

The remaining members of the group looked at each other without speaking.

'Hm!' said Diva meaningfully.

*

'Is there really a maharajah, do you think?' Georgie enquired that lunchtime, as he deftly lifted the flesh from his sea bream.

'Of course not,' Lucia replied scornfully. 'Why, she was just desperate to trump our Bellagio, and said the first thing to come into her head.'

'Yes, I expect you're right,' Georgie said. 'Jolly good bream this, Lucia.'

'One really feels very sorry for her,' Lucia sighed sympathetically. 'What a very sad woman. So given to jealousy and falsehoods.'

'A dangerous game to play though, don't you think? Like that time she pretended to be pregnant after they got married.'

'Ah yes,' said Lucia reflectively, 'dear Elizabeth's wind-egg. How well I remember it.'

'Yes, but that's exactly my point,' Georgie went on. 'After all, what happens when everyone discovers that this silly maharajah is just as much a figment of Elizabeth's imagination as her pregnancy was?'

'And why should they?' Lucia asked, as if the answer to the question was obvious.

Georgie took a pensive mouthful of his hock to think what he might have missed, but both he and the hock proved unequal to the task.

'What do you mean?' he asked lamely.

'Georgie, you can be so slow sometimes! Glebe is tucked away on its own, and there's no need for anyone to come through the town to get there if they're driving from London. So how will she ever be found out? She can just give us a detailed account of a fictitious lunch with some totally imaginary maharajah, and we'll all be none the wiser. She'd never have been able to pull a stunt like that if she'd still been living here, at Mallards.'

'I see,' said Georgie intently. 'Yes, you're right of course, Lucia.'

Lucia, who was used to being right of course, smiled indulgently.

'I say,' Georgie exclaimed, 'doesn't it make your blood boil? That the wretched woman should get away with it, I mean?'

Lucia smiled again, but this time more dangerously.

'Who said anything about her getting away with it, *caro mio?*' she said.

'Don't say you have a plan?' Georgie asked hopefully.

'I do indeed, Georgie. What could be more natural than for me to hold a tea party tomorrow afternoon and invite Elizabeth and Benjy to bring their guest with them?'

'Brilliant!' cried Georgie. 'And when she and the Major turn up alone, or make an excuse and don't come ...'

'Her maharajah will be exploded for another one of her wind-eggs,' Lucia finished for him.

'Brilliant!' Georgie said again, smiling broadly.

'Yes, I am rather, aren't I?' Lucia replied tolerantly as she rang for Grosvenor, 'And now some lamb chops, I fancy.'

Major Benjamin Flint, known – as has already been recounted – as Major Benjy, was just enjoying his second helping of toast and marmalade when the doorbell rang, though his 'enjoyment' was perhaps not as complete as it might normally have been since for the last twenty-four hours there had been a great deal of housework going on, and the house smelt strongly of bleach and beeswax, which seemed to make him want to sneeze continually.

He looked across his newspaper at his wife, pulling his watch out of his pocket.

'Who on earth can that be at this time in the morning?' he enquired.

'Doubtless we shall find out when Withers opens the door,' Elizabeth retorted icily.

'Ah,' he said, rejoining the racing results, though in a very half-hearted manner since he had for some time been denied further credit by his bookmaker.

'A note from Mrs Pillson, if you please, mum,' Withers reported, offering it on a silver tray. 'Cadman just brought it and is to wait for an answer, if convenient.'

'Ah-hah,' said Elizabeth meaningfully as she tore it open, and then 'Ah-hah' again even more meaningfully as she scanned it.

'What is it?' asked Major Benjy, digging his knife into the marmalade.

'Invitation to tea from Lucia, if you please,' she replied, dropping it casually on the table. 'And do use the *spoon*, Benjy, that's what it's for.'

'Well, that's good, isn't it?' he asked, putting his knife down guiltily. 'She does damn good teas.'

Elizabeth smiled widely and spoke to Withers.

'Please ask Cadman to tell Mrs Pillson we will be delighted to attend, and please to forgive the lack of a note given the earliness of the hour.'

Withers bobbed, said 'Very good, mum' and was gone.

The Major had noticed the smile, and it made him duly nervous. 'What's up, old girl?'

'Benjy, will you never understand the *depths* that woman will go to?'

The word 'depths' came out as an indignant cry of barely suppressed rage, and Major Benjy, deciding to treat the question as rhetorical, wisely said nothing. His wife breathed deeply a few times to control her emotions, and then elucidated.

'She doesn't believe in the maharajah, that's what's up. Her invitation includes him. We're to take him with us, because her high and mightiness thinks we won't be able to. She thinks I've made the whole thing up.'

She crumpled the note suddenly in her hand and threw it towards the fireplace with an exclamation of disgust that also doubled as a howl of rage.

'The hypocrisy of the woman! She tells such outrageous lies herself, and then accuses other people of doing the same. It does make my blood boil so! When will other people see her for what she really is: a fraud, a liar and a cheat?'

She positively spat out the last word, and then took a large swig of tepid tea in an effort to compose herself.

'How I wish now that we had invited someone else for lunch,' she said fiercely.

'But we couldn't do that Liz, old girl,' her husband pointed out, attempting to inject a note of reason into the proceedings, 'he specifically asked to speak to us privately.'

'Oh, why don't you go and play golf instead of sitting around the house all morning?' she replied tetchily. Reason, it appeared, was not a welcome caller at Grebe that day.

He glanced out of the window, noticing that it looked very much like rain. He did not much relish the prospect of getting wet through while waiting for the little tram to the golf links. Clearly the old girl would have to be mollified. He fixed his wife with a winning smile, which he had always believed closely resembled that of Ronald Colman.

'But look here, old thing, we *can* produce the article, can't we? We will just persuade HRH to pop in on some friends with us and then we'll turn up at Mallards with the maharajah in tow, what? Then who will look silly? Her, not you.'

Elizabeth stopped twisting her napkin angrily and reflected.

'Yes,' she said, a ferocious smile beginning to appear.

'Damn silly,' he proffered, picking up his newspaper again.

'Silly,' she repeated, as if trying the word out for size.

'Damn silly indeed, if you ask me,' he ended, dismissively.

She gazed at him with something close to affection.

'I don't suppose there's any more toast is there?' he asked hopefully, peering round the edge of the newspaper.

Chapter 3

Had Irene Coles, often alluded to as Quaint Irene, Tilling's only professional resident artist (though just about every self-respecting Tillingite was an enthusiastic amateur), been at work in one of her favourite positions overlooking the marshes later that morning, she would have observed a large, green Bentley sweep up the Royal Military Road, pause uncertainly before reaching the town, and then turn towards the distant marshes, heading, as it happened, for Grebe. However, as it had come on to rain half an hour or so previously, she had very sensibly curtailed her activities and gone back to her cottage, Taormina, to work instead on a distinctly shocking painting which would surely never find its way past the hanging committee of Tilling's annual art exhibition, particularly as Elizabeth Mapp-Flint was one of its three members. In any event, by reason of the same persistent rain which had driven Irene back to her indoor turpentine and linseed oil, the car had its hood up, and side windows attached, so that for even the most determined observer, Mapp herself perhaps, the identity of its occupant would have been a matter of pure conjecture. Not that this would have prevented Mapp from asserting with perfect certainty, as she once had in similar circumstances, that she had clearly identified a member of the royal family.

When the Bentley growled to a damp halt outside Grebe, it did indeed disgorge a member of the royal family, but one with its seat many miles distant from either Windsor or Buckingham Palace. The first any onlooker would have seen of His Royal Highness

Hurree Jamset Ram Singh, Maharajah of Bhanipur, was a pair of dazzling spats, which emerged doubtfully from the interior of the car and unfortunately stepped straight into the deep puddle which lay in one of the many potholes in the driveway, Mapp regarding any maintenance work to the exterior of the property as a shameful extravagance. With a sad shake of his head, the royal personage opened an umbrella, and picking his way gingerly through the more elevated, and hence drier, parts of the drive, made his way to the front door and rang the bell.

Withers said 'Oo-er' when she opened the door, tried to curtsey and bow at the same time, and asked the maharajah to come inside, though in her nervousness managed to gabble so badly as to be completely incomprehensible. 'Strange indeed,' he thought, as he politely removed his hat and wiped his feet on the doormat, 'that such rustic dialects should have survived intact. Why, I can't understand a word the woman is saying. Pure East Sussex, I presume.'

Unsure of what protocol demanded on such an occasion, the lady of the house then emerged from the living room to greet her royal guest in the hallway, somewhat discomfited by the knowledge that this could be seen as either terribly polite or terribly rude, and that she really had no idea which.

'Your Royal Highness,' she trilled, curtseying deeply. The curtsey, though thrilling and respectful, proved to be something of a mistake as getting up again turned out to be rather more challenging than going down. As she floundered embarrassingly somewhere around thigh level (the maharajah's she noticed, were clad in a rather elegant Prince of Wales check), the recently applied surfeit of beeswax polish on the floorboards undermined her. Her feet slipped in opposite directions, and she subsided sideways, coming to rest inelegantly against the hall table, upsetting a painstakingly prepared flower arrangement, most of which landed on her hair in what Quaint Irene would doubtless have recognised as a distinctly pre-Raphaelite manner.

Such was the *tableau vivant* which presented itself to Major Flint, late of His Majesty's Indian Army, as he followed his wife into the hallway.

'Now then, Liz old girl,' he said in jocular vein, 'bit early to have been at the sherry, what?'

He had to admit, as he stroked his moustache, that he had risen perfectly to the occasion, and found exactly the right words to inject a note of subtle humour into the situation. Strangely, the old girl did not seem to agree. In fact, her eyes flashed in a way that could make a chap feel rather uneasy. Obviously upset about the flowers, he thought. After all, they had cost one and six.

Fortunately, in a magnificent display of *noblesse oblige*, the maharajah struck just the right note to defuse the situation.

'Dear lady,' he said, simultaneously helping Elizabeth to her feet and slipping the flowers adroitly back into the vase, 'no formality, I beg of you. I am here strictly *incognito*.'

'I must insist, madam,' he continued, as he guided her into the living room with a hand still beneath her elbow to guard against any further beeswax-related incidents, 'that you sit down and compose yourself.'

Without quite realising how she had got there, Elizabeth found herself installed in her mother's Bergère chair, the legs of which creaked rather alarmingly in response.

'Now, my dear Major Flint,' the maharajah continued, turning towards him with outstretched hand. 'I have not seen you for many years, of course, but I recognised you at once. Why, you hardly seem a day older, my dear sir. How do you do it? Riding to hounds, perchance?'

'Sadly, no, Your Highness,' replied the Major, shaking hands in the bluff, manly fashion of a man who can be trusted to deal with Indian princes on a regular basis. 'We don't keep horses. Haven't ridden since I came back from India, actually.'

'Oh dear, that is a shame indeed,' deplored His Highness. 'Why, I remember my father telling me that you had a fine reputation as a horseman back home.'

'Pretty fair, sir, pretty fair,' Major Flint acknowledged modestly as he moved with military briskness to the Tantalus. 'Now, how about a chota peg?'

A chota peg, it turned out, would really be most welcome. As the two men gathered over the Major's steadily darkening sepia images of gymkhanas, durbars, jodhpurs, chukkas and verandas, Elizabeth wriggled herself free from between the rather constricting arms of her mother's Bergère and went to oversee the final preparations for luncheon (or should one say tiffin?). She cursed herself for not having asked Benjy in advance.

Naturally, both Major and Mrs Mapp-Flint were agog to know just what this royal visit might presage. Given the maharajah's exquisite breeding, they were not to be put out of their misery until both the fish and meat dishes had been consumed and pronounced quite excellent by His Highness. Finally, once Withers had served the raspberry fool, he looked up and smiled uncertainly.

'And now, my dear friends – if I may take the liberty of calling you so, of course?'

Elizabeth quickly indicated that, for the first and last time in her life, she was more than happy for any necessary liberty to be taken.

'How gracious of you,' His Highness murmured. 'Well, you know, dash it all, I do feel rather awkward about this, but I have come to ask you both a favour.'

Major Benjy fingered his tie nervously. Surely the chap wasn't about to touch him for his petrol money back to London? He remembered dimly having heard somewhere that the King never carried cash with him; perhaps maharajahs had the same curious custom? A sidelong glance at his wife confirmed the ominous precursor to an attack of indignation; clearly she was consumed by the same thoughts.

'What it is,' the maharajah continued, 'is my son, Ramesh. You have never met him, of course, Major. Come to think of it, he must be about the same age now that I was when you left Bhanipur.'

'Ah,' said the Major, still wondering how many miles a gallon you could get out of a Blower Bentley (not many, he reckoned).

'You see, the young fellow comes down from the summer half at Eton in a couple of weeks, and I'm really not sure what to do with him. His mother is back in India, and I have to travel abroad ...'

He tailed off, as if expecting some response from the other side of the table. Elizabeth intervened before Major Benjy could say 'Ah' again.

'But, Your Highness, can't you take him with you?'

'No, indeed, dear lady,' the maharajah wailed unhappily, 'that would hardly be' – he shot a half-smile at Major Benjy – 'convenient. I have to go and see a dear friend in Rome.'

'But your son would enjoy Rome, surely?' she persisted. 'The Forum, the Colosseum and so forth?'

Major Benjy had caught the maharajah's drift.

'Expect you'll be discussing business, though, sir? All a bit boring for the young chap. Confidential too, I dare say. Much better for you to be there on your own, I would have thought.'

His Highness finished his raspberry fool and looked gratefully at Major Benjy.

'That's it exactly, dear Major. It's really Ramesh that I'm thinking of, don't you know.'

'Tell you what,' proffered the Major, as he opened the newly stocked cigar box, 'why don't you park the sprog with us for a bit? Elizabeth would love to have a child about the place, wouldn't you, Liz?'

This last question was addressed to his wife's departing back as she went to pull the bell cord. The back in question was broad enough that the maharajah felt, rather than observed, her spontaneous shudder of horror.

'Sorry about that, sir,' Benjy hissed across the table in a stage whisper, oblivious to his wife's paedophobia. 'The old girl can be a bit slow on the uptake at times.'

'But, my dear Major,' the maharajah remonstrated, as Elizabeth returned to the table. 'I couldn't possibly ask you to take a completely

30

unknown young man into your home. No' – he held up his hand to ward off the forthcoming assurance that nothing would give them greater pleasure – 'my idea is rather different.'

He paused, and was glad to note that Mapp and the Major were now both puzzled and expectant.

'What I was thinking,' he said slowly, looking at each of them in turn, 'is that it must shortly be time for you to depart on your usual summer holiday, overseas I dare say, and that perhaps you might take Ramesh with you until it was convenient for me to come and pick him up.'

This time Elizabeth was quite grateful when Benjy said 'Ah', but the brief respite was not sufficient for her to frame whatever it was she wanted to say, so Benjy was forced to say 'Ah' again, but this time with a desperate glance at his wife. Fortunately, however, the maharajah's exquisite breeding once again imposed itself on the situation.

'Ah, my dear Major and Mrs Flint,' he said, smiling happily, 'I see that I have not expressed myself felicitously at all. Since you would be doing me such an enormous favour by having Ramesh with you, I would of course insist that your holiday be taken entirely at my expense.'

'Good God,' said the Major, quite forgetting himself.

'But of course,' the maharajah insisted. 'And if perhaps you have not yet decided where to go, I would be happy to offer you my advice, such as it may be ...'

Again he looked at them a little uncertainly. Again Elizabeth intervened before her husband could say 'Ah'.

'We had *almost* decided, Your Highness,' she replied brightly. 'We were thinking of going to Bellagio. Such a nice place, I always think.'

'A perfect choice.' The maharajah rubbed his hands in satisfaction. 'I can get there from Rome very easily once my, ah, business is concluded.'

'Now,' he said briskly, 'to details. I will instruct my bankers, Hoare's you know, to give you drawing rights on one of my accounts. Please make all your arrangements and just ask them for whatever you need. Here is my card. You will see I have a cable address where you can reach me at any time within a day or so should you encounter any problems.'

He snapped his card case shut, and returned it to his pocket as he rose to his feet.

'And now, I must be going. Thank you, dear Mrs Flint, for such a splendid lunch.'

For once Elizabeth Mapp-Flint, her mind still full of pleasurable prospects of inflicting misery on others, was not equal to remaining mistress of her situation. Before she had properly come to her senses, the door had closed behind their royal visitor and he was on his way to his car.

'Benjy!' she wailed in anguish, 'Don't let him go!'

So saying, she opened the front door again, pushed him outside and closed it behind him.

The maharajah, seeing him coming after him, paused politely and waited.

'Ah!' said Benjy.

'Did I forget something, Major?'

'Ah,' he said again. Then, realising that while this was fine as a stop-gap, it did not really serve very well to advance a conversation, 'Thought I'd come out to see you off, sir.'

'Jolly decent of you,' beamed the maharajah, getting into his Bentley.

'Wonderful bus, this,' said the Major desperately, patting the bonnet strap.

'Yes, isn't she just?' replied the maharajah, pulling out the choke and reaching for the electric starter. Then suddenly he stopped.

'I say! You've given me an idea, old boy. Can you drive?'

'But, Benjy,' Elizabeth moaned, 'now we will have to arrive at Mallards without the maharajah and everyone will think we've made him up.'

'Let anyone suggest,' the Major replied, his moustache bristling, 'that my wife is not telling the truth, and they will have to reckon with my riding crop.'

32

'No, Benjy-boy, no, *pas de tout*,' his wife screeched, though the thought of him thrashing Lucia on the front steps of Mallards while Tilling society looked on helplessly was an attractive one, not to mention strangely exciting. 'Don't you see, the more we protest, the less anyone will believe us. Oh, it's so unfair!'

'Perhaps someone saw the old boy's car?' Benjy suggested hopefully.

'Most unlikely,' Elizabeth snorted dismissively. 'He had no need to go through the town.'

They sat silently while Withers removed the last of the lunch things.

'Well,' said Elizabeth in the end, 'wait until Lady Bountiful hears about us going to Bellagio. *That* should prove we're telling the truth. Everybody knows we'd never be able to afford it for ourselves.'

'And of course,' she continued with a smile, 'it will quite spoil dear Lulu's summer. She's told everyone where they're going now. They can't change their plans without making it clear that it's because of us, and then we'll have won, won't we?'

'I suppose so, old girl,' the Major muttered uncertainly, 'though it seems a shame to spoil the surprise, what?'

'The surprise?'

'Yes, I was assuming you weren't going to say anything about it, and let Lucia just pitch up on holiday to find us staying at the same hotel, but obviously I got it wrong.'

'Benjy!' she gasped, clasping her hands together in what she felt sure was girlish glee. 'But of course – that's brilliant!'

'Eh?' he enquired.

'That's exactly how it shall be.'

Elizabeth got up from her chair and positively skipped across the room to the Tantalus, emitting a distinct creaking of whalebone as she did so. She poured a generous measure of whisky and came back to hand it to her husband, the light of adulation shining in her eyes.

'Clever boy,' she said, patting him on the cheek.

'Ah!' he responded, seizing gratefully upon this most unusual gift.

'Now,' she said, in a more traditional commanding fashion. 'Listen very carefully, and I'll tell you exactly what we'll do.'

Lucia's tea party had presented Tilling with a social dilemma. If royalty was expected, should one dress formally? What if royalty, as one understood it, was travelling *incognito*? Might not formal dress be a solecism in such circumstances? Back in Riseholme Lucia would have been able to offer assistance by writing Hitum, Titum or Scrub on the invitation, but she had not continued that practice in Tilling. Here it was generally assumed that dinner meant formal dress, though Georgie did occasionally wear a rather daring monkey jacket in the summer, while tea was usually 'come as you are', though naturally the ladies did not interpret this concession as casually as did the gentlemen.

When faced with any social dilemma, Tilling turned naturally to Mr Wyse who, having wrinkled his nose at the particularly delicate nature of the problem, said something about tweed. He had in fact merely been indicating that a tweed country suit for gentlemen might be appropriate, since this would respect the royal guest's desire for anonymity more closely than a lounge suit, but, as with all Mr Wyse's pronouncements, Tilling decided to follow them to the letter. Susan Wyse and Evie Bartlett wore sensible tweed skirts, while Diva, having discovered that the only tweed garment in her wardrobe was a winter coat, duly wore it over a summer dress, and refused to remove it. So it was that when Elizabeth Mapp-Flint arrived at Mallards she was met by an expectant group mostly resembling a fly-fishing convention.

'Oh,' said Lucia, who stood out from her grey-green tweed surroundings in a peacock blue summer dress, 'on your own, Elizabeth darling? How disappointing! We were all so looking forward to meeting this wonderful maharajah of yours.'

'Yes indeed, dear,' Elizabeth said calmly, sitting down. 'He had to go straight back to London. Such a bore.'

Everyone said 'Ah-hah' to themselves and waited expectantly for her to continue, but she showed no signs of wishing to do so.

'Come on, Elizabeth,' Diva implored, impatiently. 'Tell us all about it.'

'Nothing much to tell, dear,' Elizabeth replied, still in a very matter-of-fact way. 'Quite an ordinary little man – a bit of a disappointment really. We only saw him for old time's sake. His father and Benjy-boy were so close out in India, you know.'

'And where *is* Benjy-boy?' demanded Quaint Irene, who was as consumed with curiosity as everybody else, but determined not to show it.

'Taken the maharajah for a round of golf perhaps?' Georgie enquired innocently.

'In this weather, Mr Georgie? Hardly!' Elizabeth reached for a slice of fruit cake with an indulgent smile. 'No, if you must know I've sent the dear boy off to Thomas Cook's office in Brighton to make the arrangements for our holiday. It is that time of year, you know.'

There was a collective flutter of excitement around the room. Far from being discomfited at having been found out in her silly lie about the maharajah, Mapp was counter-attacking boldly.

'Hardly necessary I would have thought, Elizabeth dear,' commented Lucia, fixing her with a quizzical smile. 'Two second-class railway tickets to Worthing would suffice, surely?'

The company settled back contentedly. For what fun was a tea party without a steady exchange of gratuitous personal insults?

'Or a platform ticket, perhaps,' Lucia murmured very softly as she raised her cup.

This time the spontaneous 'Oh' from the audience was almost audible, and everyone lifted their cups in unison. This was a low blow. It was well known that Major Flint had been caught by a ticket inspector passing off an old platform ticket from Eastbourne as a second-class single from Hastings.

Elizabeth went rather red in the face but tried hard to adopt a look of Christian forbearance. Since such a quality was deeply alien to her nature, her attempt was not entirely successful, inducing in Mr

Wyse a sudden recollection of a deeply unpleasant childhood incident involving his sister Amelia and a set of fire tongs.

'Oh, Lucia dearest, how you make fun of us all,' she replied with a broad, though rather crooked, smile. 'Not Worthing, naturally. We should hardly need Thomas Cook's help for that.'

She sipped her tea impassively.

'Hey!' said Diva suddenly. 'Have you got a summer let for Grebe?'

Quaint Irene suddenly looked very interested as well. For years Tilling had enjoyed a unique seasonal local economy. Mapp had let Mallards for the summer, and rented Wasters from Diva. Diva had rented Taormina from Irene, and Irene had made living arrangements out in the dunes somewhere which did not bear too close examination by polite society, and were darkly rumoured to involve a hut, fishermen, Susan Wyse's daughter Isobel, and nude sunbathing.

Since Lucia had been châtelaine of Mallards, this welcome boost to various summer incomes had been sadly curtailed. Mapp had tried to reintroduce the custom, but the occasional potential tenant introduced by Messrs Woolgar and Pipstow had quailed at the substantial walk into town, and the whispers of 'flooding' and shaking of heads in the Trader's Arms whenever Grebe was mentioned.

'No dear, not necessary this year,' Elizabeth replied curtly.

Everyone looked significantly at everyone else, and then instantly regretted it and tried to pretend that they hadn't. For all were thinking the same. If Elizabeth, who never tired of telling all and sundry how depleted her finances were, was not even planning on receiving some summer rental income, how on earth could she be contemplating a holiday that was sufficiently extravagant to require recourse to Thomas Cook?

'Well now, Mistress Mapp-Flint,' the Padre intervened in the faultless Scottish brogue of a man who had lived most of his life in Birmingham, 'will ye no put us oot of oor misery?'

'Yes, do, Elizabeth,' Susan Wyse enjoined her, settling her sables more comfortably around herself. 'Just where is it you are going?'

'Do you know,' Elizabeth said with an insouciant air, 'I can't tell you. It's *un petit surprise.*'

Both Georgie and Mr Wyse, who knew that '*surprise*' was feminine, winced, though the exquisitely mannered Mr Wyse did so inwardly, the only outward sign being a momentarily pained expression that passed fleetingly across his face.

'Not from your friends, surely, Elizabeth?' Lucia pressed firmly.

'From me, dear one, from me,' Elizabeth riposted gaily with a laugh. 'I've left it to dear Benjy-boy to choose.'

'Do you mean, dear,' Lucia asked, her voice slipping an octave to mark the gravity of her enquiry, 'that you have given Major Benjy *complete* discretion?'

'Indeed,' Elizabeth replied brightly. 'Why, I've told the Major that I'm *en carte fille* with whatever he decides.'

Everyone except Mr Wyse tried not to look puzzled. Mr Wyse tried not to look shocked. He wondered whether to venture upon a gentle correction, but decided against it. There was no way of explaining to Elizabeth Mapp-Flint that she had just described herself as a registered prostitute that would not offend against at least one social nicety.

'Why, then, we shall just have to await the gallant Benjy's return,' Irene said, voicing all of their frustrations, and wondering whether she might ask Lucia for a cocktail; after all, it was gone four o'clock.

'Quite so,' Mr Wyse agreed, smiling benignly, with a brief seated bow in the general direction of Brighton.

When Major Flint returned from Brighton it was with a slightly flushed expression, partly no doubt from the excitement of his impending holiday, but partly also perhaps as a result of having imbibed a certain amount of Southern Railways whisky. He took a taxi from Tilling station, unusual extravagance though it was, and shortly afterwards strode confidently into Grebe.

'There you are, old girl, mission accomplished,' he said, nonchalantly throwing a thick package on to the sofa beside her.

With a little squeal of excitement, Elizabeth emptied it into her lap; though there were many papers, the dimensions of her lap proved equal to the task. Railway tickets, ferry tickets, hotel booking telegrams, vaccination advice, foreign exchange forms and timetables became hopelessly intermingled. With a determined expression she began to arrange them in order.

Shortly she looked puzzled and hunted through the pile, and then rummaged in her lap as though the fabric of her dress might somehow mysteriously have swallowed some missing document.

'Something wrong, Liz-girl?' enquired her husband, who had taken the opportunity afforded by this distraction to pour himself a chota peg and conceal it behind a table lamp.

'Yes, Benjy, there is. Oh, I knew I should have gone myself,' she cried in exasperation. 'I suppose you've been boozing the afternoon away in some vile pub rather than doing what you were supposed to.'

The Major tried to look as offended at this accusation as a man who had spent the afternoon boozing in a vile pub could rightfully be.

'Perhaps,' he replied stiffly, 'you might care to specify the nature of this omission.'

In retrospect he might have been better to select a silent stare of reproach as a suitable response, since the words 'specify' and 'omission' seemed unaccountably to cause him some difficulty. Fortunately his wife was too irritated to notice.

'We only have tickets as far as Paris, you stupid man!' she spat. 'How are you proposing we get to Italy – walk?'

'No madam,' he said grandly, sitting down and crossing his legs with a flourish. 'You shall be driven – and in style. A Bugatti, no less!'

'A Bugatti?' Elizabeth's eyes bulged open in surprise and then took on what Quaint Irene called 'Mapp's nasty, mean, pinched look', and what was in all honesty a rather unattractive squint.

'Where are you getting a Bugatti from?' she asked suspiciously. 'Surely they're frightfully expensive, aren't they?'

'Would be, normally,' Major Benjy replied airily, 'but not in this case. His Highness has asked if I'd pick it up in Paris at the same time as we meet the sprog, and drive it down to Italy for him. It's brand new, by the way. Been having some fancy coachwork or something done to it in France.'

Elizabeth reflected on the situation, quickly sensing its inherent advantages.

'Say nothing to anyone,' she commanded him decisively. 'Not about the car, not about where we're going, nothing.'

'In fact,' she went on, having regarded him dubiously and obviously come to a poor view of his powers of discretion, 'it may be better if we don't go into town at all for the next few days until we leave. Withers can go in for the shopping.'

'Won't that look a bit rum, old girl?' queried the Major.

Her mind flew back to an earlier episode, a happier time when she had been châtelaine of Mallards, and Lucia simply her summer tenant.

'Withers can tell everyone we have influenza,' she said, with an expression that even Quaint Irene would have been hard-pressed adequately to describe.

Chapter 4

When Major Flint answered the polite knock at the door, a very handsome fourteen-year-old boy dressed in an immaculate grey suit in Prince of Wales check, and holding a straw boater, bowed gravely.

'If you please, sir, my name is Ramesh,' he announced.

'Good to meet you, old man,' said the Major, enthusiastically wringing the hand of the reason for his unexpected sojourn at the Ritz Hotel. 'Can't tell you what a pleasure this is for the memsah'b and me. Come along in.'

'If you please, Major, I must just check that the bellboy has put my luggage in my room. He looked a most dull-witted chap. I fear for my tennis racquets, despite having given him very precise instructions in French as to their care.'

'Yes, of course, you cut along and get yourself fixed up.' The Major waved an unaccustomed cigar expansively. 'Awfully important for a chap on campaign to see to his kit, you know.'

'By the way, old boy,' he went on. 'There's really no need to speak French to them you know. If they pretend not to understand just say it again but more loudly. That's what I do – seems to work all right.'

Ramesh nodded attentively.

'I will try to remember that, sir,' he acknowledged. 'Oh, by the way, the pater's new car is downstairs. Perhaps you and your esteemed lady would care to take a gander at it while I go and check my things?'

'Absolutely, absolutely,' burbled the Major contentedly. 'Quai-hai,

Liz-girl!' he bellowed back into the room. 'The maharajah's car is downstairs. I'm going down for a recce. Coming?'

'Don't shout, dear,' Elizabeth admonished him automatically, as she finished adjusting her hat in the mirror. 'Yes, of course I'm coming, though I still think we would have done better on the train.'

The Major, however, was in no mind for such small-minded attitudes and swept her downstairs and through the lobby with much waving of arms and expounding upon the joys of the open road.

'Really, Benjy,' she gasped, for the speed of their descent had left her slightly out of breath, 'when you go on like that you do sound just like Mr Toad.'

However, this gem was entirely lost upon her husband as he propelled her forcefully through the revolving doors and came to a sudden halt outside.

'Oh,' he said simply, with much the same feeling of sudden awe and hopeless passion that had inspired a similar utterance the previous evening at the sight of a truly perfect pair of female calves at La Coupole.

Drawn up at the kerb was quite simply the most beautiful car he had ever seen. It had the most rakish of lines, the most dazzling chrome and the most perfect shade of blue paint that it was possible to imagine. The Bugatti emblem nestled coyly at the front of the bonnet, which was tied down by a leather strap polished more highly even than the stirrup strap of a Bengal lancer.

'Bugatti blue,' he murmured in a daze. He had often heard of it, but never seen it.

'It's rather small,' came his wife's objectionable opinion from beside him. He sighed. He had long since stopped being amazed by women's inability to understand cars.

'It's beautiful,' he corrected her without looking round, still unable to remove his eyes from the vision of loveliness before him. He remembered dimly that a similar inability the night before had provoked sharp words from the little woman.

'Parp, parp,' the little woman countered disagreeably.

'Liz-girl,' he said indulgently, at last deigning to turn his head, 'you will never understand cars.'

'On the contrary, I *do* understand, Benjy,' she replied with some vigour. 'I understand that it is much too small for three people and their luggage. Why, surely it must be obvious even to a simpleton like you that it's only a two-seater.'

'Well, no harm in that,' her husband responded. 'We can send the little chap on ahead with the luggage by train and meet him at the other end.'

'Tell you what,' he said, suddenly struck by an even better idea, 'we could send *you* by train, Liz, and –'

Elizabeth's expression killed this idea stillborn. Fortunately, precisely as apparent impasse threatened to come between husband and wife, Ramesh appeared, and bowed to Mapp.

'Mrs Flint,' he said. 'An honour to meet you, madam. My father has very fond memories of your splendid hospitality. He asked me most specifically to give you his best wishes.'

Elizabeth bared her teeth and beamed. After all, it was not every day that one received the good wishes of a royal personage. Then she remembered the inadequacy of their proposed conveyance and her face darkened again.

'My husband and I were just examining this car,' she said coldly, hoping that her displeasure would be clear for all to see.

It certainly was for the Major. He gulped nervously. He hoped the old girl wasn't going to cut up rough. She had already been distinctly frosty over breakfast, all because he had kissed that damn woman's hand last night. Didn't she realise, he had tried to explain, that that was what they did over here?

'Yes, she is a real beauty isn't she?' Ramesh observed knowledgeably. 'A Type 50, if I'm not mistaken – a racing version of the 46 don't you know, but with a shorter wheelbase of course.'

'Of course,' the Major concurred quickly, just to make it clear that he knew as much about Bugattis as the next man.

'The wheelbase,' said Elizabeth, suddenly sounding awfully like Lady Bracknell, 'is immaterial. Nor do I have any desire to go racing, and certainly not with my husband at the wheel.'

'Oh, I say,' the slighted driver ejaculated half-heartedly.

'Really, young man,' Lady Bracknell swept on majestically, 'I do think your father might have been somewhat more considerate in his choice of vehicle.'

Ramesh stared at her open-mouthed, as well he might. Then suddenly he smiled, and started laughing. Major Flint simultaneously applauded his courage and feared for his safety.

Being laughed at openly, rather than insulted slyly, was a new experience for Elizabeth, but while she was still struggling to come to terms with it, Ramesh composed himself.'

'So sorry, dear lady,' he said, 'but I suppose it was a natural mistake to make.'

'Mistake?' she enquired glacially.

'Yes, you see this isn't our car.'

'But ...' the Major struggled to cope with the awful pangs of loss, rejection and unrequited love twice in less than twenty-four hours. 'Your father definitely mentioned a Bugatti.'

He felt an embarrassing urge to burst into tears.

'So he did, Major, and a Bugatti is what you will have. It's parked at the side of the hotel. Come and see.'

He skipped around the corner. The Mapp-Flints followed more sedately, to be confronted by the backs of many onlookers, all staring into the street. At the urging of Ramesh, two of the hotel's bellboys courteously but insistently cleared a path for them. Reluctantly, the crowd parted.

'Oh,' came the involuntary voice of the Major once more. Then a hushed silence.

'It's rather big,' quavered Elizabeth at last.

For someone who did not understand cars, she had instantly grasped the essence of the thing. The blue paint here made but a fleeting appearance, and was much darker in colour. Overwhelmingly, the car was black, a gleaming, rather sinister black, covering the whole of the top of the bonnet, which swept forward to a large silver elephant sitting on the radiator cap. It was breathtaking. It was imposing. Above all, it was just big.

'Type 41, madam,' Ramesh concurred. 'A brand new design called the Royale. Only royalty will be allowed to own them, you see.'

'It *is* rather big, isn't it?' the Major said nervously. He was now standing beside the car and was disturbed to find that his head only reached to just above the level of the door handle.

'Indeed, Major, the bigness of it is quite overwhelming,' Ramesh agreed enthusiastically. 'The biggest car ever made, don't you know. Nearly twice as big as a Rolls Royce. The engine was designed for an aeroplane. The wheels are the same size as some railway engines.'

The crowd had drawn back respectfully and were gazing at the Major with a mixture of awe, admiration and jealousy. Having long felt that such attitudes were entirely his due, he swelled visibly, his self-confidence flooding back.

'Well,' he said rather loudly, so that all the Johnny Frenchmen who had not yet realised who the car's owner was would be left in no doubt, 'we must put her through her paces, what?'

'We should journey by rail more often, Georgie,' Lucia opined as she allowed the steward to pour her another cup of tea. 'It really is a very civilised way to travel. What a brainwave of yours to realise that we might dispense with the Rolls entirely and send all the servants off on holiday.'

'Yes, it was rather, wasn't it?' Georgie said, sounding pleased with himself. 'I thought a long sea journey so soon after your dreadful experience with those awful herring fishermen might bring back unpleasant memories for you.'

He gazed at her with such exquisite solicitude that she decided to allow him to feel pleased with himself, and merely breathed, 'Dear

Georgie, so thoughtful,' as she gazed out of the window with a suitably distressed expression, and after a few seconds wanly waved her hand briefly between them to indicate that such a painful subject need be aired no longer.

The period during which Lucia had been 'lost at sea' during a flood, in tandem with Elizabeth Mapp, was indeed not one upon which her memory chose to linger. Carried out to sea on Grebe's kitchen table in a thick fog, they had been rescued by the crew of an Italian fishing boat which, despite their entreaties, had then carried on to their customary fishing grounds on the other side of the Atlantic before returning them to Tilling some months later. Perhaps the most galling aspect of the whole saga had been that, despite Lucia's fabled fluency in Italian, she had been completely unable to communicate with their hosts (or 'captors' as Mapp had insisted on calling them).

Naturally Lucia had explained that this was because they spoke not '*la bella lingua*' but some barbarous dialect dating from well before the time of Garibaldi. While Elizabeth had equally naturally snorted with derision, a tacit agreement had been adhered to that she made no mention of Lucia's linguistic difficulties, while Lucia would not allude to the fact that a great deal of grey had appeared in Elizabeth's hair ('from stress, naturally, dear'), only to disappear on the very afternoon of their return. A dramatic return indeed, with both having been thought dead from drowning. Tilling had been treated to the entertaining spectacle of Major Benjy and his possessions being unceremoniously thrown out of Mallards, Miss Mapp's family home, over which he had claimed rights of ownership; rights, moreover, which had been exercised most assiduously in respect of the wine cellar.

Perhaps predictably, a proposal of marriage had promptly been extracted from Major Benjy, who had successfully resisted Elizabeth's overtures for several years but was now a crushed and broken man. Equally predictably, the tacit non-disclosure agreement had been honoured only on occasions when the other counterparty was actually present, so that both snippets of news had been common currency within twenty-four hours, prompting many delighted cries of 'No!' along the way.

'And of course it gives us a chance to see Venice as well,' Georgie went on happily. 'Though we'll only be there for two days,' he stressed warily, since Lucia's gloved left hand was already resting on a guidebook of impressive proportions.

His suggestion of the Orient Express had been prompted by the thought of long, hot days accompanying Lucia around the cathedrals, churches, galleries and museums of Genoa and Milan. Artfully hedged around with hints of treasures from the Byzantine Empire, and the wonder of the San Marco and the Doge's Palace, the proposal had met instantly with Lucia's approval. A perceptive observer from the table across the aisle might have wondered, though, at the secretive smile that played briefly around Georgie's lips at the mention of Venice.

Unlike the cosy little A-roads in England, their French counterparts tended to be both straight and lined with trees, in order, it was said, that the German army might more easily find their way to Paris, and march in the shade while they did so.

Major Flint, piloting an unaccustomedly large car, thought the straightness of the roads a splendid idea, since it removed the need to turn the steering wheel. He had, however, omitted to take two significant factors into consideration. The first was that any car driven in a straight line must inevitably gather speed, as it is the normal reaction of any red-blooded male to progressively depress the accelerator in such a situation. The second was that his only previous experience of motoring had been in a Morgan three-wheeler, in which the driver might almost have been sitting on the ground, thus gaining the consequent impression that one was fairly zipping along even while straining to overtake a team of shire horses ploughing an adjoining field. Its driver sitting at an eye level of about ten feet off the ground, the Bugatti created exactly the opposite impression, Major Flint being convinced that he was proceeding at a sedate and responsible pace, which would in fact arguably have been true for a racing driver such as Tazio Nuvolari on a straight road.

Alas, the Major was not Nuvolari and roads do not remain straight forever. Approaching a bend somewhere north of Lyons, the Major braked and turned the steering wheel, only to encounter something Nuvolari would have recognised instantly as understeer, accompanied by a strange sensation of sliding sideways, something which Nuvolari would just as instantly have recognised as a skid. Sadly, while Nuvolari would have swept both these minor difficulties contemptuously alongside, the Major's sporting activities had been confined largely to polo and tiger-shooting, and so the Royale veered slowly but majestically off the road, happily passing safely between two of the aforementioned trees in the process, and came to rest rather sadly in a field of onions, pointing roughly back in the direction whence it had come.

The Major remained sitting bolt upright in the driver's seat, his face still frozen in an expression of startled apprehension, as a considerable quantity of dry earth enveloped the car in a cloud of dust. Ramesh, having had the presence of mind to clutch a very elegant leather strap apparently designed for just such a purpose, had slewed sideways, but was still perched more or less on the back seat. Elizabeth, on the other hand, had fallen into the footwell and become hopelessly entangled with a travelling rug, some magazines, a Thermos flask and several egg sandwiches.

Only the car seemed relatively untroubled, standing massively and gravely in the middle of a French field, as if in mute criticism of its ignominious treatment at the hands of the human race.

Ramesh, having slipped out from the back door, came round to the other side of the car and began extricating Elizabeth, who was now emitting little gasping noises and sobs, with as much delicacy as might be achieved. Struggling upright, she fixed her husband with such a baleful gaze that it pierced the shock of the moment for the latter with all the efficacy of a cold douche.

'Good Lord,' he proffered. 'Did you see that? Something wrong with the old bus, I think. Just suddenly leapt off the road.'

Elizabeth, becoming dimly aware that her hair now seemed to contain large amounts of mashed egg which was beginning to dribble down her forehead, struggled for speech while the Major sagely shook his head.

'Damndest thing I ever saw,' he mused. 'Must be something wrong with the steering. Good job I managed to avoid those trees, what?'

He gazed more closely at his wife.

'I say,' he pointed out helpfully, 'you've got something in your hair.'

This seemed to restore his wife's vocal ability, for she now let out a wordless roar of rage, and then refilled her lungs to get on with the real business of haranguing her husband.

'The only thing wrong with the steering is the man it's attached to!' she screamed. 'I kept telling you to slow down, but you just put that screen up behind you so you couldn't hear me! Why will you never listen to me? Now you've ruined the maharajah's car, driving like a hooligan!'

At this, she sank down and sat on the running board, weeping and saying 'Oh, this is awful!' over and over again. The word 'stupid' also made several murmured manifestations, though it was unclear whether this was being applied to herself, her husband, or both of them.

Once more Ramesh was equal to the situation. Opening a beautiful walnut panel in the interior of the car, he brought forth a flask of brandy, watched with growing interest by the Major, and poured some of the contents into a silver beaker which he had unfastened from a kid-leather strap. Gradually, Elizabeth was persuaded to imbibe. Gradually, her sobs diminished until they were no more than a succession of little 'oh' noises. Gradually, and considerately, the Major finished the brandy.

'Allow me to reassure you, madam, that the awfulness of the situation appears strictly limited,' Ramesh consoled her. 'There does not seem to be any obvious damage to the car. Major, why don't you try to restart the bally old engine?'

Answer came there none, since the Major had clambered into the back of the car and was trying to open every walnut panel in sight. One swung down to become a table. Another revealed a miniature make-up cabinet, complete with mirror and silver-backed hairbrush. Frustratingly, though, none seemed to harbour fresh supplies of brandy. He was retrieved by Ramesh and persuaded to clamber with some reluctance into the driver's seat. Sure enough, the mighty engine fired up first time. Cautiously, the Major engaged first gear and de-clutched.

There were some heart-stopping wheel-spins, but slowly the great car was persuaded out of the field and back into its natural environment. They continued southwards, but at a more moderate speed than before.

The Simplon Orient Express, to give it its proper name, which distinguished it from what Lucia understood to be a much more vulgar affair which ran through Munich and some positively unmentionable places in the Balkans, finally pulled to a halt in Venice amid impressive clouds of steam and smoke. Belying their reputation for disorganisation, Italian railway and hotel employees positively bustled around the carriages, and by the time Georgie was handed down from his wagon lit by a rather nice porter and then in turn handed down his wife, their various trunks, hatboxes, hampers and art-cases were already patiently awaiting them on porters' trolleys.

At this point a very grave and important-looking individual advanced on them, and having announced gravely and importantly that he was from their hotel, bid them give no further thought to their luggage, and led them out through the station exit. It was their first sight of Venice, and rather disappointing, with no grand buildings in sight, as he helped them down some steps into a very smart motor launch with an enclosed seating area at the back, and open curtains at the windows. As if anyone would want to keep the curtains closed in Venice!

Lucia seemed successfully to have memorised that section of the guidebook which dealt with the Grand Canal. She confidently pointed out the Ca' Pesaro on the right and the Ca' d'Oro on the left. Then, as the canal swung sharply to the right, she fell completely silent, for there before them was the Rialto Bridge, and it tends to have that effect on people.

The *palazzi* on either side grew grander and grander. The canal swung slowly left again in a great curve, and they passed under the Accademia Bridge.

'Can't you just imagine them bringing Wagner along here?' Georgie asked suddenly.

Lucia shuddered, as if someone had just asked her to kiss a child, something she had successfully managed to avoid throughout an entire mayoral term.

'Oh, Georgie,' she said in evident disgust, 'how can you bring Wagner into an experience like this?'

'When he died, I mean,' Georgie persisted. 'Olga says that they brought him all along the Grand Canal on a funeral barge. Mustn't that be a wonderful way to go?'

'It is a matter of supreme indifference to me,' Lucia replied with evident sincerity.

'Though I suppose that anyone is entitled to hope for a pleasant place in which to die,' she said, after a moment's reflection.

'Even Wagner,' she added magnanimously.

Clearly, thought Georgie, Venice was already working its magic.

Most of their provisions having been spread about the inside of the car, not to mention Elizabeth's hair, the party decided to sample the fare at a roadside restaurant. It was a place of somewhat basic appearance, in which only two people were dining, both dressed in blue overalls. Both sets of blue overalls promptly left the restaurant, together with the owner, his wife and their daughter, to gaze at the magnificent automobile outside, and it was some time before one of the diners returned, drawn doubtless by the memory of his half-finished kidney turbigo, which did indeed both look and smell delicious.

The delay was unfortunate, since it had given Elizabeth a few minutes to form an appropriate conversational gambit in her mind.

'*Mon mari a craché dans les rognons,*' she announced brightly.

A most unusual expression came over the man's face. He stared at the Major, with some hostility it must be observed, then at his kidney turbigo, then back at the Major. Then he began walking towards the latter with every appearance of wanting to do him a serious injury. The Major, with the aggressive martial instincts born of a long military career, stepped rapidly backwards, took shelter behind his wife, and said 'Here, I say!'

'Run, Major!' shouted Ramesh, holding open the back door. Run the Major duly did, pursued by a Frenchman in blue overalls, now shouting aggressively but unintelligibly.

Ramesh shepherded a shocked Elizabeth out of the restaurant, past the small group of clearly bemused French observers, and into the car. Shortly thereafter the Major arrived, out of breath and red in the face. Gasping, he hauled himself into the car, started the engine, and pulled into the road, gazing anxiously into the rear-view mirror the while.

'Tripped the blighter up and kicked him where it hurts,' he explained in some agitation, 'but not sure how long it'll hold him.'

'Calm yourself, sir,' Ramesh said, looking out of the back window. 'Nobody is following us.'

Elizabeth was clearly indignant.

'If I hadn't seen it with my own eyes, I wouldn't have believed it. I had no idea they hated the English so violently. A completely unprovoked attack!'

'I am afraid, dear lady,' Ramesh explained, 'that he was somewhat angered by your suggestion that the Major had spat in his kidneys. "Cracher", you may recall, is a *faux ami*.'

Elizabeth was about to remonstrate, but quickly realised that an Indian prince in the process of acquiring an expensive private education might well know more about these matters than herself.

'I always thought my French was very good,' she said plaintively.

Etonian chivalry battled with Etonian humour, and came a close second.

'I would venture to suggest, madam,' he replied, 'that your French is jolly well good enough to be very dangerous in the wrong hands.'

Chapter 5

Lucia was enchanted by the hotel, an ancient *palazzo* which had originally belonged to one of the most distinguished Venetian families. As she gazed about her at the hammer-beam roof, the rich tapestries, and the faded portraits, she was moved to say how much it all reminded her of the dear old Hurst in Riseholme. A passing American couple, with that lack of social delicacy which must alas be expected of our transatlantic cousins, asked her if she had indeed lived in such a property. Lucia, condescending to ignore the impropriety of being addressed spontaneously by someone to whom she had not been introduced (after all, they were American and presumably knew no better), paused for proper reflection, and then gave it as her opinion that while The Hurst had been somewhat smaller and younger, it had been conceived on essentially the same schema.

Though the Americans probably had little idea what she was talking about, which had indeed been her intention, hence the use of the word 'schema', they did not seem nearly as impressed as might be expected from two citizens of a country which was only about one third as old as the building in which they now found themselves.

'Isn't it marvellous?' Lucia more chastised than enquired, the word 'marvellous' being dwelt upon, stressed, elongated, and uttered in a deep chest voice.

'It's OK, I guess,' one of the two women conceded,

'But it's kinda old, don't you think?' the other contributed. 'Why, you'd think they could afford to redecorate once in a while. This style was already out of fashion when my mother was a girl.'

'You got a point, Molly,' the first woman agreed. Shaking their heads sadly, they departed.

Lucia, for once, was speechless.

'Georgie!' she gasped.

'I'm afraid it's only to be expected, my dear,' he sympathised. 'I met some Americans while I was visiting Olga in Le Touquet last summer. They asked for iced tea with their meal, and a salad between courses.'

'No!' Lucia ejaculated, in Tilling mode.

'They jolly well did,' Georgie averred. 'In fact, if they hadn't been acquaintances of Olga I think they'd have been chucked out. Of course, the restaurant didn't have any tea, iced or otherwise. They were most put out. After they'd left, we had to explain to the *sommelier* that really we hardly knew them at all.'

'Well,' said Lucia dubiously, 'I was intending to have a cocktail before lunch as a special holiday treat, but I wonder now whether I should. It seems a little unpatriotic somehow.'

'Nonsense,' Georgie said firmly. 'It would be ridiculous to deny that at least one good thing has come out of America, and no less ridiculous to deny ourselves anything while we are on holiday. A cocktail we shall have – and then I think we shall be just in time for lunch on the terrace. I understand it has the best view in all of Venice.'

A wonderful view it certainly had. Lucia was momentarily puzzled that Georgie should have chosen a table for four, but was soon entranced by the vista of the coruscating waters of the lagoon, the chugging progress of the *vaporetti*, and the majestic, stately presence of San Georgio Maggiore on the opposite bank.

Georgie had insisted that they lunch exactly at one o'clock, even lingering over his cocktail to ensure they arrived on the dot. Lucia had thought this strange too, since Georgie was never usually one for precise timekeeping (that was more the Major's department, with much talk of 'ack emma' and 'pip emma'), and anyway they were on holiday. Yet such thoughts were soon brushed away by the beauty of their surroundings. She wondered briefly if it might be possible to have the fish pond at Mallards remodelled as a scale replica of the Grand Canal, or to have the Garden Room altered to resemble the exterior of San Georgio, but abandoned these ideas with regret. The dome might well prove quite impractical.

So engrossed was she in her thoughts that it took her a few seconds to realise that Georgie had stood up and was welcoming a guest to their table.

'Hello, Lucia,' hailed Olga in that vigorously cheerful tone of hers.

'Olga, dear,' she replied warily. 'How unexpected. I had no idea we would be seeing you in Venice.'

'I know,' Georgie said delightedly. 'I thought it would be a lovely surprise for you.'

'Indeed,' Lucia concurred. 'How thoughtful of you both.'

Olga laughed heartily.

'You are a twit, Georgie. I told you not to spring it on Lucia like this.'

'You did!' Georgie exclaimed delightedly; he always found the experience of being reproved by Olga strangely pleasurable. 'But I wanted it to be a surprise, so there!'

'Well, let's sit down,' said Lucia, and so they did.

'Tell me, dear,' she said brightly. 'What brings you to Venice? Is this a regular haunt of yours?'

'Oh, I'm just visiting some friends here,' Olga said vaguely, 'but as for the hotel, no, I don't think I've been here before.'

'Your usual cocktail, Miss Braccly,' murmured the waiter, as he carefully placed a dry Martini beside her plate.

'Well, maybe just once or twice anyway,' she continued, only slightly abashed. 'Perhaps a long time ago.'

'Then we must be grateful that the waiter has such a good memory,' Georgie said mischievously, whereupon both he and Olga burst into guffaws of laughter.

It was this aspect of Olga of which Lucia had always disapproved.

Surely there was something a little vulgar in sitting at a lunch table laughing out loud, and it pained her to see Georgie being drawn repeatedly into these excesses whenever he was in Olga's company. Say what you like about Elizabeth Mapp-Flint (and Lucia certainly made free in that regard), she had never been guilty of allowing Major Benjy to believe even for one moment that married life could actually be fun. Tolerable, yes. Amusing, perhaps occasionally, and in a suitably restrained manner. Fun, never.

While it was of course gratifying to be seen in the company of a world-famous soprano, it had to be admitted that there was something a little, well, coarse about Olga. She shuddered inwardly as she remembered Olga's penchant for the gramophone, a device about which Lucia had very strong views, having discovered that it was incapable of imparting to the slow movement of the 'Moonlight Sonata' anything approaching the deep soulfulness with which she herself imbued it. In Riseholme, Olga had even arranged dancing to gramophone records, a combination of vices of which Lucia had quite understandably been most suspicious.

She sighed deeply, but neither Georgie nor Olga seemed to notice, and so she busied herself with regarding the menu quizzically through her *pince-nez* until their unseemly mirth had subsided.

'Oh dear,' Olga gasped as she dabbed at her eyes, 'you are such a hoot, Georgie. How lucky you are, Lucia, to have him always around to keep you in good humour.'

'Indeed,' Lucia murmured absently but a trifle dubiously, without lifting her eyes from the menu. 'What is *triglia*? Do remind me, someone.'

'Red mullet, and I'm sure it's jolly good,' Olga obliged.

'Thank you dear, so kind,' Lucia said, emerging from her reverie with a slightly startled expression, as if suddenly noticing that there were two other people at the table.

'Let's order,' Olga suggested. 'I'm famished.'

'Oh, you're always famished,' Georgie chided her. 'Don't you remember that time in Deauville when you'd only just had breakfast but still polished off a whole bucket of *fruits de mer* and two bottles of Vouvray?'

'A gentleman would have pretended not to notice,' Olga said with a pout.

'There are lots of things a gentleman has to pretend not to notice,' Georgie replied archly. 'Such as that marquess, or whatever he was, you were with.'

This prompted a fresh outburst of hysterics from both. Lucia sighed again, shook her head sorrowfully, and decided on the *linguini*.

'Now then, Lucia,' Georgie said in due course, once they were sitting over their coffee, 'I have another surprise for you.'

'Shall I enjoy it, I wonder?' Lucia enquired warily.

'Indeed you will!' Georgie replied with asperity. 'I have arranged for you to spend the afternoon in the company of the most celebrated cultural guide in Venice. She has a wonderful itinerary planned. I think you're going to start over there at San Georgio Maggiore. Or is it finish? I forget, but anyway, haven't I been clever?'

Lucia had a sudden premonition that she had been out-manoeuvred. It was a feeling that she experienced but rarely, and definitely did not enjoy.

'But, Georgie,' she asked sharply. 'You will be coming with me, surely?'

'Oh, you'll be much better off without me dragging along,' he said airily. 'Anyway, I thought I might go with Olga to see her friends.'

'They're Italian, you know,' he added hastily as Lucia's brow clouded. 'Not your sort of people at all, I wouldn't think.'

Lucia gave one of her indeterminate, rather strangulated little 'oh' noises, which indicated extreme displeasure when no other obvious response immediately presented itself.

'Now then,' Georgie went on briskly, looking at his watch, 'I've arranged for you to meet her downstairs at a quarter to three, and then I thought we could all meet up in Harry's Bar for a Bellini at six. So there we are. It all works out splendidly.'

'For you perhaps, Georgie,' Lucia corrected him sharply. 'You are not the one being abandoned.'

'Not abandoned, surely?' Georgie countered, emboldened by a reasonable quantity of Pinot Grigio. 'You won't be on your own, after all.'

'Well, of course if you prefer other people's company, Georgie, there's nothing more to be said,' Lucia replied, with the tight-lipped expression of a woman who knew there was actually a great deal more to be said, and was already rehearsing it in her mind, as was revealed by the rather savage gleam that had come into her eyes.

It was time for Georgie's ace of trumps, and he played it with aplomb.

'But I had no idea you would dislike the idea so much,' he protested. 'I'll tell you what. Why don't you come with us instead? It would be a wonderful opportunity for you to practise your Italian.'

Lucia gave him a level gaze. It was the level gaze of a woman who knows that her husband has for once been successful in a bid for freedom, but is even now busy ferreting out his escape tunnel, and is confident that he will be at liberty for but a brief period of time.

'No, Georgie,' she said. 'One of us, at least, must make the most of this wonderful cultural heritage. I will have to imbibe it for both of us, that's all.'

She tried a gay little laugh, but was only partially successful.

'However,' she added grimly, 'you may cancel your arrangements, Georgie. I have no wish to be palmed off on some street urchin of a tourist guide.'

With this she rose and swept magnificently out of the room, wearing an expression of deep pain and suffering.

'Well,' said Olga quietly as she disappeared from view, 'that seemed to go quite well, Georgie.'

As she waited bleakly for the lift to arrive Lucia heard once again, though this time off in the distance, the sound of Olga's nasty, vulgar laughter.

Georgie found Olga's friends most enchanting. Arriving at their *palazzo* on the Grand Canal, they were handed up a few steps by the boatman and could then step straight through the magnificent front door into an imposing marbled hall. Here a footman bowed gravely and led them upstairs to the main living room, whereupon Olga put her head round the door and called *'Permesso?'* in fine Venetian style.

The Contessa di Alto-Brandisci ('But of course you must call me Susanna, *signor* Georgie') flowed graciously around the room as though on well-oiled castors, introducing them to her family, of whom there seemed to be a substantial number apparently spanning some four generations, most of whom seemed already to know Olga. Suddenly, Georgie glimpsed a face that he knew all too well.

'Poppy, darling!' Olga cried. 'So you could make it after all. Isn't that wonderful, Georgie?'

'Oh, yes, I mean ... well, yes,' stammered Georgie, rather taken aback.

Poppy, Duchess of Sheffield had an unremitting passion for three things in life: dressed crab, black coffee, and men with beards. In her pursuit of all three she was both tireless and incapable of deflection from her purpose. Fortunately she was blessed with the ability to take constant rejection in her stride. Indeed, even this is hardly an accurate description, for she seemed simply not to notice the most blatant of polite refusals; they were as dust beneath her chariot wheels as she ground remorselessly towards her objective. Olga said that the late duke, who had been considerably his wife's senior, had enjoyed a similar reputation with chorus girls.

Since Georgie qualified under the third of her interests, he had in the past been a constant target of Poppy's affections, which had included holding his hand under the dinner table, and stroking his beard over coffee, murmuring 'What a dear little beard' to herself in a voice of childish wonderment. Her attentions to him one summer at Le Touquet shortly after they had first met had caused Georgie to complain in exasperation later to Lucia, whom he had left languishing in Tilling with her mayoral duties, that Poppy really had been most 'forward' and 'tarsome'. On a return visit paid by Poppy to Tilling, he had resorted to locking his door at night during her stay.

Susanna showed them around the beautiful building, pointing out the family portraits and recounting how many Dalmatian pirates each of the menfolk had despatched. Olga hissed briefly to Georgie that had one of them been Major Flint then doubtless there would be Dalmatian pirate-skins on the floor of the living room. Normally he would have found this highly entertaining, but as Poppy was hanging on to his arm while they walked from room to room, saying nothing but gazing at him devotedly and coquettishly, he was feeling increasingly awkward, and not a little irritated.

Back in the living room there was prosecco with little almond *biscotti*, which Georgie pronounced quite magnificent, and then some different confectionery which was unutterably delicious in a chocolatey sort of way.

'*Capezzoli di Venere*,' said Olga knowledgeably.

Unwisely, Georgie asked for a translation.

'Nipples of Venus,' Susanna proffered briskly, at which Georgie said 'Oh' in a very pursed-up-mouth sort of way, until he caught sight of himself in a faded gilt mirror. Realising that his expression must seem somewhat strange, he experimented with trying to make it look like the natural result of needing to pronounce a particular word, but then found that he could not think of a single one which seemed appropriate. So, he slowly adjusted his mouth back to its normal shape, having spent several seconds pursing and unpursing his lips, looking rather like a pensive goldfish, as Olga unkindly said later.

Poppy, on the other hand, sighed deeply and meaningfully and reached across the arm of her chair to squeeze Georgie's hand, saying 'Mmm' and gazing at him with an air of awful expectancy. Olga produced her handkerchief, closely followed by several barking coughs which sounded to Georgie suspiciously like guffaws.

'Yes, well,' he said, distractedly removing his hand from underneath

Poppy's, 'this is all very lovely, Olga, but perhaps we should be going out to look around.'

'Oh, I agree,' Poppy said instantly, rising to her feet. 'You just wait there, you dear little man, while I go and get m'furs.'

At this there were distinct little crying noises from Olga's corner as Poppy slipped hastily from the room, but not so hastily that she was unable to glance back round the door at Georgie in mute adoration while she waved a well-manicured paw at him.

'Quick, let's go before she gets back,' he said, panic-stricken.

At this there were quick and plangent recriminations from the assembled womenfolk.

'Mr Georgie!' exclaimed Susanna, apparently deeply shocked. 'Surely you would not insult the Duchess so. She has chosen you as her companion for the afternoon. How could you possibly disappoint her?'

'Yes, for shame, Georgie,' Olga chipped in, still holding her handkerchief tightly, and doing a passable impression of Lucia, 'how could you possibly treat a duchess so?'

Even in this moment of extreme awkwardness, Georgie could not help but admire how *perfectly* she had produced exactly the deep, throbbing tone of reproof that Lucia would have imparted to the word 'duchess'.

'Only joking, of course,' he explained. 'Of course we must wait for Poppy. Delightful person. Afternoon not complete without her.'

Bewilderingly, he was now lapsing into Diva Plaistow-like telegraphese. He stopped and pulled himself together, bowing the ladies out of the room in a style that would not have disgraced Mr Wyse. By the time they had come downstairs Poppy was already waiting for them, wearing not her furs but a linen shawl.

'Decided against them,' she explained, answering their unasked question. 'Too hot.'

So saying, she clamped her hand closely around Georgie's arm, as if to prevent any further possibility of escape. He was wearing a pair of strawberry summer gloves and hoped fervently that none of the chocolate of the ... of that dessert was still adhering to her fingers.

This time they exited from the other end of the hall, passing through a much less glamorous door, and emerging in a rather drab street at the rear of the *palazzo*.

'Oh, I know where we are,' Poppy informed them, having gazed around short-sightedly for a moment or two. 'Come along.'

So saying, she dragged Georgie off in the general direction of St Mark's Square, Susanna and Olga trailing along behind.

Poppy's chosen destination was Florian's, and very charming it was too, thought Georgie, to be sitting outside in the most beautiful square in the world and sharing another bottle of prosecco. Or would have been under other circumstances anyway, without Poppy making eyes at him from across the table.

'So, *signor* Georgie,' Susanna was saying, 'I was most sad to hear you will not be staying long in Venice. Where are you going?'

'Well, I would like to stay longer, of course,' Georgie replied diplomatically, 'but we are moving on to Bellagio, you see.'

At this Susanna clasped her hands delightedly and said that she and her late husband had often spent the summer there, visiting some of their friends who owned lakeside villas.

'Yes, Olga has been before and says it is simply parfect,' Georgie said.

'As indeed it is,' she concurred emphatically. 'I can't wait to see it again.'

Susanna looked rather surprised.

'Do I understand, *cara*, that you will be going to Bellagio, *come dici* ... together?'

'Yes, of course,' Georgie confirmed enthusiastically. 'Won't it all be lovely?'

'But,' asked Susanna, greatly daring, 'I understood ... *scusi*, but I understood you were here with your wife?'

'Oh yes, of course,' Georgie explained. 'She'll be there too. We could hardly leave her behind, could we? Dear me, no. But she'll be off during the day visiting things, I expect, so I can spend most afternoons with Olga, and then the three of us can dine together in the evening. All very *molto comodo*, don't you think?'

'*Assolutamente*,' averred Susanna, gazing at him with a whole new respect. 'I can see now that you are a remarkable man, *signor* Georgie.'

'Oh, do you think so?' he asked, pleased but somewhat puzzled. He became aware that Olga had started giggling on the other side of the table, which was also rather confusing. Had he missed something?

'Bellagio,' Poppy mused, rolling the word around her mouth. 'No, I don't think I've been there. Write it down for me, will you, Olga dear? One must always be ready for new experiences.'

Georgie gave an involuntary gasp of horror, and reached for his glass to try to conceal it.

'Mustn't one, you dear little man?' she continued, softly but perfectly audibly.

Georgie choked on his mouthful of prosecco.

Susanna gave a little shake of her head, gazed at him admiringly, and repeated, 'A remarkable man.'

So it was that when Lucia arrived at Harry's Bar, decidedly after six, though she was a habitually punctual person, she was greeted by a characteristically loud Olga.

'Hello, Lucia,' she boomed, 'just as well you got here. Georgie is acquiring the most rakish reputation with women.'

'Olga, really!' he protested weakly.

'Yes, dear, really,' Lucia echoed, somewhat more forcefully. 'Decorum, please.'

She gazed disapprovingly around the table only to find herself gazing disapprovingly at the Duchess of Sheffield, whereupon she hastily recomposed her face into that of one greeting an old friend with whom one had very nearly stayed the night at her castle, being prevented from doing so only by Poppy unaccountably feigning illness to avoid such an eventuality.

What a philatelist was to postage stamps, so Lucia was to royalty and the aristocracy. She collected them with avidity. During her time in London society at 25 Brompton Square it had been said that the sight of Lucia in resolute pursuit of a Duchess brought most awfully to mind the image of a particularly determined butterfly collector. Toby, Lord Limpsfield, one of the earliest items in Lucia's collection, had once resignedly asked Adele, Lady Brixton, whether she supposed Lucia carried a killing jar in her handbag.

'Poppy, dear,' the collector trilled, 'what a pleasant surprise.'

'I dare say,' replied the duchess non-committally. This in fact marked something of a warming in their relationship, since she usually gazed at Lucia with a puzzled expression as though trying to remember who she was and simply said 'Ah, yes' to anything she proffered by way of conversation, at which Lucia would laugh gaily, and tell everyone later that Poppy was such a dear person, but so terribly eccentric.

'And this is Olga's friend, Susanna,' said Georgie by way of introduction, whereupon Lucia switched her cool, disapproving expression back on, and said 'Charmed' in a somewhat unconvincing way.

'You simply must try one of these, Lucia,' Georgie said, indicating his Bellini. 'They have the most marvellous taste of peaches, and they're not very strong at all.'

He waved at a passing waiter and pointed at his glass.

'If you say so, Georgie,' Lucia concurred. 'After all, if they are a *specialità di casa* ...'

'Ah, you speak Italian?' Susanna asked delightedly.

Georgie shot a warning glance across the table, but Lucia had no need of it to know that she was straying into dangerous territory.

'Ah, *pocissimo*, I'm afraid,' she replied, endeavouring to look both knowledgeable and modest.

'No matter,' said Susanna. 'I trust you have passed a most pleasant afternoon in our beautiful city.'

'Yes, indeed,' Lucia said decidedly. 'I put together a most instructive programme for myself. No need for a guide at all.' She shot a cold stare at Georgie.

'In fact, I can't think why anyone would bother with one at all,' she pressed on. 'They're probably all charlatans anyway, who only do it to make a change from begging on the streets.'

She noted with satisfaction that both Georgie and Olga were looking most uncomfortable. It was always gratifying when one's arrows hit the bull's-eye so unerringly.

'Most impressive,' Susanna commented. 'If only all our visitors took the trouble to prepare themselves so well, *signora.*'

'I consider it no more than my duty,' Lucia informed the table at large. 'When one is surrounded by so much culture, it can only be properly appreciated if one has made adequate preparation. For example, I had no idea the Byzantine influence was so pronounced. I fear we have been neglecting our studies, Georgie. We must put together a reading list when we get home.'

'Well, I do have Gibbon next to my bed in Tilling, actually,' Georgie protested weakly.

Lucia looked at him kindly but pityingly.

'Gibbon was Rome, dear, not Byzantium. Why, I remember reading it myself in Riseholme with poor Pepino when he was alive.'

At this point Georgie looked uncomfortable all over again, and Lucia, having laboured all afternoon under a sense of deep injustice at having been so cruelly cast aside, was able to take comfort from the fact that she had now demonstrated both her moral and her intellectual superiority in rapid succession. She raised her Bellini and sipped it contentedly.

Chapter 6

'It really is like a picture postcard, isn't it?' Georgie commented happily as he beamed at Olga.

'Oh, for goodness' sake, Georgie, do stop seeing everything in watercolour,' Olga yelled above the noise of the paddle wheels. 'Don't just observe life – live it.'

'Now you sound like Quaint Irene,' he said rather grumpily, 'but no, I can't possibly be peeved with anyone on such a glorious day, Olga, so it's no good trying.'

Olga laughed and took his arm, making him feel ridiculously proud. The trim, elegant steamer continued to chug its way resolutely up the southern leg of Lake Como, looking for all the world like a floating summer house.

'Have you told her yet?'

'About Francesco? No, I haven't quite found the right moment somehow.'

'Well, hadn't you better get a move on? We'll be at the hotel in an hour or so and you don't want her just to find about it for herself, do you?'

'I suppose not,' Georgie said distractedly, 'but it seems such a shame to take oneself away from such a wonderful view.'

'You'll have the view all day every day from now on,' Olga chided him gently. 'Why don't you just take the bull by the horns and tell her? It's nothing that she's likely to object to, anyway. It's nothing to do with her, really.'

Georgie grimaced.

'You don't know Lucia,' he countered. 'She has a wonderful capacity to get upset about anything. Why, only the other week she rebuked the Padre for speaking Scottish because it might show support for Ramsay MacDonald; she still doesn't believe that he's not a Russian spy, you know... Anyway, she's still jolly sore about us leaving her alone in Venice.'

'Oh, all right then, I'll come with you. There! She can't throw both of us overboard, can she?'

Reluctantly, Georgie turned and walked slowly forward (or, rather for'ard, as he knew they said at sea). Lucia had retired from deck to sit in the lounge, worried that her hat might be at threat from the wind, though to Georgie's mind it was nothing more than a light breeze. Having gazed briefly around her on departing the landing stage at Como, she had said cryptically, '*Manzoni*, Georgie,' and departed in search of somewhere to read her guidebook.

'By the way,' said Olga, 'I was meaning to ask you, but this is the first chance I've had. Surely Gibbon *was* Byzantium wasn't he?'

'Well, of course he was,' Georgie said crossly, 'or mostly, anyway. That's so like her. She reads the first chapter of something and then gets tired of it and starts something else, but leaves it lying around ostentatiously like Susan Wyse's OBE so that she can convincingly claim to have read it.'

Olga laughed. 'Dear Lucia,' she said, 'she really is priceless. No wonder we all love her so much.'

'Well, I'm really not sure why sometimes,' Georgie replied. 'She can be so very difficult, you know.'

'Yes, but magnificent with it,' cried Olga. 'Hello, Lucia. Enjoying the view? Isn't it marvellous?'

'Most dramatic,' averred Lucia. 'One can see why Shelley was so impressed. Divine Shelley! I feel we have been neglecting him, Georgie. Something else to put on our reading list when we get home.'

So saying she produced a slim notebook from her handbag and

proceeded to make a small, painstaking note, presumably about Shelley.

'Oh, yes, well, look here, Lucia, I just wanted to tell you something, actually.'

Lucia looked up quizzically from her still open notebook.

'You see, you know we had to leave Foljambe and Grosvenor and everyone behind? Well, Olga's found me a valet for the holiday. There now, isn't she clever?'

Lucia gave one of her tight little noises that were intended to convey that if she could deign to consider so trivial a matter she would surely disapprove.

'Yes, he's called Francesco, and he's waiting for me at the hotel,' Georgie said quickly. 'Oh look, a kingfisher, I think. No, it's gone. Oh, what a shame. Perhaps we'll see another one in a minute.'

'Well, if you think it's necessary, of course, Georgie,' Lucia said, treating this transparent change of subject with the contempt it deserved. 'It does seem rather extravagant somehow.'

'Yes, but we are on holiday, you know,' Georgie responded, while still scanning the horizon intently for further avicular treats, 'and you know how lost I am without Foljambe.'

Lucia was silent for a few moments, and then turned to Olga with an expression of studied casualness.

'Olga, dear,' she enquired, 'I don't suppose you were similarly thoughtful as to the provision of a lady's maid, by any chance?'

'Indeed I was,' Olga assured her, 'the hotel said they would be happy to arrange it for you. I'm afraid I don't know her name, but she should be awaiting your arrival as we speak.'

'Probably dusting your chest of drawers with *pot pourri*, or something,' Georgie ventured unnecessarily.

'Yes, thank you, Georgie,' Lucia said sharply, 'I am sure the woman is perfectly competent.'

'I wonder what Francesco will be doing?' mused Georgie. 'I say, you know this is all rather exciting. I've never had a valet before.'

Before marrying Lucia, Georgie had lived very simply with just the trusty Foljambe to cook and clean for him. 'Trusty' in the sense that she was the only person allowed to handle his bibelots, though 'trusty' only to a limited degree, since she had callously decided to leave him to his own devices by marrying Cadman, Lucia's chauffeur. Since Lucia had just decided to stay on in Tilling rather than go back to Riseholme, this had left Georgie distraught at the prospect of having to return to Riseholme to live there alone.

Georgie had sprung into decisive action, writing to his solicitors to cut Foljambe out of his will. This did something to relieve his feelings, but nothing to resolve his situation. He had then attempted to bribe Cadman away from Lucia's employment, an attempt which failed and left him in danger of exposure to Lucia. He had then announced that he was selling his house in Riseholme and was off to lead a cavalier bachelor existence in London, a brilliant stratagem marred only by the fact that Lucia refused to believe him. Bowing to the inevitable, he had agreed to stay on in Tilling too, and in due course, once proper arrangements had been made for the safekeeping of his bibelots, he and Lucia had finally got married, thus resolving the servant problem to everyone's satisfaction. Georgie often wondered if servants really appreciated just what sacrifices their employers made for their benefit.

Georgie had only ever had one other member of staff: a chauffeur in Riseholme, whose name nobody could remember and who, both Georgie and Foljambe were at pains to stress, 'slept out'. Lucia had surmised early on in their friendship that Georgie was not good with servants, since he was unduly devoted to Foljambe and was careful never to cross her, while he engaged in light-hearted banter with his chauffeur, calling him a naughty boy when he went the wrong way (which seemed to happen remarkably often). Georgie had given up both car and chauffeur before leaving Riseholme, and Lucia had been careful to train Georgie in behaving properly towards Cadman, whose reaction should he be called a naughty boy and have the back of his hand slapped could be all too easily imagined.

The steamer chugged and splashed its way through a long curve to the right ('starboard', Georgie thought to himself) and suddenly Bellagio came into view, with its pink and yellow buildings climbing up the hill, and its landing stage for the various lake steamers, whose routes radiated outwards in all directions, across to Argento, which was now astern of them, or right up to the northern end of the lake beyond Dongo and Gravedona.

'Look!' said Olga, pointing to a large building on the extreme left. 'There's our hotel. See – there's their luggage cart waiting for us on the jetty.'

'Giuseppe!' she shouted, as the ferry docked, waving to a man in morning dress, who bowed gravely in reply, but was unable to refrain from bursting out in a smile at the same time.

As they alighted, Giuseppe's minions were already seeking out their bags and loading them on to the trolley. Georgie rather daringly stepped across a gap of at least three or four inches just to show what an accomplished naval voyager he was, but was disappointed that nobody seemed to notice. He thought briefly about going back on board on the pretext of having dropped his handkerchief just so that he could disembark again to a more appreciative audience, but decided against it. He remembered an occasion in Le Touquet when his leather soles had slipped on some wet planking with very tiresome consequences for his pink Oxford bags. So he contented himself with settling his lavender cape about his shoulders and smiling benignly as he looked around.

Olga had come up trumps, not that he had ever doubted her. Bellagio was simply enchanting, he thought, as they walked along the front, between hotels on the right and open-air restaurants by the lake on the left. Whereas the sunlight in Venice had been reflected by the water, as if flashing on the jewellery of an ageing courtesan, here it seemed to be soaked up by the soft stone, and then gently exuded along with a general air of welcome. To the right, flights of steps rose up between the hotels flanked by little shops and cafes. To the left was the stunning spectacle of Lake Como, the more distant steamers seeming like dabs of white gouache applied to cobalt water, with the *terre verte* and burnt sienna of the hills rising in the background. Bellagio, he decided at once, was by far the nicest place he had ever been. He sighed contentedly as he followed Lucia's parasol towards the hotel.

As they entered the gate and started walking up the driveway, Lucia suddenly halted her stately progress and Georgie nearly bumped into her. Olga, too, stopped in her tracks and gave a very vulgar whistle.

'Brother!' she said. 'What gives, Giuseppe?'

'Yes,' Lucia followed up, in a tone that could be disapproving but one couldn't quite be sure, 'what is that monster of a car?'

Georgie knew full well she was hedging her bets. If it turned out to belong to royalty or nobility she would affect to admire it, while should the owner be revealed as a common-or-garden millionaire she could simply sniff sadly and walk off.

'That, *signora*,' said Giuseppe proudly, 'is a Bugatti Royale. Built only for royalty, you understand. It is an honour for us to have it here.'

Lucia perked up at the prospect of being able to add a princess or two to her collection of duchesses.

'Do I understand,' she purred, 'that you have royalty staying with you at present?'

'Not at present, no,' Giuseppe conceded reluctantly. 'The lady who came with the car is somehow connected with royalty, although the precise nature of the relationship is obscure. Normally, of course, one would assume ...'

He broke off, unsure how to express so delicate a sentiment to so refined a nature as Lucia's.

'But not in this case?' Olga proffered, eager to help him out of his difficulty.

'*Definitely* not in this case,' Giuseppe said with feeling.

'So, what's she like?' asked Olga, consumed with curiosity.

'She is an English lady, Miss Bracely, travelling with her husband and a young man. The young man *is* allegedly royalty, though he refuses to confirm this.'

'Yes, but what's she *like*?' wailed Olga.

Giuseppe pondered how best to respond.

'She is a lady of very decided views,' he said, after due consideration. 'Very decided. She decided, for example, that she wanted the Royal Suite which, as you know, dear lady,' with a bow to Lucia, 'is reserved for you and your husband. So determined, in fact, that she left one of our receptionists in tears for quite some time. She then offered the manager a very large amount of money to shift you into another room. She claimed that you would not know the difference, *signora*, and so there would be no harm done, as she put it.'

'No!' said Georgie, reverting to Tilling 'Any news?' mode in the shock of the moment.

'Obviously the woman must be taught a lesson,' Lucia said dismissively. 'I look forward to meeting her.'

Georgie and Olga looked at each other with a mixture of anticipation and foreboding.

'Well,' Olga murmured to him as they followed Lucia into the hotel, 'at least it will give her something to do.'

At this point an extremely handsome man with dark hair and a moustache emerged from behind the grand staircase and bowed to Georgie.

'Mr Pillson, sir? My name is Francesco. I must tender my apologies for not meeting you at the landing stage, but I was preparing your room.'

'Oh,' said Georgie rather uncertainly, not having rehearsed the correct form for greeting a new valet, 'yes.'

'When you are ready sir, I will show you the way.'

'If you would simply give me your passports, sir and ladies, I will take care of all the formalities for you,' Giuseppe offered. 'I am sure you would all like to go up to your rooms.'

'Thank you,' Lucia replied, gazing at Francesco with disapprobation. Unabashed, he bowed politely to her and stepped aside to let the three of them pass. Olga peeled off on the first landing with a cheery 'See you downstairs for lunch', and they headed to the front of the building.

A pair of large gilded doors took them into a generous living room, far larger than that at Mallards. The front of the room dazzled with glass from floor to ceiling, looking out over the terrace restaurant and the swimming pool to the lake beyond.

A door gave off on each side of the room. By one, a maid stood; she curtseyed to Lucia. Francesco opened the other and gave Georgie a welcoming smile.

Georgie's room was almost as big as the living room had been. He gazed out of the window with delight. Then he turned, smiled at Francesco and said, 'Oh, this is quite *parfect* – everything is so nice!'

Francesco was already unpacking Georgie's things, carefully removing the tissue paper stuffing from the arms of his jackets.

'It is indeed a beautiful location, sir,' he agreed.

Georgie sauntered back into the living room and sat down on a couch. There was a large mirror opposite which was really very convenient, for when he crossed his legs he could see that his trouser crease was straight, and that he was showing the right amount of sock. He made a mental note to ask Lucia if the same effect might be arranged at Mallards.

Francesco came back into the room.

'Excuse me, sir, but it is just midday. May I mix you a cocktail?'

'Oh, yes, thank you,' said Georgie delightedly. 'Perhaps a gin and it?'

'An excellent choice, sir,' Francesco said gravely, 'but as you are in Italy I wonder if I might suggest a Negroni? It is only a slight variation, but one which I venture to suggest you will enjoy.'

'Oh well, yes, thank you,' Georgie said weakly. Being in the same room as Francesco was rather like being in the company of a film star. From his warm, dark eyes to his dazzling white teeth he was as near perfectly beautiful as any human being has a right to be. He flashed the dazzling teeth now as he opened one of the full-length windows.

'There is a balcony, sir, if you care to sit in the open air.'

He settled Georgie into a chair and then left to mix his drink, which

73

on delivery proved quite excellent, though perhaps a trifle large. He was struck by a sudden thought.

'I wonder, Francesco,' he ventured, 'if you might telephone Miss Bracely's room and ask if she would care to join us here for a drink before lunch?'

Miss Bracely said she'd be jolly well delighted, and ordered a sidecar in advance. Before long, she and Georgie were happily ensconced on the balcony, waiting for Lucia to join them.

'Oh, Olga,' he said contentedly, 'thank you so much for suggesting all of this. I just know everything is going to be wonderful.'

He took a large mouthful of his Negroni, rolled it appreciatively around with his tongue, and then added, 'And I do like Francesco.'

'Mm,' Olga concurred enthusiastically, 'so do I.'

Chapter 7

Lucia was some time joining them, and when she did so the reason for the delay became obvious as she had completely changed her outfit.

'Lucia, how gorgeous!' Olga exclaimed. 'Aren't you wonderful?'

'Now you sound like Quaint Irene again,' said Georgie mischievously.

'May I prepare you a cocktail, madam?' Francesco enquired.

'Thank you, no,' Lucia replied, rather coolly Georgie thought, and then, 'if you two have finished your drinks, perhaps we might go down to lunch?'

Giuseppe fussed around them on the terrace, installing them at a shady table.

'I find, Georgie,' Lucia said rather sharply after Giuseppe had given them their menus, 'that we appear to be in something of a backwater.'

'Surely not?' Georgie queried in surprise, looking around the terrace. 'I believe this is by far the best restaurant in Bellagio. The menu looks superb. But if you would like to go somewhere else ...'

'Don't be obtuse, Georgie,' Lucia said sharply. 'I refer not to the restaurant, but to Bellagio itself. My guidebook is strangely silent, mentioning only this hotel as a point of interest. I presumed it to be an oversight, but on consulting my maid, I find that apart from one small church there is nothing here at all – no cathedral, no galleries, nothing.'

'Well, there is a rather fine cathedral in Como,' Georgie said. 'You saw the outside of it as we came from the station to catch the steamer. That would make a fine outing for you one day.'

'Oh, Lucia,' Olga cut in breezily, 'Bellagio offers a very different sort of holiday. We are surrounded by wonderful villas with beautiful gardens all up and down the lake. Why, if you want to, you can take a different steamer every day and travel around to your heart's content.'

'I cannot help noticing,' Lucia remarked tightly, 'that you both refer to what I might do, but that the first person plural is strangely absent. May I ask what you two are planning to do, while I am undertaking these daily excursions?'

'Well,' said Georgie uneasily, 'I thought I might try some watercolours – maybe from the balcony of our room. There's a wonderful view from there.'

'Indeed,' Lucia said in an even tighter voice. 'I was hoping, Georgie, that we might spend at least *some* of our holiday together.'

'Oh, but you will, of course,' Olga assured her, kicking Georgie under the table. 'Why, we should all go up to Gravedona one day, or perhaps across to Cernobbio.'

'Hm,' said Lucia, but barely mollified. 'I can't help thinking, Georgie, that this is another attempt to get rid of me. Perhaps you have some other stray beggar to palm off on me as a guide?'

'Oh, Lucia, really,' replied Georgie, in a scandalised tone. 'I'll have you know it was Susanna, actually, and we all had a jolly good laugh about it, when we told her that you'd thought she was a street urchin. Really, I was only thinking of you. I thought you might enjoy her company as she showed you around.'

'She's a countess, of course,' he went on airily, 'so it's a good job she has a good sense of humour. Why, she might have been offended and never spoken to us again.'

'Only an *Italian* countess, Georgie,' said Lucia, provoked beyond endurance. 'Why, they're two a penny you know, positively everyone out here is some sort of countess. You meet them all the time. It's probably no different from being on the parish council of your local church back in England.'

76

She suddenly noticed that Olga, who was facing the hotel, was staring back over Lucia's shoulder with a very surprised expression on her face.

'Why surely it can't be ...? Yes, it is. Lucia, Georgie, surely those are your friends from Tilling, aren't they?'

Lucia turned to find Mr and Mrs Wyse bearing down upon them, Mr Wyse in a natty linen suit and what looked like a bee-keeper's hat without a veil.

'Dear lady,' he said, whipping it off and bowing, 'forgive the intrusion. Miss Bracely, Mr Pillson.'

Further bows.

'But what on earth are you doing here?' asked Lucia. 'I thought you were going to Capri as usual.'

'Cholera, dear,' Susan Wyse said, rolling her eyes alarmingly. 'Fortunately we heard about it as we approached Naples, turned straight round and headed north again. They're talking of quarantine and fever hospitals. Too ghastly!'

'Then of course we had to decide what to do, where to go,' Mr Wyse explained, 'and straight away we naturally thought of joining our good friends in Bellagio. So, we phoned ahead for rooms and here we are.'

He beamed at the assembled company.

'Wonderful,' Lucia pronounced determinedly. 'Why, how wonderful to have some of the grand old Tilling crowd around one. Giuseppe, could you please bring two more chairs?'

'Oh, three please,' Susan said. 'We are travelling with Algernon's sister Amelia.'

'Oh, another Italian countess,' Georgie commented. 'Well, tum-ti-tum. So common at this time of year, I find.'

Lucia forbore to respond.

Amelia, Contessa di Faraglione, emerged through the French windows and greeted them without any unnecessary show of emotion such as might disturb her eye-glass.

'But Amelia, dear,' Lucia enquired as Georgie and Mr Wyse hastened around the table seating the ladies, 'Susan said something about quarantine. How did you escape?'

'In a fishing boat,' Amelia boomed. 'Had to bribe the coastguard, of course. So silly. Why, there hasn't been cholera in our family for years.'

'But isn't it infectious, rather than hereditary?' asked Georgie.

'Nonsense,' Amelia asserted, 'and anyway my cheroots would keep any infection at bay. Cheroot smoke is very sterile, you know.'

A sudden suspicion struck Lucia.

'That isn't your Bugatti outside, by any chance?' she asked casually.

'No, dear,' said Susan. 'Why, we have the Royce as usual.'

'The owners are British but something of a mystery, I understand,' Mr Wyse interjected. 'We have yet to meet them as we arrived late last night and went straight out for a walk this morning.'

'It's, well, big, isn't it?' Georgie said, turning slightly to look at it in the driveway.

'Too big, I fancy,' Susan said. 'Too big for Italian roads, anyway. Didn't you notice how many dents and scratches it has? My chauffeur is of the opinion that it's had quite a few *contretemps* on the way here.'

'Bounced off a few things, is what he said,' Mr Wyse contributed, while breaking a bread roll in a particularly exquisite manner.

'Then tutted and shook his head, poor man,' Susan continued. 'I think seeing such a fine car in such a sorry state really upset him.'

'I dare say we'll meet them this evening,' Olga ventured.

'Indeed,' Lucia said grimly. 'I am looking forward to it.'

The Wyses both looked rather surprised at the vehemence of Lucia's utterance, and both said 'No!' in a highly gratifying manner when the full extent of the unknown woman's perfidy in attempting to purloin Lucia's accommodation was explained. There was then a rather awkward pause, which Mr Wyse characteristically sought to alleviate.

'How typical of you, Mrs Pillson, to have chosen such an exquisite location for your holidays. Such taste. Such refinement.'

'Well, one had read so much about it,' Lucia replied, 'and I decided at once that this was just the place for us. So glad I managed to persuade Georgie. The very surroundings inspire an almost tangible feeling in one of enduring beauty, don't they? Shelley, you know, and Manzoni.'

She drew a deep, quavering breath as though inhaling copious amounts of enduring beauty and testing its perfume.

'Manzoni?' queried Mr Wyse in some puzzlement.

'*I promessi sposi*,' Lucia intoned gravely, making it sound like a religious incantation.

'But that's set mostly in Milan, surely?' he replied, before he had a chance to consider that questioning the châtelaine of Mallards' literary knowledge was against every rule of polite Tilling society.

'Lake Como,' Lucia averred. 'I remember it distinctly.'

Amelia had no knowledge of the rules of Tilling society, and would probably have had little time for them even had she done so.

'Yes, dear, but only the first chapter,' she said dismissively.

After lunch Lucia interrogated the concierge at some length as to local places of interest and shortly afterwards departed in a motor launch to visit a renowned private garden to which the hotel had been able to obtain access for her. Georgie thought of pleading fatigue, but a stern glance from Olga, coupled with Lucia gazing distractedly into the distance, was sufficient for him to express a wish to accompany her with an almost credible level of enthusiasm.

The Wyses departed in search of a shady spot, Mr Wyse to attempt a two-day-old *Times* crossword, Susan to read the latest Rudolph da Vinci. Rather thrillingly, the author had visited Tilling as the summer tenant of Grebe, but rather less thrillingly had turned out to be a perfectly ordinary middle-aged woman called Susan Leg, who during the course of her stay successfully resisted Lucia's sustained efforts to persuade her to write a book set in Tilling and featuring its lady mayor as the central character.

Olga departed by motor launch in a different direction, in search of some friends who were staying in Cernobbio.

After some gentle hours had passed, during which the Wyses had slumbered decorously, Lucia had passed slowly around the garden of a lakeside villa gravely writing the Latin names of many plants in her notebook, Georgie had waved away many a marauding wasp, and Olga had shared cocktails with a marchese, various Italian film actors and at least two millionaires, the various guests of the hotel began to filter home, rather like social moths being drawn to the candle of the magnificent sunset which was displaying its full glory above the mountains to the west.

Georgie really *was* rather fatigued now, but at Francesco's invitation lay down on the bed while his new-found faithful retainer massaged peppermint oil into his temples, which revived him tremendously. Francesco then handed him into his evening dress, even tying his bow tie for him.

'I hope you approve of your cufflinks, sir,' he said quietly. 'I polished them while you were out.'

'Oh,' replied Georgie, mightily impressed, 'yes, thank you, Francesco.'

'May I get you a glass of sherry, sir, while you wait for Mrs Pillson?'

'No,' said Georgie, feeling truly reckless on his first evening by Lake Como, 'I will have a Negroni.'

'Very good, sir.'

Francesco went to busy himself at the cocktail cabinet while Georgie sat down and admired his cufflinks. Francesco brought the Negroni which Georgie sampled, and pronounced quite excellent. Then he practised crossing his legs for a while in the mirror, and found that if he concentrated really hard he could nonchalantly shoot his cuff at the same time as he straightened the crease on his knee.

Finally, after Georgie had finished his drink and was considering another, Lucia's door opened, and she appeared, a vision in silver-grey silk.

'I say!' he said. 'Don't you look wonderful? Is that new?'

'Thank you, Georgie,' she replied graciously, 'and yes, it is.'

'Do you notice anything different about me?' he asked, and shot one of his cuffs to convey the broadest of hints.

Lucia glanced quickly to check that his toupée was on straight and said distractedly, 'No, dear, shall we go down?'

Crestfallen, Georgie said, 'Oh, yes' in a very sad little voice, and offered her his arm.

'Why, Georgie,' Olga cried as he came downstairs with Lucia, 'I do declare! You've had your cufflinks polished.'

'Oh,' he said, mightily pleased, 'you noticed.'

'No, actually Francesco told me,' she whispered as she leant forward to give him a little peck on the cheek.

Then she took Lucia's arm and said, 'Come on, Lucia, I need a drink,' as the three of them moved into the charming little lounge area, where a piano trio was playing.

'Why there are the Wyses and Amelia,' Lucia said. 'Good evening everyone, good evening ...'

Her voice faded away as she noticed that the Wyses and Amelia were all sitting there wearing very strange expressions. Amelia jerked her head so violently in the general direction of the terrace that her eye-glass fell out and dangled, neglected, on its cord.

'Lucia dear, how lovely to see you,' Elizabeth Mapp-Flint broadcast to the room at large as she swept into the room from the terrace. 'And Mr Georgie *and* Miss Bracely. Goodness, so many lovely people. The Wyses of course we have just met on your way through to the terrace to take the air. Joy unconfined, dear. How wonderful all to be together like this. Why, it'll be just like Tilling, won't it? Except that Benjy-boy and I will be *in situ* as it were, and not have to travel all the way in from draughty old Grebe. Joy unconfined! Joy, joy, joy!'

She clasped her hands before her and beamed widely and fixedly as if to make explicit just how unconfined her joy really was. In doing so she bared her teeth, which Georgie and Mr Wyse, both being of a somewhat nervous disposition, found distinctly alarming. Susan's face showed embarrassment, Olga's deep shock, and Amelia's an involuntary but sincerely felt grimace of distaste.

Lucia was in danger of being rendered speechless. Unfortunately Mapp made her speech of welcome just that odd second too long, allowing Lucia to recover, parry and riposte.

'Elizabeth!' she marvelled, 'and Major Benjy! Good evening, Major.'

'Good evening, dear lady,' he responded warmly. 'And I see we are to be blessed with the company of Miss Bracely. What joy indeed!'

'Why, Elizabeth, what a surprise,' trilled Lucia in wonderment. 'But of course, I should have guessed it was you, when I heard about that business with the rooms.'

A frisson of uneasiness rippled through the company.

'Sorry, dear?' Elizabeth's smile became if anything a trifle more fixed, leaving a lasting impression of gums and neck-wrinkles.

'My suite, dear,' Lucia chided her gently. 'Really, how very naughty of you to try to make them give you my accommodation. But then, how very like you. Fortune favours the bold, don't you always say?'

Mr Wyse, well practised in being an onlooker in such situations, blanched inwardly at the force of Lucia's assault. There was not so much an edge to the conversation as a stiletto blade.

'Sorry, dear, not with you at all,' Elizabeth said briskly, as if in a hurry to get off to the kitchen to bottle some of her celebrated marrow jam, and unprepared to tarry for social trifles. 'Some trouble with your rooms was there? Sorted out now, I trust.'

'Perfectly, *grazie tanto*.' Lucia raised a hand as if acknowledging the forehead-knuckling of a gathering of yokels. 'Everything was, as you say, sorted out. Before we arrived, in fact.'

She paused and gazed levelly at Elizabeth.

'As soon as the hotel realised that the person claiming my rooms had in fact no right to them at all.'

'You speak in riddles, dear one,' Elizabeth protested gaily. 'Why, how very complicated it all sounds.'

'I refer to the Royal Suite, Elizabeth,' Lucia informed her

remorselessly. '*My* suite, which you tried to persuade the hotel to give to you.'

'Why yes, I do remember some confusion or other now that you come to mention it,' Elizabeth conceded graciously. 'So silly! Because the maharajah had booked our rooms, they naturally thought the royal suite was for us, I suppose. Luckily we managed to put them right.'

'The maharajah?' Lucia queried, looking around the room theatrically. 'But where is he, Elizabeth. Is he not coming down to dinner?'

'No, dear,' Elizabeth said equably. 'Not quite.'

'No?' exclaimed Lucia in disbelief. 'Dear me, what a shame, Elizabeth. Why, I thought you had become firm friends. I thought you might be travelling together.'

'Not quite,' Elizabeth repeated, savouring the moment. 'With his son.'

'His son?' Lucia echoed blankly. Elizabeth's lunge and attack had been perfectly timed and elegantly executed.

'Yes, dear, Ramesh. Lovely boy. Lovely manners. Eton and all that, you know.'

At this moment the object of her description came hesitantly into the room, dressed in immaculate evening dress, and stood politely beside her.

'Why there you are, your highness,' she warbled. 'You must allow me to introduce you to my friends.'

'Elizabeth, Elizabeth,' chided Lucia gently. 'One does not introduce royalty to one's friends, one introduces one's friends to royalty. Perhaps you would permit me, your highness?'

So saying, with an elegant curtsey, she took charge of the situation, introducing everyone in turn, her young royal charge protesting repeatedly that everyone must please call him 'Ramesh'.

As he begged everybody to be seated she drew him expertly to the sofa beside her. So busy had she been with her introductions that she could not possibly have been expected to notice that this left everyone grouped around facing inwards in a loose rectangle with her at its centre. Likewise it was surely a coincidence that the rectangle contained two seats too few, thus accidentally excluding the Mapp-Flints altogether, who were left hovering uncertainly on the periphery between two equally distant tables.

Naturally this caused Mr Wyse acute distress and he rose at once to remedy the situation, and there was much fussing around and calling of waiters to move chairs and tables. While all this was going on Elizabeth protested that nobody should trouble themselves on her account, dear Mr Wyse must be seated, dear Susan was in danger of knocking her drink over, and perhaps it was time for dinner anyway, all in an increasingly shrill tone of voice.

'Of course, dear,' Lucia's voice rose above the genteel chaos, 'if you're on your way in to dinner then of course we mustn't detain you. So nice to meet you, Ramesh, perhaps we can talk tomorrow.'

Suddenly everyone was seated again exactly where they had been a few seconds previously and the Mapp-Flint party found itself borne away into the restaurant by a giant bubble of expectation, with Lucia smiling sweetly and waving a wan little hand at the sorrow of their having to part so soon after they had encountered each other.

'Well!' gasped Georgie a few seconds later. 'What do you think of that?'

'Typical Elizabeth, dear,' Lucia enlightened him briskly. 'Dog in a manger. Cannot bear to see anyone have fun, and so drags poor Major Benjy here to try to spoil it for us all.'

'Not *spoil* it, surely?' Susan tried gamely.

'Well, what would you call it?' Georgie retorted, rather shortly. So shortly, in fact, that he apologised immediately.

'Oh, I'm sorry, Mrs Wyse, but really! We go to all the trouble of choosing this wonderful place only to find that Elizabeth Mapp, of all people, will be sharing it with us.'

'A coincidence, perhaps?' Mr Wyse ventured, making a final effort to pour oil on troubled waters. 'I cannot believe that Mrs Mapp-Flint would deliberately set out to spoil anyone's holiday.'

Even as he said it, he realised how lame it sounded. Why, it was he himself who had discovered how only a few years previously Miss Mapp had put the Major literally in fear for his life when she suspected that another woman might be stealing his affections, notwithstanding their 'understanding' – an understanding, it must be admitted, that was distinctly one-sided.

Amelia, who was of a much less charitable disposition, snorted in derision.

'Don't be a fool, Algy, of course she would. Remember that business with the cakes.'

Everyone knew that shortly before Lucia's arrival in Tilling (strange that although of course Georgie had accompanied her everyone still thought of it instinctively as 'Lucia's arrival') Elizabeth Mapp had first surreptitiously turned up the heat in Diva Plaistow's stove in an effort to ruin her entry in a cake competition and, when this first tactic had proved unsuccessful, had then shamelessly sneaked into the church hall to switch the name flags around, thus passing off Diva's efforts as her own and vice versa. Again it had been Mr Wyse who had discovered her deception. Then as now, it had been Mr Wyse who struggled in vain to find some innocent explanation for it.

'I would believe anything of that woman,' Amelia declared firmly, and glared at her brother, daring him to contradict her. In fact he had dared to contradict her only once, when they were children together, and after that very distressing resulting incident involving a pair of fire tongs had wisely never sought to do so again.

'She is a pill and a blister,' Amelia continued, thus revealing for all to hear that her recent reading matter had included P.G. Wodehouse. 'In fact,' she continued, hitting her stride, 'I would go so far as to say that she is a major blot on the landscape.'

She sat back triumphantly as Mr Wyse protested weakly, 'Oh, I say.'

'I am forced to agree with Amelia,' Lucia said, in a voice which likewise brooked no disagreement. 'It is a low trick, and sadly typical of Elizabeth.'

'Then let us rise above it,' Olga broke in. 'Just because she's trying to spoil our holiday, it doesn't mean we have to let her, does it? For example, we know they've just gone into dinner. They're likely to be there for an hour and a half or so. We shall simply wait until they've finished, sitting here having a chat and a few drinks.'

'Oh, Olga,' Georgie said admiringly. 'You *are* wonderful. You always know exactly what to do to make things right again.'

Lucia made one of her characteristic little strangulated noises which, as always, was perfectly modulated, this time conveying similar approbation but with an accompanying modicum of disappointment that nobody had thought to wait for her to make exactly the same suggestion.

'Tomorrow,' Olga went on decisively, 'I'll speak to Giuseppe. He can wait each day until they book for dinner and make sure we don't overlap. That way the worst that can happen to us is that we have to put up with them here in the lounge for a few minutes either before or after dinner. There – what do you say?'

'I say a large dry Martini, please,' Amelia said decisively, 'and a sandwich to keep me going for the next hour or so.'

Chapter 8

B reakfast the next morning was a rather awkward affair, the various parties of extended Tilling society wishing each other a hearty 'Good morning', and then sitting determinedly at separate tables almost perfectly triangulated around the edge of the room. Mr Wyse was unable to attempt the crossword as yesterday's *Times* had not yet arrived by train from Milan. Georgie was feeling somewhat under the weather as the extra wait before dinner had resulted in him imbibing one or two more Negronis than was altogether wise, and he had been obliged to bring his Kruschen salts down to breakfast with him and mix them with hot water.

'Really, Georgie,' Lucia said disapprovingly as she watched him raise the glass to his lips with a slightly trembling hand, 'I hope you are not going to adopt Italian habits while you are here.'

She made the word 'Italian' sound redolent of the worst social excesses: gluttony, sloth, and perhaps even polyamory.

'Certainly not,' he replied primly. 'This is just a precaution. Probably something I ate, I expect.'

Lucia darted a meaningful glance across the room at Major Benjy and then back at her husband. As meaningful glances go, it was eloquent. Major Flint (she still could not get used to thinking of them as the Mapp-Flints) was famous in Tilling for the variety of explanations offered for 'feeling not quite the thing' in the morning, usually taking the form of some recurrent and debilitating tropical ailment picked up while serving the King, God bless him, in foreign climes, at which point he would gravely tug the peak of his cap, gaze briefly into the distance as though reviewing serried ranks of sepoys, and walk off with a slightly unsteady military tread to the little tram that ran down to the golf links.

Olga meantime had been speaking Italian to Giuseppe over the breakfast buffet and now came back to join them.

'All fixed,' she said briefly, setting down a large plate of scrambled egg. 'They've booked for seven-thirty, so Giuseppe will reserve tables for us and the Wyses at nine.'

'Thank you, dear,' Lucia said with feeling. 'Though it pains me that such subterfuge should be necessary.'

'Yes, really!' Georgie agreed. 'Why, even by her standards she's surpassed herself this time. And those lies she told about the rooms! Why, everyone must have realised she wasn't telling the truth, yet she didn't seem at all abashed.'

'It's at this stage,' Olga said, looking up from her scrambled egg and adopting a Scottish accent, 'that the Padre would say, "Charity, Mister Pillson", and then something about having to "Ging awa' to the wee wifey".'

'Indeed, dear,' Lucia concurred abstractedly. She had been about to expound at some length on Elizabeth Mapp-Flint's many deficiencies of character, and did not appreciate the course of the conversation being deflected into the relatively harmless byways of Tilling pastorale.

'Oh, how much I miss Tilling,' Olga went on. 'All those lovely people! I wonder if I should get myself a little cottage there, like I did in dear old Riseholme.'

'Oh, Olga!' Georgie exclaimed. 'What a wonderful idea! Why, it would be simply parfect. I could come round and play for you in the evenings – we haven't tried any Schubert for ages, you know.'

'Not in the evenings, Georgie,' Olga said quickly, with a glance at Lucia. 'In the afternoons perhaps, if Lucia is busy with her committees and things.'

'How thoughtful, dear,' Lucia broke in, gazing sharply at Georgie, 'but quite unnecessary of course. Why, you know that you are welcome as a house guest at Mallards any time, no matter how long you care to stay.'

'Darling Lucia!' Olga replied with heartfelt affection. She put down her knife and fork and was about to reach out and take her hand, but remembered just in time that Lucia had a horror of being touched. 'How kind you are.'

'Now you sound like Quaint Irene again,' Georgie murmured.

Lucia, who never breakfasted on anything more substantial than tea and sliced fruit, was already finished, and planning the day ahead.

'I really must replant the garden on our return, Georgie,' she said decisively as she flicked through the several pages of neat handwriting which detailed her garden visit of the day before. 'Why, I see now how desperately unadventurous we have been.'

'We?' queried Georgie with raised eyebrows, but Lucia swept on regardless.

'Stocks and nasturtiums indeed. Stuff and nonsense, more like. We must be bold, Georgie. We must be adventurous. Above all, we must be Italian.'

'Oh, I thought you had reservations about the Italians,' Georgie said innocently.

'Some Italians, naturally, Georgie,' Lucia replied, looking over her reading glasses rather sternly. 'It would be asking altogether too much to approve of the entire race. Machiavelli, the Borgias, Nero, Caligula. No, no.'

'Yet where it comes to gardening, now, Georgie, that is another matter entirely,' she went on. 'Really, I feel quite inspired. I will have colour, colour, and more colour.'

'Oh well, that does sound nice,' Georgie said complacently. 'I do know what you mean, Lucia. Personally I have always found stocks rather dull.'

'I have fallen in love with rhododendrons,' Lucia announced

dramatically. 'I will create several banks of them behind the lawn. I have quite decided.'

She put her notebook away in her handbag with the air of momentous decisions having been taken. She glanced at her companions and was disappointed to find that they were both occupied in signalling the waiter for more toast, strangely uninterested in her having just changed the horticultural standards of Tilling at a stroke.

'So what is it today then, Lucia?' Olga asked. 'More gardens?'

'Possibly,' Lucia replied, 'but to be honest I'm not sure, dear. We're taking the ten o'clock steamer to Gravedona, and we will see what transpires. I have no settled plans at all. I hear there is a charming little church there, and then I thought we could have a light lunch somewhere, Georgie, before starting back.'

'We?' Georgie asked again, but this time Olga kicked him under the table, so that he said 'Ow' before he had time to stop himself.

'We-ow?' Lucia queried. 'Is that some new Italian expression Francesco has been teaching you, Georgino?'

'Sort of, yes,' he replied testily. 'Well, that sounds fun, doesn't it, Olga?' he continued, shooting the diva a despairing glance.

'Tremendous fun, Georgie,' she nodded, 'a nice little trip on one of those pretty steamers and then a good lunch somewhere. Who could ask for more?'

'Yes, I'm sure you're right,' he said. 'Why don't you come with us?'

Lucia made one of those noises that always sounded like a wounded animal moaning softly in the distance, but which on this occasion seemed to be reluctantly invitational in nature.

'Can't be done, I'm afraid,' Olga responded. 'Susanna has cabled asking me to meet some visiting American millionaire at lunchtime. Anyway, you two must have time to yourselves. You don't want me tagging along all the time.'

'Too thoughtful of you, dear,' Lucia murmured.

*

The church at Gravedona was at least cool, if uninteresting. Even the combination of Lucia and the guidebook were unequal to the task of justifying a visit of more than ten minutes, though Lucia did her best, gazing at what Georgie thought to be quite unremarkable areas of stone or glass and saying 'Ah-hah' intently. He was reminded of a performance of *Zauberflöte* he had once attended at which a very pretentious man from Hampstead (or perhaps it was Hammersmith, he could never quite remember) had insisted on laughing loudly in all the wrong places to try to prove that he spoke German better than anyone else in the audience.

On leaving the church, Georgie looked around desperately for a cafe, only to be swept inexorably onwards by Lucia's regal progress. As he had feared, her new-found interest in gardening then resulted in them wandering around the grounds of another villa in the mounting heat while she peered through her glasses at labels tied to plants and then said, 'Why Georgie, do come here and look at this,' in tones of unbridled enthusiasm, before striding energetically to the next.

'Oh, look,' he said weakly at last, 'another plant.'

Lucia looked at him severely.

'Georgie,' she reproved him, 'where is your pride in your English heritage? Why, gardens are as much in our blood as the sea. Drake, Raleigh, Hawkins, you may say.'

Georgie was about to say, 'But you don't much care for the sea,' but she swept on in growing declamatory mood.

'Capability Brown, *I* say! Why, what would Blenheim Palace be without Capability Brown? Or Hatfield House without John Transcendent?'

Georgie had never even heard of the latter, and so contented himself with saying meekly, 'You're right of course, dear,' which somehow always seemed an appropriate response when conversing with Lucia. He took out his handkerchief and mopped his forehead. At this stage Lucia, who if truth be told was beginning to feel a trifle warm herself, even though she had taken certain liberties with her undergarments, became a model of solicitude.

'Why Georgie,' she said, pouting, a sure sign that she was about to lapse into baby talk, 'is ickle oo hotty?'

'Oh, yes,' Georgie replied gratefully, 'me is poor ickle boy. So hotty-wotty.'

Major Flint, had he been present and overheard discourse of this nature passing between Lucia and Georgie, would at this point have experienced a spontaneous feeling of nausea, and reflected on his relative good fortune. At least with Liz-girl, God bless her, there was never any need to descend to such repellent dulcification.

'Then oo must have cool dwinkie at once,' Lucia continued. 'Naughty Lucia to be so thoughtless. Oo should scold me.'

So, with Georgie trotting gratefully in her wake, her path led finally to two chairs and a table in a shady corner outside a cafe, and two large Italian lemonades, which were truly tart and refreshing in a way which English lemonade never seemed quite to achieve. Presumably because the lemons were so fresh, they agreed.

Refreshing lemonade notwithstanding, it was with a feeling of great lassitude that Georgie finally came safely back to the landing stage at Bellagio that afternoon. Lucia spied Olga sitting in the lounge with her American millionaire and inserted herself swiftly and expertly into the conversation. As she began talking intently of consols, yield curves and growth stocks, Georgie slipped away upstairs, pleading a headache.

'Good afternoon, sir,' Francesco greeted him gravely, 'and how was Gravedona?'

'Oh, all right, I suppose,' said Georgie distractedly. 'well, not very much to see, actually, only lots of plants. Rather too many plants, if you must know, particularly on a warm day.'

'Perhaps a tepid shower might answer, sir?' Francesco asked, to which Georgie replied that a tepid shower might answer very nicely.

'If you were to remain on your balcony this afternoon, sir,' Francesco suggested, 'there would be no need to wear a collar.'

'Oh, yes,' Georgie enthused, 'I see the thing immediately. Perhaps my lilac cravat? And ...' He hesitated. 'Would it be too wicked to wear my silk dressing gown in the middle of the day, do you think?'

'Not at all, sir,' Francesco reassured him. 'Why if you were to sit out here with your paints, it would surely be most appropriate. Very artistic, in fact.'

'It won't be too hot, you don't think?' Georgie asked dubiously.

'Not under the awning, sir. I took the trouble to extend it while you were in the shower.'

'Oh, yes,' Georgie fretted, 'but do I feel in the mood for painting, I wonder? I do still have a very tarsome feeling. What is it, I wonder? Not exactly tiredness because I don't feel sleepy, but ...'

'Lassitude perhaps, sir?' Francesco prompted discreetly.

'Why, yes, the very word,' Georgie marvelled. (He actually said 'ward', but Francesco seemed instinctively to have mastered this particular form of Tilling patois and understood immediately what he meant.)

'And they don't market anything for lassitude, do they?' he mused gloomily.

'On the contrary, sir,' Francesco replied, taking out a cigarette case from his jacket pocket. 'Perhaps you might care to try a Turkish cigarette? I have them made up to my own recipe in Beirut. They have various ingredients which exercise a very calming effect.'

He lit one for Georgie, who inhaled experimentally and then, with an appreciative murmur, more deeply.

'How very unusual,' he commented. 'What is that lovely smell? Jasmine, perhaps, or honeysuckle?'

'You will understand, sir,' Francesco said apologetically, 'that I would prefer not to reveal the precise combination of ingredients, as it is a secret of my own invention, but you are correct in identifying various floral extracts.'

While Georgie sat in his armchair and smoked his cigarette, Francesco deftly set up a chair and easel on the balcony and laid

Georgie's painting materials readily to hand. Georgie, feeling suddenly much better, wandered out and surveyed the lake in a rather lordly fashion, almost as though he owned it.

'You know,' he said decisively, 'I *do* feel like painting after all, Francesco. What wonderful cigarettes those are – why, I feel quite relaxed all of a sudden.'

'Then perhaps I could leave you another, sir, for later? I am told they are a wonderful aid to the concentration.'

Francesco left a bottle of mineral water and a glass within reach, laid another of the cigarettes alongside a box of matches, and slipped discreetly away. Georgie, feeling ready to commence reducing Lake Como to watercolour on grain torchon, contemplatively smoked the second cigarette as well, but at some point while he was still to reach for his brush his lassitude became overwhelming and the next thing of which he was aware was Lucia coming out on to the balcony some considerable time later.

'Why Georgie, there you are,' she said. 'Have you been painting?'

'No, sleeping, I'm afraid,' Georgie said drowsily, coming to with an effort. He became aware that he was very thirsty and, reaching for the glass, filled it, and drank greedily.

Lucia sat down beside him and said, 'I really must tell you about the most fascinating discussion I've been having –' but broke off abruptly. 'Why, Georgie, what on earth are you talking about? You *have* been painting – look!'

Georgie stared at the paper uncomprehendingly.

'But I could have sworn I'd been asleep,' he protested feebly. 'The last thing I remember is smoking a cigarette while Francesco went back inside ...'

Lucia was staring intently at the picture.

'This is very unlike your usual style, *caro mio*,' she opined somewhat uncertainly.

Georgie too was having problems coming to terms with what he saw.

'Was the water really that violent purple colour?' Lucia asked.

'Why no, I don't think so,' he faltered. 'I'm sure it must have been pretty much as it is now.'

There was a pause while Lucia examined something.

'And what is this, pray?' she asked rather coldly.

'It looks like some kind of sea-monster,' Georgie said nervously.

'I was referring to whoever, or whatever it is that is wrestling with the sea-monster,' she pressed him, still more coldly.

'Well, I suppose it must be Neptune,' he admitted reluctantly. 'See, look at those huge muscles and – oh!'

'"Oh", indeed,' Lucia said briskly, turning the paper over. 'Too much shellfish at luncheon perhaps, Georgie. I have heard that it can do strange things to Englishmen who are unused to the heat of an Italian summer.'

'Yes, I suppose it must have been that,' Georgie said fixedly, staring out at the lake. 'I really must be more careful with my diet. More Kruschen salts, perhaps.'

Perhaps fortunately Francesco looked out through the French windows at that point and said, 'Good evening, sir, good evening, madam. I wonder if I could interest you both in a drink while you change for dinner?'

'Oh, what a good idea,' Georgie said with relief. 'Perhaps a Negroni?' He glanced enquiringly at Lucia.

'Prosecco for both of us please, Francesco,' she said authoritatively. 'Mr Pillson has decided to be more careful with his diet. It seems that Negronis may have an unfortunate effect upon him.'

'I am indeed sorry to hear that, madam,' Francesco said smoothly. 'Allow me to order a bottle of prosecco immediately. There is one in the cellar that I can particularly recommend.'

By the time the ice bucket arrived with its inviting foil-covered contents, Lucia had already departed to begin her evening toilet, but a discreet knock on the door summoned her maid, who carried in a glass full of precious foaming liquid. Georgie, for his part, was enjoying a luxurious bath. He was still feeling most relaxed, but understandably puzzled by the events of the last few hours.

'Francesco,' he enquired, as he emerged into his bedroom in his underwear, 'can you paint at all?'

'Not to save my life, sir, as I believe you say in England,' his valet answered with regret.

'So, you didn't paint anything on the balcony this afternoon? While I was asleep, I mean?'

'Why no, sir, of course not,' Francesco said, smiling at Georgie. 'On the contrary, I took the liberty of slipping away to take coffee with Frau Zirchner's maid. A charming girl, though rather short of conversation.'

'So I painted that ... scene?' Georgie enquired, still nonplussed.

'I did not see the painting in question, sir, so cannot answer for its authenticity,' Francesco replied cautiously, 'but when I looked on to the balcony a couple of times to see if you desired anything, I did indeed notice you painting.'

'Oh,' said Georgie.

'If I may say so,' Francesco ventured, 'you appeared very happy, sir. Perhaps you should paint more often while you are here.'

'Oh,' Georgie said again.

While this conversation had been going on, Francesco had been helping Georgie into his evening clothes. He now gave a discreet cough.

'I did happen to mix a Negroni, sir, almost by accident, you might say. If you would care for it, it is concealed inside your hatbox.'

'Oh, I say,' said Georgie, much taken with the idea, and then, it sparking an obvious connection in his mind, 'you don't happen to know Major Flint, do you?'

'I believe there is a gentleman staying at the hotel by that name, sir, the gentleman with the Bugatti Royale unless I am mistaken. A gentleman with a military background, I believe, whose wife does not understand him.'

'Really?'

'So I understand from Frau Zirchner's maid, sir,' Francesco said gravely.

'Frau Zirchner? Is she that rather angry-looking Swiss lady who is travelling with a companion? The young English lady?'

'Indeed, sir, the young English lady who has such a very fine figure, though it is not of course my place to notice such things.'

'And the Major told Frau Zirchner's maid that his wife didn't understand him?' Georgie asked in some bewilderment. What on earth had Major Benjy been doing talking to someone's maid, he wondered.

'No, sir, I understand he told the young lady, Miss Flowers, after dinner last night. Frau Zirchner happened to overhear, and her maid witnessed her mistress warning the young lady – in no uncertain terms, I understand – not to have anything more to do with the Major.'

'Oh,' said Georgie again. A knock at the door signalled that Lucia was now waiting in the living room, and he drained his Negroni. Francesco opened the door with a bow and Georgie swept out on a cloud of gin, sweet vermouth, bitters and gardenia toilet water to join his wife.

'Why, how wonderful you look, Lucia,' he greeted her, as indeed she did. This was yet another new outfit, but this time in a fetching kingfisher blue.

'*Grazie tanto, caro mio,*' she said graciously with a little curtsey, and took his arm.

As they went downstairs she had an air of being distracted, and finally she asked him something suspiciously casually.

'Georgie,' she proffered off-handedly, 'had it by any chance struck you that your Neptune's face bore an uncanny resemblance to Francesco?'

'No,' he said at once, very determinedly. 'It hadn't struck me at all.'

Chapter 9

No sooner had Georgie and Lucia entered the lounge than they were swept into a group comprising the Wyses, Olga and Mr Brabazon Lodge, the American millionaire with whom Lucia had already had such an interesting conversation that afternoon, and was clearly contemplating many more.

'Glad to meet you again, Pillson,' Brabazon greeted him heartily with a crushing handshake which caused poor Georgie to wince involuntarily. 'What are you in?'

'Evening dress, naturally,' Georgie gasped, wringing his hand, and confused by the question, 'though we sometimes call it "hitum", you know.'

Lucia gave a gushing laugh.

'Mr Lodge is referring to investments, dear,' she clarified.

'Oh, gilts, actually,' Georgie said uneasily. He could not help but feel there was something not quite right about discussing one's finances in public. As his gaze darted around he caught sight of the Wyses, who clearly shared such views, looking distinctly uncomfortable.

Mr Lodge's lip curled in much the same manner that it might be imagined it would if Georgie had just told him that he was in the habit of eating two or three babies every evening grilled with lemon juice, but before he could say anything Mr Wyse cut in.

'Dear lady,' he cried, with a bow to Lucia, 'we are all waiting to hear of your latest garden inspection. What new ideas do you have in store for us when we visit Mallards next summer?'

How like Mr Wyse, Georgie thought, to be able to detect potential embarrassment and deflect it so deftly almost in the same instant. As he looked at him in admiration, Mr Wyse caught his glance and for once, very uncharacteristically, gave a subtle, almost furtive nod of the head in acknowledgement. Really, Georgie thought, Italy was working its magic on everyone.

'Little new today, I fear,' Lucia replied, taking her notebook from her handbag, 'though,' – her pencil paused judiciously as it ran down the page – 'there was a rather nice little chionodoxa that might do very well in the rockery.'

'But we don't have a rockery,' Georgie interjected unhelpfully.

Lucia looked at him in much the same way that Julius Caesar might have reacted to the Thirteenth Legion responding to his order to cross the Rubicon by objecting that they might get their sandals wet.

'A relevant consideration, I grant you, Georgie,' she said, fixing him with a steady gaze while holding her pencil in the same position on the page, 'but hardly an important one.'

Olga made a gurgling noise and then, as everyone looked at her, recovered herself.

'Really, Georgie,' she chided him, 'you really must learn to stop concerning yourself with trivial practicalities. Lucia is clearly being visionary.'

'Quite, dear, the big picture,' Lucia agreed, 'the broad sweep ...' she stopped and gazed dreamily upwards into the distance. After a few seconds during which everyone unconsciously held their breath, she gave a little sigh and cast her gaze downwards again as if suddenly becoming aware of the mere mortals around her who were not privileged to share her Olympian heights, nor the lofty vision which they afforded.

'... the grand design,' she concluded, bestowing upon the word 'design' a vibrancy which made it sound positively thrilling.

Brabazon Lodge, clearly deeply moved, took a pull at his whisky before venturing an opinion, but when he did so it became distressingly evident that he may not have been following Lucia's visionary process as closely as she might have hoped.

'Gilts are all very well for widows and orphans,' he said contemptuously, 'but from what I can see from this chair, Mr Pillson, you are neither a widow nor an orphan.'

It was a slightly jarring moment, and Olga could have sworn that Mr Wyse gave a little wince, although of course such a thing was altogether impossible. However, even Mr Wyse's sensibilities were being tested to the utmost. It was as if the runaway train which he had deftly diverted on to an uphill branch line to spend itself noisily but harmlessly until it ran out of steam, had been suddenly picked up by some malevolent Gargantua and placed firmly back on its original course, heading towards a level crossing crowded with children on a school outing.

'Oh,' said Georgie, at a loss to know how to respond, or even to know whether he was expected to respond or not, 'well, I suppose I am an orphan, actually. Both my parents are dead, you know.'

There was another near-wince from Mr Wyse, who gathered himself to interject some fresh social banality, but Brabazon Lodge pressed on mercilessly.

'Are you a widow or an orphan, sir? That is the question I wish to address to you. Are you a child, that you need protection?'

'Well,' said Georgie, faltering again. He had been Tilling's most dashing young man for some years now, and Riseholme's most dashing young man for many more years before that, but claims to childhood would clearly be going too far. Perhaps Mr Lodge meant the question rhetorically?

Fortunately it appeared that this might indeed be the case, for his interrogator now let him off the hook by answering his own question.

'No!' he exclaimed, jutting his jaw aggressively. 'You are neither a widow nor an orphan, sir. Neither a simpleton nor an old woman either, I'll be bound.'

There was an uneasy silence as everyone stared at him, waiting to hear what would come next.

'So why, sir,' he asked, having first drained his whisky, 'invest like an old woman?'

He gazed triumphantly around the group, clearly conscious of having scored some sort of disputative bull's-eye. Lucia made one of her indeterminate noises that sounded to Georgie suspiciously as if she was about to add her condemnation of her husband to elderly spinsterhood to that of Brabazon Lodge, and he glared at her directly. The noise tailed off, modulated into a minor key, slipped up a couple of tones, and then became more confidently meaningful as Giuseppe approached with some menus, as if his imminent arrival was really what she had been trying to intimate to the company all along.

He gazed mournfully at them.

'*Signori, signore*, a thousand pardons, but I am afraid we have no tables for seven available at the moment. One for four, which we can stretch to five, yes, and one for two, but in different places so we cannot push them together.'

'Oh, indeed,' Lucia commented rather disagreeably.

'If you would care to wait, *signora*,' Giuseppe suggested, 'perhaps in thirty or forty minutes it may be possible, but not at the moment.'

He glanced quizzically around the group.

'Well, I'm jolly well not going to wait,' Olga said decisively, in a tone that brooked no argument. 'I'm starving. Don't worry, Giuseppe, two tables will be fine. Put me with Mr Lodge.'

There was a collective gasp, quickly stifled, and everyone tried not to catch anyone else's eye. This was gallantry well over and above the call of duty which Olga was exhibiting, the sort of blind courage which won VCs, though often posthumously.

'No, dear, no need,' Lucia broke in, beaming at her and the Wyses. 'If dear Mr and Mrs Wyse will forgo their privacy tonight, I would welcome an opportunity to continue my conversation with Mr Lodge. Georgie, you can take Olga in and look after her, can't you, *caro mio*?'

Georgie murmured that indeed he could.

'Then that's settled!' Lucia exclaimed, with an air of finality.

Giuseppe inclined his head respectfully.

'It shall be exactly as you wish, *signora*. Please to give me just a few minutes. The people who have your table for four at the moment are just leaving, but we need to re-lay it for you.'

He vanished backwards, instantly blending seamlessly into the surroundings with that knack which all the great head waiters seem to possess. One moment there they are recommending the fish of the day, the next they have disappeared as if through an invisible trap-door.

As they began to peruse their menus, the Mapp-Flint party appeared, first Mapp, beetling along in the van, then Major Benjy as the main body, waving a cigar expansively, then Ramesh acting as rearguard, and expertly but unobtrusively preventing the Major from blundering into the dessert trolley.

'Ah,' said the Major as the gentlemen stood, 'here you all are.'

'Elizabeth, dear,' Lucia trilled, 'so sorry to miss you.'

'Indeed,' Elizabeth replied with a bright, fixed smile. 'I assumed we would all be eating at seven-thirty as usual. I hadn't realised you were going to adopt such Italian customs as dining late. Really, Lucia, I do think you might have told us.'

'A whim,' Lucia responded, waving a hand wanly as if she had been much too occupied throughout the day to give so trivial a matter as dinner any thought whatever. 'Perhaps it is the influence of the surroundings, but I find myself gently tugged in different directions all day as if by the shifting currents of the lake.'

Elizabeth took a few moments to consider this image. She briefly imagined Lucia hopelessly out of her depth and drifting downwards towards the bottom, but it was no good, she was unable to do the thought proper justice with its object standing in front of her and very clearly in no danger whatever of an imminent lonely death by drowning. Still, she tidily stored the scenario away to comfort herself with it on another occasion.

She suddenly realised that there was a stranger in their midst and smiled unctuously, saying, 'I don't believe we've met,' with a meaningful glance at Mr Wyse.

'I'm so sorry, dear lady, where are my manners?' that worthy cried in genuine distress. 'Mrs Elizabeth Mapp-Flint and Major Mapp-Flint, Mr Brabazon Lodge.'

'From America,' he added significantly, with a bow westwards.

'Glad to meet you, old man,' the Major said effusively. 'This is our young companion, Ramesh. Looking after him for his pater, don't you know.'

'How do you do, sir,' Ramesh said politely.

'How was your dinner?' Olga enquired.

'Quite adequate, I suppose,' Elizabeth said dubiously. 'For abroad, anyway.'

'Mrs Flint is a jolly excellent cook herself, so my father tells me,' Ramesh cut in smoothly, 'so it is inevitable that any meal should suffer by comparison when judged by her own high standards.'

Elizabeth Mapp-Flint's not inconsiderable bosom began to swell spontaneously with pride at these words – royalty could always be relied upon to find the *mot juste* – but was still only half-swollen when it was cruelly deflated by Lucia's next comment.

'Oh, indeed!' she agreed emphatically. 'Why, her jams are the talk of East Sussex.'

Elizabeth gasped in outrage. She deeply resented accusations that a jar of her jam (greengage, she insisted: marrow, Diva Plaistow averred contemptuously) had once given the Padre food poisoning. Surely anyone with an ounce of sense could see that they were vile lies spread by Quaint Irene. Why, if any further proof were required, Irene had herself once claimed to have mistaken a pot of Mapp's famous marmalade for chutney, clearly a laughable contention.

'Tell you what,' the Major said to nobody in particular, brushing aside domestic dramas of suspect preserves and midnight stomach-pumping, 'if you get a chance do try the Amarone – it's superb.'

'Would you agree, Mrs Mapp-Flint?' Amelia asked.

'I wouldn't know, Contessa,' came the response, with a dark look at the Major. 'I didn't have any.'

'Fair's fair, old girl,' he protested. 'You were having fish, so you stuck to the white.'

'Do you mean, sir,' Brabazon Lodge enquired slowly, 'that you have just drunk an entire bottle of Amarone unassisted?'

'Not at all, old man,' the Major replied, 'I had the assistance of a bottle of Barolo. Jolly good it was, too.'

This news was greeted with stunned silence, tempered by a grudging admiration that the Major was still both upright and coherent. It was broken by Mr Wyse.

'Shall we?' he enquired, with an apologetic bow to Elizabeth.

Amid a general murmur of acquiescence and hunger the seven who had not yet dined moved away in search of their respective tables.

'Jolly decent of Lucia, I must say,' Olga opined as Georgie held her chair for her, 'to take care of that blister Lodge. My heart positively quailed at the thought of having to sit through a whole dinner alone with him.'

Georgie strongly suspected that Lucia, who did not number altruism among her many sterling qualities, merely wished to get some tips from the blister Lodge on how to make even more money, but the presence of the Wyses prevented him from saying so.

'You know, something quite remarkable happened earlier,' he said instead. 'I fell asleep on the balcony this afternoon, or at least I thought I did. It transpires that I wasn't really asleep after all, and that I'd painted a picture without realising I'd done so.'

Mr Wyse, who was a great devotee of Conan Doyle, looked interested.

'How very intriguing,' he commented.

'Yes, isn't it?' Georgie said. 'The most remarkable part of it all, though, is that when I looked at the picture, well, Lucia looked at it really, it wasn't at all in my usual style. In fact, it looked as though it had been painted by someone else entirely.'

'Perhaps it had?' Amelia enquired in a matter-of-fact manner.

'Yes, I thought of that too,' Georgie conceded, 'but the only other person there was Francesco and he can't paint – I asked him.'

'Fascinating!' Mr Wyse commented with admiration. 'Why, Mr Pillson, you have given us a conundrum to solve, and no mistake.'

'Now, now, Algernon,' said Susan, who knew only too well that once her husband began to wrestle with a puzzle, whether acrostic or otherwise, he could rapidly become lost to the world, 'let's concentrate on the menu instead, shall we?'

At the other table Lucia and Brabazon Lodge were locked in financial discussion. Mr Lodge had heard about, and marvelled at, Lucia's daring foray into Siriami gold, and her subsequent experiments, largely successful, with a number of the London Stock Exchange's lesser-known growth stocks.

'Mrs Pillson,' he said judiciously after a while, 'I do declare you are by far the most sophisticated and knowledgeable amateur investor it has been my pleasure to meet.'

While Lucia was naturally flattered by such sentiments, though dear Mr Lodge was of course doing no more than stating the obvious, she was nonetheless slightly discomfited by one word, and said so.

'Amateur?' she queried.

He waved his hand rather more dramatically than Lucia had done earlier, but conveying a similar message of faint apology.

'I intend no disrespect,' he stated. 'What you have achieved has been truly remarkable. But have you never felt that there is somehow another level of investing waiting just out of reach, out of sight?'

'A sort of "next step", do you mean?' Lucia asked thoughtfully.

'If you like, yes.'

'As a matter of fact,' Lucia said, gazing at him wonderingly, 'I have. How clever of you to realise that, Mr Lodge.'

He shrugged modestly.

'In fact I thought I recognised in you something of myself fifteen or twenty years ago, Mrs Pillson. Fortunately I met someone who was prepared to show me what I needed to do to take that next step.'

Lucia crumbled her bread unheedingly, her gaze fixed firmly upon Mr Lodge.

'Perhaps ... ,' she began hesitantly.

'Yes?'

'Perhaps you might be prepared to be that person for me, Mr Lodge. A sort of adept, if you will, who shows the poor acolyte the way to wisdom.'

Lucia's eyes were fixed upon his own so intently, and had become suddenly so soft and dewy, that Mr Lodge could hardly now be expected to demur. He did not.

'I would be honoured and delighted,' he declared, 'but only if you are truly prepared to go all the way.'

'Oh, I am, I am,' Lucia cried earnestly. 'My dear Mr Lodge, I place myself entirely in your hands. Only show me what to do, and I shall endeavour to satisfy your expectations completely. Why, I realise suddenly that I have been looking for someone like you for a long time now. My efforts recently have left me strangely unfulfilled.'

Mr Lodge nodded sagely and understandingly, while the waiter who was pouring their Pinot Grigio made a mental note to tell his colleagues after dinner that the rich English lady who had arrived with Miss Bracely was not after all nearly as straight-laced as she appeared.

As the larger group had disappeared into the dining room, Elizabeth was left seething in the lounge. She sat down heavily on the sofa which the Wyses had just vacated and said, 'Well, what do you think of *that*?'

'Think of what, old girl?' the Major enquired, sitting down beside her.

'Lady Bountiful, of course. A whim, indeed! She deliberately changed the time when she was planning to dine, yes, and forced poor Susan and Mr Wyse to go hungry as well, just so she didn't have to pass the time of day with us.'

'Be fair, Liz,' Major Benjy replied. 'I was damn hungry. If they want to wait until some ridiculous continental time to have dinner, let them, say I. Their loss, not ours.'

This did not serve to mollify his wife at all. On the contrary, she seemed hardly even to notice that the Major had said anything at all. Appearances in this case would not have been deceptive. She was in fact lost in thought. Suddenly the frown cleared from her face.

'I've got it!' she exclaimed. 'We'll wait.'

'Wait for what?' asked the Major, uncomprehending.

'Oh, wait here of course. Do pay attention, Benjy. Lulu has set out deliberately to avoid us. She believes she has succeeded. Very well, let her, but when she finishes dinner and comes in here for her coffee she will find us comfortably ensconced and even she won't have the gall to ignore us. She will simply *have* to come and sit with us. Mr Wyse will insist.'

'Perhaps nonetheless, dear lady, I may be excused?' Ramesh asked. 'I shall just take a short walk outside and then retire for the night, if you have no objection.'

'No objection at all, Ramesh. Off you go by all means.'

She beamed contentedly and sat back. Major Benjy beamed contentedly and sat up straight, for he had just spotted Frau Zirchner and Miss Flowers at another table.

'Whatever you say, old girl,' he concurred. 'Sure you're right, as usual.'

'Of course I'm right,' Elizabeth snapped.

'Well,' the Major said, 'since we're going to be here awhile, why don't we make ourselves comfortable? I'm sure they must have a pretty decent brandy tucked away somewhere behind the bar. I'll just go and ask them.'

He stood up and moved towards the door. He realised of course that this would take him past Frau Zirchner's table, and was just planning his next move when providence came to his aid. Having returned from a drinks break, the band struck up a tune.

'Good evening, ladies, good evening,' he hailed them as he drew level. 'Frau Zirchner ma'am, perhaps you would care to dance?'

Frau Zirchner, as he had hoped and planned, looked even more disagreeable than usual and begged to be excused. A touch of indigestion, she explained.

'Oh, what a shame,' replied the Major sympathetically. 'Then perhaps you, Miss Flowers?'

Before she had a chance to reply he took her hand in what he thought was an unmistakeably gallant manner and urged her gently towards the dance floor. To Frau Zirchner it looked much more as if he had roughly dragged her companion bodily from her chair, and she opened her mouth to protest against this outrage, but marginally too late. With all eyes upon them, since they were the only couple who had taken the floor, Major Benjy led Miss Flowers into a waltz of almost exaggerated perfection, his frame bent backwards in classic style and his gaze fixed a trifle foggily over her right shoulder. He couldn't help noticing that Liz-girl was looking a little pained away in the distance. Perhaps she too was suffering from a touch of indigestion.

As the evening wound towards its later stages, Mr Wyse could not help but keep returning to the puzzle of Georgie's painting, though Susan kept changing the subject with increasing desperation. Ramesh was rather dashingly buying a drink for an Italian girl two years his senior (he had lied convincingly about his age) at a bar at the other end of town. Mr Lodge was asking Lucia if she had ever heard of a 'control premium'. Miss Flowers was confiding to Major Benjy that she much appreciated his efforts to relieve her of Frau Zirchner's company. Elizabeth and Frau Zirchner were independently radiating discontentment.

As the second dinner sitting drew to a close several of these narrative threads became abruptly tangled together, as the later diners returned to the lounge to find the earlier diners still in occupation.

Frau Zirchner had by this time retired rather pointedly for the evening, and Miss Flowers, having promised to follow shortly, had shamelessly broken her word by remaining downstairs to dance with the Major (she would claim rather lamely the next morning that she had not been wearing her watch and had lost track of the time).

As expected, Mr Wyse instantly insisted that everyone should sit together and Lucia, murmuring 'Delightful' and 'How wonderful that you stayed, dear', could only rally round and show willing. Elizabeth could have hugged herself that her plans had worked out so well.

Only one thing was not as she would have liked it to be. She had envisaged Lucia and the others emerging from the dining room to find her and the Major in rapt domestic conversation, from which they could have been aroused with starts of surprise, having noticed neither the new arrivals nor that so much time had elapsed since they began their tête-à-tête. This effect had been rendered impossible to achieve by Major Benjy's insistence on dancing with that scrawny girl who clearly needed to be told discreetly that her skirt was far too short for polite society.

So instead Elizabeth chose to gaze at the pair in rapt attention, her fingers fixed to her chin, a delighted smile playing around her lips (an effect which Mr Wyse found vaguely disturbing without quite knowing why), and beating time to the music distractedly with her other hand as she crooned the tune to herself.

This *tableau vivant*, though neatly contrived and deftly executed, was not however proof against that dreadful Lulu's snide carping.

'Not dancing with your husband, Elizabeth?' she marvelled.

'No dear,' Elizabeth replied, beaming if anything more beatifically than ever.

'Oh, but how very understanding of you to allow him to dance with someone else,' Georgie slipped in mischievously.

'On the contrary, dear Mr Georgie, I positively encouraged it,' Elizabeth enlightened him.

'Really?' Lucia queried, with arched eyebrows. 'Why, how very modern of you, Elizabeth. If I had such a *manly* husband as the Major, I'm sure I wouldn't let him out of my sight.'

'Well, he isn't out of sight,' Mr Wyse pointed out in a very matter-of-fact manner. 'He's just on the other side of the room.'

'Why yes, of course, so he is,' Georgie concurred. He crossed his legs and shot out his cuffs perfectly at the same time, and was disappointed that nobody appeared to notice.

Both Mapp and Lucia could feel the energy beginning to drain away from the badinage. There is a tide in the affairs of a really disagreeable exchange which, if taken at the flood, leads on to that most gratifying of conclusions: the realisation that one has caused genuine pain and unhappiness to another. This conversation, though, was definitely on the ebb, and in another second or two the underlying menace would have drained completely away. They both knew that this would never do, but it was Elizabeth who found a way to recharge the pregnant pause with a fresh injection of sincerity.

'It's just that he is such a wonderful dancer,' she confessed coyly, 'and I feel that I let him down when I partner him myself. That's why, Mr Georgie, I encourage him to dance with other women. Why should only I have a chance to experience dancing with dear Benjy-boy?'

She cupped her chin in both hands now and leant forward on the table, which gave an ominous lurch. The assembled company, totally vanquished, fell silent. It was a time now to fall silent triumphantly, and savour the taste of a tactical success. Instead, Elizabeth decided to go for that rarest of military phenomena, a truly decisive victory, and in doing so fatally over-reached herself.

'Doesn't he waltz divinely?' she breathed girlishly.

Lucia cupped her chin in both hands and gazed at Major Benjy with equal rapture.

'Yes indeed,' she breathed girlishly, 'but what a shame the band is playing a foxtrot.'

Chapter 10

The next morning at breakfast Olga had another chat with Giuseppe in Italian, confident that even if she was overheard nobody would understand what she was saying. She came back to the table grinning broadly.

'They've booked for the second sitting this time,' she informed them gleefully, 'so I've booked us all in for the first. Golly, isn't this exciting? It quite reminds me of the old times in Riseholme. Such intrigue! Such cunning schemes!'

Since Olga and Lucia had frequently been ranged on opposite sides of whatever cunning scheme was currently being hatched in Riseholme, Lucia contented herself with saying, 'Yes, isn't it?'

In truth the choosing of sides had been Lucia's doing, not Olga's. Lucia had attempted to 'run' Olga whereas Olga had no intention of being 'run', and had anyway been introduced to Riseholme as Georgie's friend, not Lucia's. Despite previous mistakes (not that they were ever acknowledged as such) by Lucia in attempting to run people, not least an Indian guru whom she had stolen from Daisy Quantock, Lucia had not learned her lesson, and it was only slowly, and thanks to Olga's unremitting good humour, that a *modus vivendi* had been arrived at over the years. That Olga sang Wagner Lucia came finally to accept with gracious magnanimity, since it could at least be excused, if not actually forgiven, on the ground that it was a requirement of Olga's professional career. That Olga possessed a gramophone, gave hugely successful impromptu parties, and could actually speak Italian, were glaring shortcomings less easily overlooked.

Incidentally, Lucia's Indian spiritual guide had turned out to be a runaway alcoholic curry chef, who had absconded from Riseholme one night in fear of discovery from Georgie's sisters (they being habituées of the Indian restaurant in question), taking Georgie's bibelots and a considerable sum in cash with him. Undaunted, Lucia had given it out that he had been called away by his astral masters to fresh spiritual pastures, having now set his Riseholme followers' feet surely upon the way to enlightenment.

Georgie, however, was more forthcoming.

'Yes, isn't it just? Oh, Lucia, how it all takes me back!'

'Indeed, Georgino,' Lucia replied with a noticeable lack of interest, 'but how long ago it all seems.'

She gazed dreamily into the distance, an unmistakable sign that the conversation had come to an end and that the subject might now be changed.

'But what happens tomorrow, I wonder?' Olga mused. 'Will they dine early or late? Bluff or double bluff? It's rather like that old game of stone, scissors and paper, isn't it? What fun!'

'I rather think I know what dear Elizabeth will do tomorrow,' Lucia said suddenly, with that quick little smile that Georgie loved so much.

'Do tell!' he urged her.

'I don't think I will,' she said archly. 'But let's just say I have a contingency plan.'

She giggled to herself, and Georgie said, 'Oh, aren't you wonderful?' in a very gratifying fashion, so gratifying in fact that, just for a fleeting moment, she almost felt guilty that she didn't actually have a contingency plan at all. Thankfully Olga was hungrily attacking some poached eggs, or she might have ruined everything by asking what it was.

'You know, that Mr Lodge is a fascinating companion,' Lucia said suddenly, making clear what had really been on her mind all along.

'It takes meeting someone like that to make you realise how small your own ambitions have been.'

Knowing that nobody could ever accuse Lucia of harbouring small ambitions, Georgie looked startled. Olga, with a mouth full of poached egg, looked startled. Had Mr Wyse been present, perhaps even he might have looked startled, though guiltily and momentarily.

'Really?' said Georgie in genuine surprise. 'Surely not.'

'Yes, Georgie, yes,' Lucia contradicted him decisively. 'My views have been narrow and un-enterprising. I have been content with so little, when I could have been encompassing the world. I must resolve to be bolder in future.'

'Bolder? How?' asked Georgie, looking puzzled. 'Look at Siriami – that was bold, surely?'

'Oh, Georgie, really!' Lucia said with a fond smile. 'Siriami was nothing. Why, how much of my fortune did I hazard? The merest, smallest part of it. No, a real investor must be prepared to risk everything on one throw.'

'Gambler, more like,' Georgie said sourly. 'I do wish you would put all this speculation out of your head, Lucia. What would happen if you *did* risk everything on one throw, and lost it? Where would you be then? I certainly don't think you'd like to live on my money, in a little cottage with just Foljambe to look after us.'

'I have no intention of losing it all, *caro mio*,' Lucia said sharply. 'Of course I would weigh all the risks before investing.'

'But still, Lucia,' Olga protested feebly, 'I know it's none of my business, but why would you want to risk losing everything, all in one go?'

Lucia was silent for a moment, as though asking herself the same question and finding herself surprised that she did not know the answer.

'I think it is a question of knowing that I can go further,' she said finally. 'Of being able to hold my head up in the company of men like Brabazon Lodge. Anyway, I think I have taken my present style of investing as far as I can. I need a further challenge.'

'But what do you have in mind, Lucia?' Georgie asked. 'You're surely not planning on going into the casino and putting everything on red?'

'Of course not,' Lucia replied sharply. 'What I have in mind is a soundly researched investment scheme, proposed by Mr Lodge himself, but it represents a sea change in how I act as an investor. You see, dear ones, instead of investing in lots of different companies, I am going to sell all my holdings, all of them I say, and invest in just one.'

'But ...' Georgie gasped. He groped for the word he had heard so often when Lucia had been lecturing either him or someone else on investment, and finally found it.

'But what about *diversification*?' he challenged her. 'Why, you're always saying how important it is, that it takes away the risk of investing in any one single company.'

'Yes, that's what I thought,' she admitted, 'but you see I was wrong. Or, at least, only half right. Yes, of course it's true that if you concentrate your entire portfolio in one company it is much riskier, but I was overlooking the control premium.'

Georgie and Olga looked at her blankly.

'The control premium,' she repeated, her eyes shining. 'Mr Lodge explained it to me, and suddenly everything fell into place. You see, if you actually own all the shares in a company, or at least most of them, then you control it. The directors have to do what you say. Effectively you run the company, not them. So in fact there is no risk at all because you can stop them doing anything rash or imprudent.'

'But don't public companies cost rather a lot?' Georgie asked. 'Surely you couldn't buy a whole company, Lucia? Not even you.'

'Not alone I couldn't, no,' she confided with the air of a magician just about to reach the *dénouement* of a card trick, 'but if my money was mixed together with lots of other people's, then yes. You see, Mr Lodge is setting up a limited partnership in America to buy a bank, and he's invited me to participate. The minimum subscription is half a million dollars, and by coincidence that's almost exactly what I've got.'

'But why would you want to own a bank, Lucia?' Olga asked innocently. 'Or, rather, to be a very small part-owner of a bank?'

'Mr Lodge says there is a boom in asset prices going on in America of unprecedented proportions,' Lucia enlightened her, ignoring the sting in the tail of Olga's question. 'He says the best way to get into it is to buy control of a bank, then borrow money in the inter-bank market, and then lend it out to property companies to buy office blocks in Manhattan.'

'But then don't you just end up with the interest on some loans?' Olga queried.

'No, Olga dear, you end up with the interest on *lots* of loans,' Lucia enthused. 'That's the clever bit, you see. Because only a few people at a time need to take their cash out of the bank, you can lend out all your depositors' funds, and all your shareholders' capital many times over, perhaps even a hundred times over. Then you rake in the money, pay yourself dividends as shareholders, and then use those dividends to invest in property yourself. You see? From now on I am an investor no longer. From now on, I shall be a capitalist.'

A silence greeted the conclusion of this peroration. Georgie and Olga looked at each other.

'Do you mean,' Georgie asked at length, 'that for every pound, or dollar rather, that somebody deposits with a bank, the bank can go out and lend a hundred dollars?'

'Yes, exactly,' Lucia said simply. 'Isn't it clever?'

'But surely it's hugely dangerous?' Georgie persisted. 'What happens if all your customers turn up on the same day and want their money back?'

'But they don't, you see, and they won't,' Lucia said. 'Why, think, Georgie. Have you ever had more than one or two people in the queue with you in the bank while you are waiting to cash a cheque?'

Georgie was forced to admit that he had not.

'Well, there you are, then,' Lucia concluded triumphantly. 'It's called fractional reserve banking. Mr Lodge has promised to lend me a book about it. Why, talk of the devil, there he is. Mr Lodge! Do wait for me, there's a dear.'

With that Lucia rose from the table, looked around, said 'Lunchtime, possibly,' rather vaguely to Georgie, and set off in pursuit of her fellow capitalist.

'Well!' said Georgie in exasperation, once she was out of earshot. 'That's all we need! Lucia in the grip of a new craze.'

'Mmm,' Olga sympathised, 'but look on the bright side. She can't be in two places at once. While she's off discussing high finance, she can't be dragging you around endless gardens, can she?'

'You're right,' marvelled Georgie. 'Of course! I hadn't thought of that. Why, this new idea might even drive the whole gardening thing out of her head altogether.'

'And of course,' Olga said archly, 'we can always spend some time together – if you've got nothing better to do, that is?'

'What could be better than spending time with you?' Georgie asked, gazing at her adoringly.

Olga laughed and patted his hand.

'Thank you, Georgie dear, that was naughty of me.'

Georgie finished his last piece of toast and faced the day ahead with a new-found resolution.

'Goodness me, a day without Lucia, what shall we do?'

'Well, a morning anyway,' Olga warned him. 'There's no saying what she'll want to do this afternoon.'

'Yes, well, a morning then,' Georgie conceded. 'What shall we do?'

'Well,' Olga said, glancing up at the clock, 'I have an appointment with a charming man who's flying over from Lake Garda. Why don't you meet him too? To tell you the truth, I'd be very glad of your company, Georgie. I strongly suspect he has designs upon whatever shreds of my virtue may remain.'

'Oh,' exclaimed Georgie, 'the bounder!'

Olga laughed again.

'Dear Georgie,' she said, 'I'm sure I will be quite safe in your presence.'

At this moment a faint humming sound began to make itself heard, which grew into the unmistakable note of an aircraft engine. Presently, as people began to crowd to the windows and look out, a speck appeared in the sky away to the east, which grew rapidly into the shape of a biplane with floats attached. It dropped a streamer and then circled the lake slowly, presumably to judge the direction of the wind, before making a long landing run and touching down immaculately, and finally taxiing to a halt at a point just off the hotel's swimming jetty.

'Oh, it's him,' Olga cried. 'Damn the man, why does everybody except me always have to be on time? Quick Georgie, let's go. I have to run upstairs before I can meet him.'

Georgie strolled out on to the terrace to watch. A small splash showed where an anchor had been thrown out of the plane. At the same time, the hotel's launch was being unmoored and started up, with much shouting and waving of arms. It approached the plane, and the pilot stepped in from the float on which he was standing in a sprightly manner. It was now that Georgie became aware of a growing buzzing, and feared the onset of a swarm of his dreaded wasps. As he looked around nervously, he realised that every man, woman and child in Bellagio was running, positively running, towards the jetty, completely ignoring the fact that the gardens were of course private property, some of the men waving their hats as they did so. He was reminded of the scene in *Cavelleria Rusticana* when Alfio comes in on his wagon, and all the villagers run out to meet him.

The person who stepped out of the trim little launch ten minutes later and strode through the gardens was a sharp-featured, balding man with a moustache. Though he was slight in stature, the effect of his approach was electrifying. People crowded to shake his hand, so that his approach grew slower and slower until finally it ground to a halt altogether, and he was overwhelmed by a sea of well-wishers, raising his hat to the ladies and shaking hands with the men.

Georgie watched in fascination as, through the hubbub of cries and shouts, a particular pattern began to make itself heard, until it became a rhythmical chant. Suddenly he recognised it, and everything fell into place.

'D'Annunzio! D'Annunzio! D'Annunzio!'

'My God!' he gasped as Olga reappeared beside him. 'It's Gabriele d'Annunzio.'

'Yes, of course it is,' she replied in a very matter-of-fact fashion, 'why else would they be shouting his name?'

Slowly, very slowly, the light-infantry *mêlée* that was d'Annunzio and his admirers reached the terrace. As it did so, it separated, and the object of their adoration was able to step forward and kiss Olga's hand. There was a little murmur of envy from the female contingent of this crowd which had appeared from nowhere.

'Miss Bracely, an honour,' said the little man with the waxed moustache.

'My friend, Mr Pillson,' Olga said, waving at Georgie, who essayed a bow of which Mr Wyse would have been proud.

D'Annunzio looked Georgie dubiously up and down, before proffering a hand. Georgie was unsure whether to shake it or kneel and kiss its ring, but, being English, wisely chose the former course. The crowd now gazed admiringly on Olga and Georgie; clearly any friend of the great man was deemed to have absorbed at least a little of his radiating glory.

'To Fiume!' a man shouted boldly from somewhere back in the garden, and this prompted a fierce growl of support and a few impromptu handclaps.

'Too late for that, my friend!' d'Annunzio called back, which prompted another growl from the crowd and a female yelp of 'Shame!' from somewhere over towards the herbaceous border.

The great man lifted his aquiline features towards the east, placed his hand in his jacket, and flexed one knee in a gesture which was demonstrably Napoleonic. The crowd suddenly fell quiet. Was he about to address them?

No. Having held the pose, and the tension, for a palpable ten seconds or so, he relaxed, turned to Olga and said, 'It was a cold flight from Lake Garda, Miss Bracely. Perhaps you could revive me with a cup of coffee?'

The crowd, sensing that they had somehow been cheated of their moment, nonetheless broke into spontaneous applause as d'Annunzio laid one hand lightly on each of Olga and Georgie and, as Giuseppe obsequiously bowed and walked backwards, magically without bumping into any of the furniture, advanced into the lounge. An army of waiters descended upon them, moving chairs and tables, proffering and lighting cigarettes, and whisking in fresh, hot coffee. Over in the corner the German couple who had actually ordered the coffee looked first bewildered, then angry, then resigned. After all, what could you expect from a nation that thought sausage was just something to put on a pizza?

D'Annunzio looked dubiously at the proffered cigarettes.

'I prefer Turkish,' he said, looking round expectantly.

'Oh, let me get some from my valet,' Georgie said importantly. He was still getting used to the idea of having a valet. A waiter was duly despatched in search of Francesco and Turkish cigarettes.

'You know, Olga and I play your songs all the time,' Georgie gushed, 'and to think now that I've actually met you.'

'Tosti's songs, you mean,' Olga corrected him gently.

D'Annunzio inclined his head graciously.

'Tosti is a fine composer,' he averred. 'I believe his music almost does my poetry credit, but it is natural that it is my name that you should remember. Tell me, sir, which is your favourite?'

'Oh, there are so many,' Georgie enthused, 'but I think perhaps "*L'alba separa*". So thrilling, you know. Such magnificent words.'

'And so wonderful to sing,' Olga interjected.

The poet nodded sagely. 'A great poem should always make a great song. It's all a matter of the stresses in the line. When I compose verse, I think of a rhythm.'

'And what about Schubert?' Georgie pressed on. 'What about "*Winterreise*"? Isn't it divine?'

D'Annunzio shuddered theatrically.

'So cold. So depressing. And anyway, Müller is a most inferior poet.'

'Oh,' said Georgie in surprise, but was prevented from continuing by a slight but determined shake of the head from Olga.

'Do tell us, *maestro*,' she cut in, 'what you are doing here? To what do we owe the honour of this visit?'

He looked genuinely surprised.

'It should not be necessary for a beautiful woman to ask why a man has come to visit her,' he replied, 'and it is you who honour us, Miss Bracely, not me.'

'That's very sweet of you,' Olga assured him, 'but surely there must be some other reason? After all, you spoke of lunch, and it is only ten-thirty.'

D'Annunzio laughed deprecatingly.

'Well, you have found me out, Miss Bracely, as you say in England. In fact there is a small errand which I should run, but perhaps you would care to accompany me?'

'I'd be delighted, but where to?'

'Just up to Como. We can do it easily in ten minutes or so in my plane. There is a lady there, quite an old woman actually, who is the mother of one of my men who was killed during the war.'

'What a nice thought, to go and visit her,' Olga said admiringly. 'Why, I am sure she will be very touched that you have made the effort.'

'Yes, I dare say,' d'Annunzio replied in an offhand manner. 'In fact the main reason for visiting her is that she has a photograph of me which her son took, and I want it for my museum.'

'He was a photographer, then?' asked Georgie.

'Yes, to be exact he was my personal photographer, at least for a short while. I insisted that photographers should be attached to my unit. It was good for morale.'

'Whose morale?' Georgie wondered inwardly.

'How did he die?' asked Olga.

'It was unfortunate. I knew the nation would want a picture of myself against the backdrop of some captured enemy trenches. This meant that the man, I forget his name, had to expose himself to enemy fire briefly while he set up his tripod and camera and worked the shutter. He objected that it was too dangerous, but of course I ordered him to stop whimpering and do his duty. I was proved right, as always. He managed to take the photograph with at least a second to spare before he was shot.'

'Not good for the photographer's morale, then,' Georgie thought.

'Oh no!' Olga cried. 'How horrible! What happened next?'

'We waited until dark to retrieve the camera and his body. Luckily the plate was undamaged. It would have been all too easy for it to have been broken by a stray bullet. So the image was preserved for posterity.'

D'Annunzio sipped his coffee reflectively.

'But I don't understand,' Georgie said. 'How does the photo come to be in the possession of the man's mother?'

'My fault entirely,' d'Annunzio said, waving his hand in front of him as though swatting a fly. 'I visited her to show her the historic picture, the heroic picture I should say, which her son had captured. I told her that his last thoughts had been of her.'

'Were they really?' Georgie marvelled.

'Indeed. In fact, he spent at least an hour crying out for her while he bled to death. However, while I was describing all this to her she became very agitated – quite hysterical in fact – and I thought it best to leave. In my haste, I left the photo behind.'

There was a pause while he despatched his empty coffee cup with a lordly wave to a hovering waiter. Georgie struggled to think of something to say, but failed. Fortunately Olga, as always, came to the rescue.

'You mentioned a museum, *maestro*, a museum to the war perhaps?' she ventured.

Again the great man looked genuinely surprised.

'No, to me, naturally.'

'But you're not dead,' Georgie blurted out without thinking, whereupon Olga gave him a very stern look indeed.

This time the wave of the hand was as if from the lofty slopes of Mount Parnassus.

'Anyone, my dear sir, can have a museum dedicated to them once they are dead. That is so common an occurrence that it can hardly be considered an achievement. In my case it is fitting that the museum should take shape as quickly as possible. I am no longer a young man, despite what my figure may suggest to the contrary, and the nation demands it.'

'Oh,' Georgie goggled.

A fresh cup of *espresso* arrived and d'Annunzio sniffed it appreciatively before disposing of it in a single gulp.

'Naturally I have designed it myself,' he went on.

'Naturally,' gasped Georgie. 'Such a task could hardly be left to anyone else.'

'I see you understand entirely, sir,' the poet said approvingly. 'There shall be one room for me as a great novelist, another for me as a great poet, and another for me as a great journalist and public speaker. An aeroplane of some description will commemorate me as a war hero in the sky, and a torpedo boat as a war hero on water. What I am after today is something for the room – or perhaps it may be several rooms, I have not quite decided – which will commemorate me as a war hero on land.'

'Perhaps you should feature a memorial to all your photographers who died in action?' Olga suggested innocently.

'I had not considered it,' d'Annunzio replied thoughtfully. 'After all, it is a museum to me, a national figure – an international figure, I should say more correctly – but perhaps there is something in what you say. A small tablet, perhaps. Not intrusive. Tucked away somewhere. Yes, I will think about it.'

At this point a waiter proffered Georgie a silver tray with a note upon it. As he unfolded and read it a frown crossed his face.

'Not bad news, I hope, Georgie?' Olga enquired, clearly worried.

'No, nothing really. It's just that we seem to be out of Turkish cigarettes. So sorry.'

'It is of no consequence, sir,' d'Annunzio pronounced magnanimously. 'Come, dear Miss Bracely, let us go. Perhaps we shall see you for lunch, sir, yes?'

While Olga and d'Annunzio posed for photographs outside arm in arm, Georgie went upstairs in search of Francesco, who was waiting shamefaced in the middle of the living room.

'Now then, Francesco,' Georgie demanded, more puzzled than cross. 'What on earth did you mean in your note when you said that you are not at liberty to come downstairs?'

'Forgive me, sir,' Francesco pleaded. 'I know it was unpardonable of me to disobey you, but you see it would not have been possible for me to come face to face with ... that man.'

'Why ever not?'

'It is difficult to explain without betraying a confidence, sir.'

'Oh, I see,' Georgie said awkwardly.

'I will tell you as much as I can without embarrassment, sir. I owe you that.'

'Very well, then,' Georgie replied. He sat down but was so agitated that he forgot to check his trouser crease as he crossed his legs.

'You see, sir, that man and I shared some experiences together. In fact at one time I knew him very well. He would certainly have recognised me immediately had he seen me.'

'But why would that have been a problem?' Georgie asked.

'Our time together did not end well, sir,' Francesco said hesitantly. 'In fact, I think it fair to say that we did not part on good terms. Harsh words were exchanged. Hurtful words, certainly, on his part.'

'I see,' Georgie said, but by no means sure that he did. There was a pause during which he hoped that Francesco might elucidate, and then on reflection rather hoped that he might not.

'Oh, well,' he said at length resignedly, 'let's say no more about it, shall we?'

'Thank you, sir,' Francesco said quietly, bowing deeply. 'It is very good of you to be so understanding. May I get you anything, sir?'

'No. I don't think so,' Georgie mused. 'In fact, I think I will go for a walk before lunch.'

'Perhaps I could recommend the second flight of steps from the main street, sir? There is a particularly fine silk shop. I think you would find the ties interesting.'

Then, as he opened the door for Georgie to go out, he said quietly, 'And may I thank you again, sir, for your understanding. If I may say so, it is no more than I would have expected from such a kind gentleman as yourself.'

Chapter 11

Lucia arrived alone for lunch, Brabazon Lodge having departed to Milan for an important business meeting. As she entered the lounge she felt her social antennae beginning to vibrate. There was a strange air of expectancy about the place, a sort of pleasurable tension, she was sure of it. She sensed that somehow something was afoot, and her instincts rarely let her down.

She walked towards the terrace, and stumbled upon Georgie and Olga in conversation with a rather nondescript-looking man, whom she took for a bank manager, or perhaps a passed-over civil servant.

'Oh good, there you are, Lucia,' Georgie greeted her. 'We've been waiting for you to go into lunch.'

'Yes, I have passed a perfectly pleasant morning, thank you, Georgie,' she said a little sharply.

'Oh yes, well now,' he replied, affecting to ignore the implied rebuke, 'may I introduce *maestro* d'Annunzio?'

His eyes sparkled at her expectantly. He knew her *penchant* for rubbing shoulders with the rich and famous.

'*Signora* Pillson,' d'Annunzio murmured, leaning over her hand. 'A pleasure, madam.'

'Very nice to meet you,' Lucia said distractedly. 'Olga, dear, I trust you had an enjoyable morning?'

This with a sharp glance at Georgie.

'Yes, thank you, Lucia,' Olga replied. 'I do so enjoy flying.'

'Flying?' Lucia echoed. 'Yes, I saw an aeroplane earlier. Don't say that was you?'

'I had the great honour of flying Miss Bracely to Como,' d'Annunzio announced, handing Olga her wrap, which had been lying over the arm of her chair. 'Shall we go in, ladies?'

Lucia noticed that Giuseppe bowed very low as they stepped outside on to the terrace, and the waiters scurried around in a most obsequious fashion. She wondered if Georgie had over-tipped the previous evening. Really, lira were so difficult; all those zeros taxed even her agile mind.

They sat down and Giuseppe handed them menus. Then, with a flourish, he presented the wine list to d'Annunzio and said '*Altezza*'.

Lucia's ears pricked up and she gazed at d'Annunzio in some confusion.

'Am I mistaken,' she asked hesitantly, 'or did Giuseppe just refer to you as Your Royal Highness?'

The great man waved a hand magnanimously, graciously, condescendingly.

'The King made me a prince,' he acknowledged, 'but I rarely use the title. The name Gabriele d'Annunzio is honour enough for anyone to bear.'

'Your name is familiar certainly, Your Highness,' Lucia temporised, glancing meaningfully at Georgie. He detected her difficulty at once and rode to the rescue.

'I should jolly well think so,' he cut in. 'Why, you hear his poetry when Olga sings those wonderful Tosti songs we love so much.'

'Of course!'

Lucia smiled warmly and clasped her hands in joyful remembrance.

'What an honour to meet the poet of "*Ideale*". It has always been my favourite.'

This was true, since it also happened to be the only one she could remember. She viewed Tosti's songs with some mistrust, partly because they were Italian and might for all she knew contain all sorts of vulgar references if only one could understand the words, and secondly because they were something which Olga and Georgie pursued together, and after Lucia had mistaken Schubert's cradle song for the prayer from Cortese's *Lucrezia* one evening she had thought it better to feign a complete lack of interest in song as an art form. After all, when a discerning person decides to take no interest in a subject then ignorance simply becomes a rather superior form of discriminating disregard.

She glanced across warmly at Georgie as though to convey an impression of long winter evenings happily shared poring over Tosti on the duet stool, only to notice that his mouth had acquired a curiously pursed look, as it had on that dreadful day when Major Benjy had spilled red wine on one of Georgie's treasured fingerbowl doilies.

'That was Errico,' d'Annunzio said dismissively. 'A most inferior poet. Now, Miss Bracely, what do you say to a Vernaccia di San Gimignano? It is from a very fine estate. I know the proprietor.'

As lunch progressed, d'Annunzio regaled them at great length with stories of his exploits as a novelist, a poet, an orator who had brought Italy into the war, a soldier who had won great victories on land, a pioneering aviator who had led his squadron to Vienna and back and given the sight of one eye in the service of his country, and a fearless sailor for fear of whose torpedo boat the entire Austrian battle fleet had remained bottled-up in port. Any acknowledgement of contributions by other people to the great events of the twentieth century was notable by its absence.

A second bottle of Vernaccia came and went, followed by a Brunello di Montalcino ordered up specially from the manager's private cellar. Growing yet more expansive, he waxed lyrical about his plans for a museum to himself, at which point Lucia suddenly looked very thoughtful indeed.

Making any interjection into d'Annunzio's flow seemed somehow unmannered, given its imposing prose and measured cadences, but Georgie finally managed it after the *antipasti* and pasta courses had given way to the main business of the meal, and the one-eyed poet was inserting a piece of veal into his mouth.

'I do so just adore those steamers on the lake,' he said, introducing a note of bathos into the epic drama that was their companion's lunchtime conversation. 'They are so very beautiful, aren't they?'

The veal seemed to disappear all too quickly.

'They are typical of our Italian veneration of beauty, of style,' d'Annunzio replied, gazing pointedly at Olga, who pretended to be terribly busy with her *osso buco*. 'In Germany or Austria you would doubtless find something dumpy and unappealing, you only have to look at their women to know that.'

'For shame!' Lucia chided him, laying down her knife and fork with a girlish air. 'Such ungallantry!'

He shrugged.

'I return all my fan mail from Germany and Austria unopened,' he said simply. 'It reduces the strain on my secretary, and it avoids unpleasant experiences. You would not believe the things some people send me in the mail. One deranged woman from Salzburg sent me a dead rat. What can the poor woman have been thinking of?'

'What indeed?' Olga concurred innocently. 'What a shocking want of respect.'

He shrugged again, this time in the manner of a man who can nobly bear any indignity that life cares to throw in his direction, particularly if stamped with a Salzburg postmark.

'I am sure,' Lucia countered coquettishly, 'that Italian ladies do not show such disregard for your fine qualities.'

'Certainly not,' he assured her. 'Mostly they write to offer marriage. Often they enclose some of their underwear as a token of their longing. Understandable of course that their enthusiasm should take such a form, but it does raise the awkward problem of what to do with it all.'

He put another piece of veal into his mouth and masticated rather sadly.

'Oh –,' said both Georgie and Olga together, both having had the same idea at the same time. They looked at each other and then quickly looked away again, like a pair of naughty children caught out in a mischievous prank. Georgie stared very hard at his plate and tried to hold his breath. If necessary, he decided, he would start coughing.

'But of course you must display it all in a cabinet at your museum,' Olga proffered enthusiastically. 'Or rather, several cabinets since there is so much of it. Just think, women will flock from all over Italy just to identify their own, and then go home to be feted by their town as someone for whom you had so much feeling as to treasure and display their underwear.'

'Surely the nation would demand it?' Georgie managed to get out, before he was consumed by a fit of coughing.

Lucia was much discomfited by all this talk of underwear. Really, the combination of both Olga and Italy acting upon Georgie was producing some most unfortunate consequences. He would never have been so coarse at home. She tried saying, 'Well, really' a few times, and then 'Olga, dear', but d'Annunzio was nodding sagely as he weighed this new suggestion.

'It shall be done,' he announced solemnly. 'As you rightly say, *Signor* Pillson, anything concerning my relationship with the Italian people is a matter of national importance.'

'Not just national, surely?' Olga asked. 'After all, *maestro*, you have acted upon so many great events in international affairs that I would imagine people would come from all over the world to view the exhibits.'

He nodded again, but Lucia was beginning to suspect Olga of poking fun at him (those sly, secretive glances between her and Georgie spoke volumes), and that would never do. She had not even started to think about the various ways in which such a great personage might be fitted into her present and future plans, and she could not afford the slightest possibility of him taking umbrage and disappearing, never to be seen again.

'I understand from the concierge,' she cut in smoothly, 'that one can actually hire a steamer for the evening and go wherever you like. You can even have your own little dinner party on board.'

'Oh!' Georgie was captivated instantly. 'What a wonderful idea, Lucia. Yes, let's do it!'

'Trust you to think of something like that, Lucia,' Olga said admiringly, sounding yet again like Irene. 'You have such style!'

Such sentiments were of course gratifying, and Lucia acknowledged them by a wan gesture with a gloved hand.

'It shall be done,' she announced brightly, looking around the table with a smile, and for a horrified moment wondered if d'Annunzio might think that *she* was poking fun at him. Yet no, he was beaming at her and nodding. She breathed a sigh of relief. One had to be so careful with these Italians.

'Perhaps in, say, three nights' time?' she enquired. 'It will probably take time to make the arrangements.'

She pulled her notebook and silver pen from her handbag and furrowed her brow in concentration. Now it was Georgie's turn to breathe a sigh of relief. Lucia was so very much more amenable when she was planning a project of some kind, and one also tended to see much less of her, as she would be out running around, organising people. He reflected happily that he could probably look forward to at least two undisturbed afternoons on the balcony.

'And of course you must come, *maestro*,' Olga said suddenly, cutting in on Georgie's pleasant thoughts.

He sat up, aghast. Had the woman taken leave of her senses? He glared at her, and she shrugged imperceptibly, as if in mute apology.

'Oh, I'm sorry, Lucia,' she went on humbly, 'what terribly bad form me inviting someone to your party.'

'Not at all, dear,' Lucia cried warmly with a little giggle, her eyes gleaming, 'why, I was just about to say the same thing myself. Do come, please, dear Prince.'

'Yes do,' Olga urged. 'You could fly over in the afternoon and stay the night here. I'm sure they must have a free room.'

He looked dubious.

'This week is very difficult, I fear,' he relied, and Georgie's heart leapt. 'I am writing my annual letter of self-nomination for the Nobel Peace Prize, and the deadline is fast approaching.'

Lucia was distraught at the prospect of losing her star guest, but rose to the challenge.

'Of course I do understand the many pressures on your time, Your Highness. Why, at home I suffer from them myself. How everybody works me so.

'No,' she said decisively. 'You must tell us what is most convenient for you, and we will arrange everything for that date. Perhaps you might telephone me here at the hotel tomorrow?'

D'Annunzio thought that perhaps he might, and the meal petered out with dessert and coffee. D'Annunzio departed for his plane in the hotel launch, having first kissed both ladies' hands, in Olga's case in what Georgie viewed as an unnecessarily lingering manner. Despite the amount of alcohol which he had consumed over lunch, the floatplane lifted off without incident and climbed away down the lake to the east.

Lucia disappeared at once in search of the concierge, leaving Georgie and Olga together in the lounge.

'Well really, Olga,' Georgie protested. 'What on earth were you thinking of? Why did you have to invite that awful little man to dinner?'

'Because I could see that Lucia wanted to but wasn't sure how to go about it herself,' she replied, smiling at him kindly, 'and I wanted her to be happy.'

She sat down and picked up a magazine from a coffee table.

'And anyway,' she said apologetically, 'it seemed like the least I could do after I was sick in his aeroplane earlier.'

With Lucia off busying herself with the arrangements for her steamer trip, Georgie was left to his own devices, and was much looking forward to spending another quiet afternoon on the balcony, particularly as so much wine at lunchtime had left him feeling pleasantly drowsy.

Francesco had anticipated this request and helped him off with his collar and into his dressing gown and cravat. The former was bright red and embroidered with a giant Chinese dragon on the back, while the latter was a delicate mixture of gold and puce. As he gazed at himself in the mirror, he could fancy himself positively ablaze with colour.

'My, aren't we looking fine?' Olga marvelled, echoing his thoughts. 'I hope you don't mind me coming in – the door to your suite was open.'

'Not at all,' Georgie said. 'You don't think it's too much, do you? I wasn't quite sure about the puce.'

'Tommyrot!' Olga exclaimed. 'Why, you'll drive any passing woman into a positive swoon of passion, Georgie. In fact, I'm not sure if it's even safe for me to be in the same room as you.'

'Oh, really,' he protested weakly.

At that moment Francesco re-entered the room, having laid out Georgie's painting kit on the balcony table.

'Good afternoon, Miss Bracely,' he said suavely. 'You know, if you will forgive the impertinence, I would like to congratulate you on your Brunnhilde last year at Bayreuth.'

They both looked at him in some astonishment, so he went on quickly.

'I can see you are wondering how I could afford to attend such a festival,' he said with a smile. 'The explanation is quite simple. A gentleman friend whom I met while he was taking the waters in Baden-Baden very kindly invited me to stay with him during the festival, and it so happened he had a spare ticket for the *Ring*. I was indeed most fortunate.'

'Indeed you were,' Georgie agreed. 'Why, you know, I thought of going myself, but when I looked into it I found it would be ruinously expensive.'

'Georgie, dear one,' cried Olga in dismay. 'Why didn't you tell me you wanted to go? The singers always get given free tickets, you know.'

'Oh well, maybe next time,' Georgie said. 'Anyway, I saw you in *Siegfried* at Covent Garden.'

'Next time I perform a *Ring* anywhere in the world,' Olga said decisively, 'you must come with me, Georgie. You can be my *repetiteur* or something, or just come as my guest.'

'Oh,' said Georgie humbly. He was about to say something, and then stopped. They exchanged glances and each knew the other was thinking back to the time when Olga really had asked Georgie to come away with her on tour, quite out of the blue one day while he was drying his paintbrushes. There had been no earthly reason why he should not have agreed. Lucia was married to Pepino, and Georgie was resolutely single, cutting his usual dash as Riseholme's long-standing debonair young man. No reason except the most important one of all.

He had shaken his head, not trusting himself to speak.

'Why can't you come?' she had asked.

He had looked her straight in the face and said, 'Because I adore you.'

Neither of them had ever spoken of it again. Yet now, as they stood close together years later in a hotel bedroom on Lake Como, the resolute Italian sunshine forcing its way between the slats of the shutters and showing them life for what it really was, just a constantly shifting sequence of light and shade, they were reminded, poignantly, of what might have been.

Georgie opened his mouth to say something, and so anguished was his expression that Olga said, quickly and brightly, 'Why don't we sit on the balcony together and have a cigarette?'

'Yes,' he said quietly. 'Let's.'

There was a discreet cough from Francesco.

'If you please, sir, I have already placed two chairs on the balcony and left you a box of my favourite Turkish cigarettes on the table.'

'Thank you, Francesco,' Georgie replied. 'That all sounds quite parfect.'

Once they were settled on the balcony, Francesco brought a carafe of water and then disappeared backwards with a bow.

They both lit up and gazed contentedly out at the lake while they inhaled. As he allowed the smoke to drift slowly out again, Georgie darted a sideways glance at Olga.

'Would you like to know what I was thinking just then?' he asked.

'I'm not sure,' she replied after a pause. 'Are you certain you want to tell me?'

'Oh, I don't think it can possibly matter now after all these years,' he said, taking another puff.

He felt a deep inner mellowness beginning to flood through his body and felt that in this mood, and this setting, he could tell Olga anything. The world itself seemed to be flowing past more slowly, almost as if it were giving him a chance to catch up and jump on.

'Go on then,' she said with a smile.

'I was just thinking,' he said slowly, seeking to choose exactly which words he needed to convey his precise meaning, 'or, rather, realising, I suppose ...'

'Yes?'

'I was just realising,' he said much more firmly, having now seen exactly what the truth of it was, 'what a very great shame it was that I have spent so many years lurking inside in the shadows, afraid to step out into the sunlight.'

'Oh, Georgie,' she said gently. 'My poor dear lamb.'

Returning to the suite some hours later, looking forward to a restorative bath, Lucia stopped dead as she came into the living room. Georgie and Olga were on the sofa, locked together in what seemed to Lucia very much like a passionate embrace. She wondered whether to creep out of the room again and affect not to have noticed anything, but she was not a woman to shirk a challenge and anyway she wanted her bath. Just at that moment she noticed her maid's frightened face peering round the door to her bedroom, which meant there was no longer any choice in the matter.

'Please open the shutters,' she said as if nothing in the world was out of the ordinary, 'it is so very dark in here.'

As the maid scurried to comply light flooded into the room and it became apparent that Georgie and Olga were in fact fast asleep. Georgie was sitting upright at one end of the sofa, with one arm around Olga's shoulders. She had presumably originally been sitting next to him, but had fallen sideways so that her face was now resting against his chest and emitting, it must be admitted, some most unladylike snores.

As the shutters clattered back into their resting place the noise awoke the slumbering pair, who gazed around them in some confusion. Olga gave Georgie an affectionate little pat and then pulled herself upright.

'I assume,' Lucia said icily, 'there is some explanation for this unseemly display?'

'Oh,' said Georgie, looking totally bewildered. 'Lucia.'

'Yes, Georgie,' said that worthy. 'Lucia. Your wife.'

The last two words were loaded with unmistakable reproach, and he floundered for an explanation, but found none.

'I really don't understand,' he said lamely. 'I don't even remember coming in from the balcony. Olga, what are we doing in here?'

'Blowed if I know,' she replied. 'I'm in the same boat as you. Last thing I remember we were sitting out there looking at the lake.'

She walked rather stiffly over to the French windows and stepped on to the balcony. Four or five cigarette butts had been stubbed out in the ashtray. Suddenly she picked one up and smelled it, teasing it with her fingernail as she did so. Then she started laughing.

'I am glad, dear, that you should find all this a cause for amusement,' Lucia commented glacially. 'Personally I fail to see the joke, but then perhaps I am at a disadvantage in not moving in Bohemian circles where such behaviour is openly condoned.'

'Oh, I'm sorry, Lucia,' Olga said contritely. 'It's not like that at all. I'm laughing at us, Georgie and me, for being so naive. Here – smell this.'

She thrust the mangled stub under Lucia's nose. She recoiled slightly, gazing at Olga uncomprehendingly. Impatiently Olga snatched it away and, crossing to the sofa, pushed it at Georgie. He took it and sniffed it gingerly.

'What is it?' he asked. 'Gardenia perhaps, or honeysuckle?'

'It's hashish, you chump!' Olga cried. 'We've drugged ourselves.'

'But why would Francesco do such a thing?' Georgie asked, stupefied. 'Why, he told me they were relaxing.'

'So they are in small doses,' she concurred, 'but not if you smoke two or three, and particularly if you're not used to taking the stuff in the first place.'

'That man is an evil influence upon you, Georgie,' Lucia declared. 'I have thought it from the first. There is something not quite right about him. Something I admit I can't put my finger on, but now you have proof positive for yourself. He has tried to turn you into a drug addict.'

'Oh, surely not,' Georgie protested weakly. 'These cigarettes are in common usage in the Levant.'

'Allow me to point out the obvious, Georgie,' Lucia said tartly, 'but we are not in the Levant. Nor do I, for one, have any wish to go there, and I certainly have no intention of being carried off there against my will in a narcotic haze.'

There was a silence while Georgie and Olga tried to imagine Lucia being stuffed unconscious into a laundry basket by two sinister Orientals and smuggled out of the hotel to a waiting lorry. Unaware of the grainy black-and-white film unfolding in their minds, Lucia enjoyed the silence with satisfaction while she prepared her parting shot.

'If I were you, Georgie,' she announced in her best Elizabethan manner, 'I would dismiss the man on the spot.'

So saying, she turned smartly on her heel and entered her bedroom, and the door closed behind her with a click of finality.

Chapter 12

That evening the Mapp-Flints strolled into the lounge in preparation for their dinner some hours later than they were accustomed to. Major Benjy had in fact been complaining loudly for some time.

'Dash it all, Liz-girl, I really don't see why we should have to eat at the same time as everybody else. I mean to say, I'm starving, what?'

Liz-girl gave him a despairing look. For all his moral support, freely offered and accepted both before and after their marriage, the Major had never been able properly to appreciate the sheer intense pleasure which his wife experienced in knowing that she had made someone else even the teeniest bit uncomfortable, let alone actively unhappy. Faced with her master-plan to discomfit the Wyses and annoy Lucia, all the poor lamb could do was bleat about how hungry he was and how he 'couldn't half murder a beef sandwich'. Eventually she had relented and ordered him one to be brought up to their room. This he pronounced 'just the thing to give the troops', and ordered up a bottle of Bardolino to accompany it.

However, no sooner had they entered the lounge, the Major glancing around for Miss Flowers in what he hoped was a sufficiently surreptitious manner to escape the attention of his wife, than it became apparent that Elizabeth's master-plan had fallen at the first hurdle, for from the dining terrace came the unmistakable sound of Olga's hearty laugh. In truth it had of course been doomed from the outset, the opposing forces having had the benefit of superior intelligence, but Elizabeth was not to know this.

As they sat down with Ramesh, she did something with her teeth of which her dentist would certainly not have approved, but contrived to smile sweetly as she was handed the menu. The waiter in question looked first startled and then apprehensive: the sweeter Mapp contrived to make her smiles, the more menacing they seemed to innocent bystanders.

After five minutes or so Lucia and her party emerged from the terrace, laughing gaily amongst themselves.

'Elizabeth, dear!' Lucia greeted her, and Elizabeth pinned on her smile even more sweetly.

'So naughty of you, dear one,' Elizabeth remonstrated with her, 'to change the hour of your dining without informing us. Why, we would have loved to join you.'

She noted with a glimmer of satisfaction that the Wyses looked somewhat embarrassed at this news. At least her stratagem had not been entirely wasted.

'Why, dear,' Lucia replied innocently, raising her eyebrows. 'We usually dine at 7.30, you know. Naturally we assumed that you would too, as you did last night.'

Mr Wyse, looking yet more embarrassed, seemed about to interject. Suspecting, correctly as it happened, that he was about to venture that they might agree on the spot a time at which they might all dine together the following night, Lucia hastily and firmly said, 'I see your table is ready', at which point there was nothing for the Mapp-Flint contingent to do but move off. Lucia breathed a sigh of relief, thanking her lucky stars that she had not been cursed with Mr Wyse's excessively charitable nature. As they began to move towards the terrace, the piano trio struck up.

'Ah,' said the Major, pausing to listen for a moment with the debonair smile of an accomplished dancer, 'a polka, I fancy.'

Lucia laughed that bright silvery laugh of hers that was designed to make everyone fall silent and listen to what she had to say next, for it was likely to be terribly clever.

'Oh dear, Major,' she said. 'I can see I shall have to educate you about triple time.'

As Mr Wyse gravely bowed Lucia, Susan and Amelia into their chairs they looked around themselves contentedly for a few minutes in that pleasant feeling of slight over-fullness that so often seems to follow hard upon the heels of an Italian meal. The waltz (for indeed so it was) drew to an end and a little desultory applause broke out. The violinist could then be observed bending over and talking to the pianist, albeit with less agitation than when a couple had recently requested, and danced to, an Argentinian tango. Whatever the nature of his suggestion, the pianist seemed strangely reluctant to comply, but was finally propelled across the room in the manner of the most easily bullied member of a group of boys being sent next door to ask if they could have their ball back.

'Miss Bracely,' he importuned, with a bow worthy of Mr Wyse. 'Might you favour us with a song?'

Many a *prima donna* might have refused such a request outright, and had the man dismissed for his temerity into the bargain. Olga, however, was a diva of the people, literally so; she had once deeply shocked Lucia by disclosing not only that she had been brought up in an orphanage, but that she would have greatly preferred the gutter. Though Lucia suspected that some perverse humorous intent lurked behind the words, she could hardly help but find them appalling. She would later hint, as delicately as possible, that this might go some way to explaining why Olga had inexplicably committed the social solecism of not having had calling cards printed when coming to stay in Riseholme.

As it was, Olga simply said 'Why not?' and, as Georgie was giving a little 'Oh' of anticipation, grabbed him by the hand and started stalking towards the piano, whereupon he gave another little 'Oh', this time of apprehension.

'But Olga,' he protested weakly, 'we don't have any music with us.'
'Don't worry about that,' she said briskly, 'just play whatever you can remember.'

As she walked to the curve of the piano and stood looking out into the lounge, a total silence fell. As if drawn thither by the telepathic impulses of some musical *gestalt*, all sorts of people seemed suddenly to have appeared, standing expectantly around the edge of the room, most of the waiters among them, abandoning their responsibilities on the terrace.

Everyone stood looking at Olga. Olga stood gazing calmly out into the middle distance. Georgie sat motionless at the piano. The silence threatened to become oppressive. Somebody coughed, and was instantly shushed.

Then, without really realising what he was doing, Georgie found his fingers moving across the keyboard in the jaunty little opening of *'Widmung'*. Olga entered, her voice filling the room, and suddenly he knew that everything was going to be all right, that the accompaniment would now run like some clockwork music box. He had started his fingers moving in the right order and they would now continue with a momentum of their own.

Olga sang with all the urgent longing of a young girl, redolent with adolescence and romantic notions. Then came the magic moment when the music changed to mark the passage from innocence to knowing, and the girl's voice changed with it, now passionate, wondering, satisfied. The final section drew the work to its triumphant close amid applause, and a round of *'wunderschöning'* and *'pracht'* volleying from the German contingent.

Olga let fall her mask of the young girl, and ran round to Georgie, laughing with sheer delight.

'Another!' she called, resting her hand on his shoulder.

They both knew what it had to be. Firmly but sweetly, his fingers found the notes of *'Ideale'*.

*

Out on the terrace the Major was growing restive that nobody had come to take his wine order, Ramesh was daydreaming silently about the potentialities of his new-found friend Corinna, and Mapp was fulminating against Lucia.

'The unmitigated dishonesty of the woman! She knew that we wanted to eat with them and deliberately changed their reservation so that we would miss them.'

'Eh?' responded the Major.

'*That* woman! Lady Bountiful!'

'Ah!'

On a good night Major Flint could pass an entire dinner merely interjecting 'Eh?' and 'Ah!' into his wife's conversation, he having learned over many years of practice to endow the latter syllable with as many different shades of meaning as any foreseeable situation might require. This, however, was destined not to be one of those evenings.

'What do you mean – "Ah!"?'

'Well, look here, I mean dash it all, Liz, how do you know she actually changed her reservation, after all? Maybe she was always intending to eat at 7.30 and last night was just – what do you call it?'

'An aberration?'

'That's the johnny,' the Major acknowledged gratefully.

'*She* is an aberration,' Elizabeth said, still trembling visibly with rage. 'It was a sad day for Tilling when some well-intentioned person invited her into our midst.'

The Major knew that the well-intentioned person had been none other than Elizabeth herself, though she had been motivated more by the prospect of a summer tenant for Mallards at a thumping great rent than by altruism, so he said 'Ah' in what he hoped was a warmly sympathetic sort of way.

'To think that I could have allowed myself to be so totally taken in by her,' she continued with the merest hint of a sob.

The Major gazed at her in some alarm. The old girl's waterworks were bad enough when endured in the privacy of one's own home, but to be deplored even more when sitting in public surrounded by foreigners and still waiting for someone to bring you a drink. 'You're a victim of your own good nature, Liz-girl,' he said in an uncharacteristic burst of fluency. 'Told you about it before. Too good-natured by half, don't you know.'

To his horror this seemed only to make matters worse.

'I know, I know,' she said, beginning to whimper into her handkerchief. Out of the corner of his eye the Major saw Ramesh's gaze fixed resolutely at a spot somewhere halfway up the nearest wall.

At this point Major Flint usually said 'Now, now' and if he found that did not answer, as generally it did not, his wife being a lady who enjoyed developing any minor irritation into a full-scale disaster, suitably dramatically rendered, then tried 'There, there'. If this latter abjuration too proved futile then he would usually gaze around Glebe's drawing room helplessly for further inspiration and, it failing him, depart for the golf links. Sadly, such tactics seemed entirely unsuited to the terrace of an Italian hotel.

'Don't give her the satisfaction of getting you upset,' he hissed in a sudden flash of brilliance. 'Rise above it, that sort of thing, what?'

Elizabeth teetered on the edge of a full-blown emotional outpouring, considering her options for what seemed to her dinner companions an eternity, and then drew back from the brink. With a final broken sob into her handkerchief she returned it to her handbag, and said 'Yes', gulping visibly with barely suppressed emotion.

'There, there,' the Major finally dared to say, but this time in the rather smug tones of a man who has finally been able to bring the little woman to heel in time to avoid spoiling one's dinner. 'Now, why don't you take a look at the menu?'

'I couldn't eat a thing,' Elizabeth snuffled. 'Really, Benjy, how could you expect me to?'

'You really should try to anyway, dear lady,' Ramesh said, having clearly finished counting the bricks in the wall. 'I must say your courage in the face of such extreme provocation is jolly well an example to us all.'

Such solicitousness and comfort were balm to Elizabeth's injured feelings, especially springing from so royal a source, and she mentally resolved to essay another such quite spontaneous, yet authentically touching, display in due course.

'Ah,' said the Major with satisfaction as a waiter finally approached. 'About time too, I must say.'

As a man in search of immediate food and drink the Major was, however, about to be disappointed.

'Pardon me, *signora*,' the waiter said to Elizabeth, 'but are you the English lady who has ordered the party? On the steamer?'

A scrupulously truthful person would of course have replied in the negative at once, but Mapp knew it to be the sign of a truly developed sense of propriety that truthfulness was a quality best applied selectively, since it could have quite unforeseen consequences if handled clumsily.

'Ah yes,' she said, lifting her voice very slightly at the end so that she could comfort herself with the thought that all she was really doing was asking a question rather than confirming a fact.

Perhaps it was the sight of both the Major and Ramesh gazing at her dumbfounded, though, which gave the waiter further pause for thought.

'The private party on Thursday evening, madam? Is that you or have I made a mistake?'

Having learned all she needed to know, Elizabeth could afford to be gracious.

'Indeed you have,' she said kindly with one of her sweetest smiles, causing the waiter to recoil involuntarily.

'Rum thing,' thought the Major, 'how it has that effect on everybody.'

'I believe the lady you seek is Mrs Pillson,' Elizabeth intoned unctuously. 'The last time I saw her she was in the lounge. Listening to that delightful singing, I'll be bound.'

The waiter bowed and left, bearing with him the curious sensation of having been magically reprieved from some deeply unpleasant experience. Elizabeth was grateful for his departure, for the effort of holding the smile in place was taxing her deeply.

'Oh!' she ejaculated, putting the menu down very firmly on the table so that all her cutlery clattered, and people looked up from their dinners.

'Now, now,' the Major ventured, warningly.

'That woman!' seethed Elizabeth. 'The duplicity! The selfishness! The utter gall!'

'Don't get you, old girl,' the Major said, rather wishing that she would be quiet so he could concentrate on choosing between an expensive bottle of Amarone and a very expensive bottle of Amarone. 'Surely someone's entitled to have a party if they want to?'

'A party,' his wife pointed out icily, 'to which we have not been invited, Benjy.'

'Well, that's all right, isn't it?' he replied infuriatingly. 'I mean, it's not as though you like the woman or anything.'

'Oh well,' came the prompt response. 'If that's going to be your attitude then I can see there's no point in discussing it.'

The handbag and handkerchief made an unwelcome reappearance at this stage. The Major and Ramesh gazed at them in mounting alarm.

'Surely, my dear Mrs Flint,' Ramesh said soothingly, 'all you have to do is to invent a prior engagement. Something that would keep you from attending?' He wisely bit off the words 'even if you had been invited'.

Elizabeth sat very still, her handbag open and her handkerchief halfway to her face. Suddenly she put it back and said firmly, 'That is exactly what we will do.'

She beamed triumphantly at the two of them and was gratified to see that they still had no inkling of the sheer genius of what had just occurred to her.

'We shall have a party of our own,' she crooned, hugging herself at her own brilliance. 'On the same evening. Here at the hotel. A magnificent party. Drinks, food, music, everything. You can host, of course, Benjy, and Ramesh will be guest of honour.'

'Here, I say,' protested her husband, becoming dimly aware that his own drinks bill could possibly be seen in a certain uncharitable light already to be slightly excessive, 'we can't pledge the maharajah's credit for that sort of thing, old girl.'

'Nonsense,' came the crisp rejoinder from the old girl. 'If you remember, Benjy, the maharajah was gracious enough to say that we could have anything that we wanted.'

'Yes, but here, I say ...' the Major floundered uneasily.

'Apart from anything else,' Elizabeth continued, 'I am sure his Highness would expect us to entertain a few select guests on behalf of his son. Isn't that right, Ramesh?'

Ramesh's face acquired a sphinx-like inscrutability.

'I am sure, dear lady,' he replied carefully, 'that my father meant exactly what he said.'

Elizabeth gave a little 'Hah!' of triumph, hurled generally in her husband's direction, and said sharply to the nearest waiter, 'Please fetch the manager at once.'

The man who appeared a couple of minutes later in response to the waiter's urgent summons looked worried. He was all too aware that most of the serving staff had neglected their duties quite shamelessly to listen to Miss Bracely in the lounge.

'*Signora, signor, Altezza*,' he bowed.

'Is anything wrong?' he enquired artlessly.

'Well, now you come to mention it,' the Major said, looking up the wine list, 'we do seem to have been waiting a damned long time for someone to take our order.'

The manager made an almost imperceptible gesture with his head and Giuseppe appeared as if wheeled smoothly into position, with his notepad and pencil poised.

The manager bowed again, said, 'So sorry for the delay,' and turned to go.

'Wait!' Elizabeth said imperiously.

'That wasn't it at all,' she said, glaring at her husband. 'We wanted to ask if we might have a party here at the hotel on Thursday evening.'

'A party in your room, *signora*? But of course. Wine and sandwiches, perhaps? Nothing easier. We would be delighted to make the arrangements for you.'

'No, no,' said Elizabeth crossly, 'that won't do at all. I meant a *real* party, perhaps there in the lounge, with dancing and champagne, and perhaps some caviar.'

The Major gulped, but to his relief heard the manager explain that, with great regret, such a request was impossible to accommodate.

'The lounge is for the use of the hotel's guests, *signora*,' he explained to a disgruntled Elizabeth, who looked like a seven-year-old who had just been told that she would have to wait until next Christmas for the china doll she had been admiring in Santa's grotto in Selfridge's. Actually, wetting herself while seated on Santa's lap at Selfridge's aged seven after he had told her exactly that happened to be one of Mapp's earliest memories, as well as one of the happiest.

'If perhaps it was not high season, we might be able to make an exception,' he went on with a shrug, 'but as it is we are fully booked.'

'Perhaps if madam was to invite the whole hotel?' Giuseppe offered jokingly.

The Major was about to say 'That's a good one, eh?' but the chortle died stillborn as, with total incredulity yet a sense of awful inevitability, he heard his wife say calmly, 'Why of course that is exactly what we have in mind. So sorry if I did not make that clear.'

The manager gaped, as well he might.

'You are aware, madam, that we are fully booked?'

'Of course I am,' Elizabeth said dismissively. 'You just said so.'

'And that we have over a hundred rooms?'

'Naturally,' came the airy response. 'Everyone knows that.'

The manager and Giuseppe exchanged meaningful glances. The

Major gurgled incoherently. Ramesh's expression grew, if anything, yet more inscrutable.

'I'm sorry, madam,' the manager said uncertainly, 'but do I understand you correctly? You wish to host a party for about two hundred people – everyone currently staying at the hotel in fact? With champagne and caviar? And a dance band?'

'Certainly,' Elizabeth assured him. 'That is exactly what I wish to do. On Thursday evening.'

'Then it shall be exactly as you wish, madam,' the manager said. 'Perhaps you would be so kind as to ask for me tomorrow morning so that we may finalise the details?'

'I shall indeed,' she replied, smiling ferociously. 'Good night to you. Now then, Benjy, for goodness sake let's order.'

The Major had still not regained the power of speech, but as Giuseppe bent over him enquiringly he jabbed his finger at the very expensive Amarone. Suddenly nothing seemed to matter very much any more.

Chapter 13

The next morning Olga's conversation with Giuseppe seemed to take longer than usual. Rather than a crisp, though elegant, exchange, it seemed to evolve into a lengthy confabulation, replete with much shrugging and gesticulation by Giuseppe. Olga returned to the breakfast table wearing a serious expression.

'What's up?' Georgie enquired.

'I think she's got us this time, the old trout,' Olga replied, sounding worried. 'When Giuseppe asked her what time she would like to take dinner she said she'd like to keep it flexible and would decide nearer the time.'

'Indeed?' enquired Lucia sternly, looking up from the newspaper over her *pince-nez*.

'Fraid so,' Olga confirmed. 'Apparently the word "whim" was mentioned.'

'Indeed?' Lucia repeated, this time in a tone heavy with exasperation. 'Really, does Elizabeth never have an independent thought?'

'But surely you can see what she's up to?' Georgie asked crossly.

'Of course I can, Georgie,' Lucia said sharply. 'It is really quite obvious. Elizabeth intends to hang around in the lounge all evening until we arrive, and then rely on the Wyses inviting them to join us.'

'Which they will, of course,' Georgie concurred. 'Really, how very tarsome. Wretched woman!'

'They will if given an opportunity, yes,' Lucia replied calmly, and then maddeningly buried herself in her newspaper again.

'Hmm,' she said, as if to herself, 'I see that industrials have hit a new high. I wonder if this is the time to be selling after all?'

'Well, you know my views on *that*,' Georgie said firmly.

'I'm sorry, Georgie?' Lucia enquired, looking up from her newspaper with a little sigh at being disturbed. 'Did you say something?'

Georgie was about to say something really rather sharp, but then was suddenly struck by a new thought.

'I say,' he said slowly. 'You said yesterday you had a contingency plan.'

'Did I really?' Lucia asked distractedly. 'Dear, dear, well I never.'

'Yes, you jolly well did,' Georgie insisted. 'Now come on, Lucia, out with it!'

'Yes, do rescue us, Lucia,' Olga pleaded, adding her entreaties. 'Come up with some stroke of genius like you always do.'

'Really, how you all work me so,' Lucia said in resignation. 'Well, if you must know, I do think it is time for a change of scenery. I suggest we try one of the restaurants outside the hotel, perhaps that one down the road past the steamer station.'

'Brilliant!' cried Olga. 'Lucia, what a wonder you are.'

'Yes, well,' Georgie said, wondering why he had not been able to think of this for himself, 'brilliant indeed. I'll ask the concierge to book us a table after breakfast. What time would suit?'

Lucia made one of her tight, lingering yet quavering noises which indicated very clearly, as it was intended to, that Georgie really had not kept pace with her racing intellect after all.

'No?' Georgie queried uncertainly.

'I think not, *caro mio*,' Lucia said, as further explanation seemed to be called for. 'Much better if you go for a stroll there yourself a little later and make the arrangements. Remember, Elizabeth seems to have established the custom here already of offering large sums of money to the staff ...'

'Oh, yes,' Georgie cried hotly. 'Of course she has! How right you are, darling, as usual. Perhaps we could go there for a drink before lunch?'

'You will have to go on your own, I'm afraid, dear,' Lucia said, returning to her newspaper. 'Mr Lodge is leaving for America this afternoon and I need to discuss all the arrangements of our forthcoming transaction with him. Really, so much to think about.'

She could hardly say 'How you all work me so' again quite so soon, so she contented herself with a sad little shake of the head.

Georgie was by now contemplating what colour spats he should wear for his outing in the town. He was wearing a pair of mustard yellow Oxford bags, whose knife-edge creases would afford him lots of opportunities for really stylish leg-crossing, in which case his spats would be sure to come prominently into play. Perhaps the lilac ones? Yes, the lilac. Or perhaps the magenta? Oh, how tarsome. He would have to ask Francesco. He would be sure to know.

'Oh, then perhaps I could come with you, Georgie?' Olga asked. 'I've got a few letters to write, but that will only take an hour and a half or so.'

'Yes, do dear,' Lucia said. 'In fact, why not have lunch together somewhere as well? I do want to make the most of every minute I have left with dear Mr Lodge.'

'Parfect,' Georgie said delightedly.

'What about the Wyses?' Olga asked suddenly.

'Much the best thing if we tell them at the last moment, don't you think?' Lucia suggested. 'Perhaps a note to their rooms at about six o'clock ...?'

'Brilliant!' Olga cried again. Georgie thought, a little sourly, that she was in danger of becoming quite a bore on the subject.

'By the by,' Lucia said casually, 'it might be an idea to book a table for nine o'clock on the terrace, Georgie. Just as a back-up of course. Olga, dear, you can always tell Giuseppe that we are unlikely to need it if you like, but just so long as it is written in the book.'

Georgie gasped despite himself at this fresh demonstration of spontaneous genius.

'Oh yes,' he breathed. Then, although he already knew the answer, 'And what time at the restaurant ...?'

'Oh, I think about seven, don't you?' Lucia replied breezily. 'That way we can always be back in the lounge for a drink or something around nine. After all, it would be a pity to miss poor Elizabeth altogether.'

As Georgie was loitering outside the front door some time later, waiting for Olga, he noticed Major Benjy similarly engaged.

'Good morning, Major,' he called, raising his rather natty boater with the dark blue ribbon which Francesco had insisted would go perfectly with his lilac spats – yes, it had been the lilac ones after all – but the Major seemed unwilling to be drawn into conversation. Rather splendidly attired in a Prince of Wales check lounge suit (brand new, surely, wondered Georgie) and a pale grey fedora, he raised the latter with a curt 'Morning, Pillson,', and resumed his loitering.

Suddenly Miss Flowers appeared, dressed for tennis and carrying a racquet. As she strode into the Italian sunshine, her hair swept back and her white tennis dress dancing above her knees, she could only be described, though it would be the most dreadful cliché, as a vision of loveliness. The Major gave an involuntary exclamation of admiration and sprang into action.

'Hello,' he said, falling into step beside her. 'Off to play tennis?'

'Yes, I am.'

'Do you like tennis?'

'Not particularly.'

'Good,' said the Major without any pause in the tempo of the conversation as he took her racquet and handed it to a startled passing hotel worker. 'Let's go for a drive.'

So it was that in the space of only a very few seconds since exiting the hotel Miss Flowers found herself being handed into the most magnificent motor car she had ever seen, displaying her legs fleetingly but delightfully in the process. As the Major clambered in beside her and pressed the self-starter she found herself thinking how very masterful he could be, and wondered whether she found that attractive in a man or not. As they drove out of the gate with an ominous scraping noise from the offside pillar he said, 'Lunch somewhere?' in a nonchalant sort of way, and she decided suddenly that she did.

'Well!' Georgie said to Olga as she appeared slightly too late to appreciate this romantic vignette, 'What do you think of that?'

'What?' she asked, as well she might.

'The Major has just swept Miss Flowers off somewhere in that enormous Bugatti of his, or rather the maharajah's. Too scandalous!'

'Georgie, dear, you are a dreadful old prude,' Olga replied with a laugh. 'Is this really the man who was discovered by his wife only yesterday in the arms of another woman?'

'You beast!' Georgie cried, colouring deeply, 'You promised you wouldn't mention that ever again.'

Olga laughed again, tucked her hand into his arm, and they set off down the drive. After walking along 'the front', as Georgie insisted on calling it, they found a nice shady spot where they could drink a Negroni and watch the Como steamer come in, which Georgie enjoyed enormously, crossing his legs casually and expertly whenever anyone glanced in their direction after their companion had commented that surely that woman over there was a famous opera singer.

Then they continued on to the restaurant where they had *vitello al tonno* and a crisp *verdichio*, with they both pronounced an excellent combination on what was becoming a rather warm day. Not forgetting to make a reservation for six people that evening, they strolled back to the hotel in a leisurely fashion.

Georgie by this time was feeling the heat, and retired to his room, where he found his faithful retainer waiting to minister to him. In a matter of minutes he was out of his clothes and in a tepid bath, which he found most delightful. Then once again he daringly wore a shirt with no collar as he began to settle himself on the balcony for the afternoon.

'Now then, Francesco,' he said, having been plucking up courage to broach the subject since the previous evening, 'I wanted to talk to you about these cigarettes of yours.'

'I can easily give the address of my supplier, if you wish, sir,' he replied, 'though I cannot of course allow him to reveal the precise combination of ingredients.'

'Yes, well, it's the ingredients I wanted to talk to you about, actually,' Georgie said in what he hoped was a very severe tone of voice indeed. 'Am I correct in believing them to include hashish?'

Francesco shrugged.

'A little harmless essence of poppy sir, yes. Many gentleman find it very relaxing, you know, more so even than the tobacco itself.'

'Yes, well, I do think you might have told me,' Georgie said, feeling as he did so that he really should be taking an altogether sterner line. 'My wife, you know ...'

He faltered, and Francesco raised his eyebrows.

'Your wife, sir?'

'Well, actually, she found Miss Bracely and me on the sofa together after we had both been smoking them.'

Francesco raised his eyebrows again.

'My compliments, sir. Miss Bracely is a very attractive woman.'

'That's not the point,' Georgie snapped, stung now into genuine outrage. 'It was all most embarrassing. My wife ...'

'Took it amiss, perhaps, sir?'

'Yes, and ...'

Francesco sighed.

'That is the trouble with wives in my experience, sir, if I may be permitted to say so. They leave a man all too little ... discretion.'

'Yes, well,' Georgie said, and then it all came out in a rush.

'If you must know, she wants me to dismiss you. She says you are a bad influence upon me.'

He found that Francesco had lit one of his Turkish cigarettes for him, and drew heavily on it to calm his agitation. It did indeed seem to have a very relaxing effect.

'And are you going to dismiss me, sir?' Francesco asked with a worried frown.

'Oh, no, I suppose not,' Georgie said unhappily. 'Oh, blast Lucia! Why does she have to be so tarsome about all this?'

Francesco brought an ashtray over to the balcony table, and leant close to place it beside him, so close that Georgie could clearly smell his perfume. He wondered if it might be one of those new French colognes, and what it might be like to wear a daring cologne himself rather than just boring old toilet water.

'I did enjoy your recital with Miss Bracely, sir,' his valet murmured respectfully. 'I had no idea you were such a talented pianist in addition to your painting skills.'

'Thank you,' Georgie replied awkwardly into Francesco's shirt front. He found his heart was suddenly beating more quickly, doubtless as a result of his agitation.

'Tell me, sir,' Francesco enquired softly. 'You are clearly such a sensitive gentleman. Do you possess any other particular ... artistic tastes?'

This at least was an easy question to answer.

'Why, yes,' Georgie said brightly. 'How clever of you to guess. Actually, do you know, I'm very fond of needlepoint.'

Francesco moved away and said, 'Indeed, sir' as he gently closed the French window.

Unlike Georgie's balcony, Mapp's looked out over the side of the hotel, and so she was able to observe, as Georgie could not, the return of the Royale and its occupants. It now bore a very different appearance to that which it had enjoyed a few hours previously. One front wing was hopelessly crumpled, and the headlight on that side of the car was leaning over at a drunken angle. 'Drunken' is perhaps an unfortunate choice of words. Let us content ourselves with the merest factual outline, which is that the Royale had come together rather briskly with a lorry travelling in the opposite direction after the Major had enjoyed an excellent lunch and was driving one-handed. With the other hand he was stroking Miss Flowers' knee in what he hoped she would understand to be a companionable and reflective sort of way, while she was exercising as much effort to arrest the progress of his hand as might decently be expected of a young lady, without deterring a gentleman altogether.

Elizabeth observed them get out of the car and stand side by side inspecting the damage, noting with disapproval that the young woman was wearing what could only be reckoned a very short dress indeed.

She then observed, with mounting grimness of countenance, Miss Flowers take the Major's arm, stand on tiptoe to kiss him quickly, say something to him and then skip away giggling into the hotel. The Major, still blissfully unaware that he had been the object of his wife's beady gaze for some time, beamed, stroked his moustache, set his fedora on his head at a jaunty angle, and strode into the hotel in a debonair, man-about-town sort of way that in other circumstances Elizabeth might have found indescribably attractive, but now forced from her a spontaneous scream of rage.

On entering their suite the Major found himself at the epicentre of a storm of ever-increasing ferocity which ended only when his wife became quite literally speechless and retired to the bedroom, banging the door behind her, to collapse prone in noisy, racking sobs on the bed. The Major was unable to retire to his own room to nurse his wounds, as the Mapp-Flints' suite was somewhat smaller than the one which Mapp had attempted nefariously to purloin, and ran only to a bedroom and a living room. In ordinary circumstances this would have posed no difficulty, since the Mapp-Flints were in the habit of sharing not only the same bedroom but the same bed, something which polite Tilling society privately thought was taking matrimony altogether too far. Since he now felt a strong urge to leave the room, however, the only place left to go was the balcony. Seizing a bottle of whisky and a glass, he stalked morosely on to it and sat down to contemplate, over a comforting chota peg or two, the many unfairnesses of the world, his reflections gradually becoming dimmer and dimmer until finally his chin sank on to his chest and they faded altogether. The lopsided headlamps of the Royale gazed up at him in mute reproach as he slumbered.

In a different room of the hotel, Frau Zirchner was at this moment haranguing Miss Flowers both for neglecting her duties as a lady's companion and for displaying an unseemly eagerness for male company. Fortunately, as she grew angrier she lapsed spontaneously into Swiss-German, a language which Miss Flowers understood hardly at all and which seemed to consist largely of umlauts with a verb at the end every now and then. So she stood in her little white tennis dress with her eyes cast down demurely, and said '*Das tut mir leid*' at intervals until the torrent abated.

Frau Zirchner then became the second female occupant of the hotel in quick succession to burst into tears, explaining at great length that she felt responsible for her companion's moral welfare, and that this must inevitably be deeply compromised by her going off alone in a motor car with a married man. Miss Flowers now switched to '*Entschuldigung sie mich*', which seemed to answer quite well until, mercifully, it grew time to dress for dinner.

Back on the Pillson balcony, Francesco gently woke Georgie from his slumbers.

'Time to dress for dinner, sir,' he murmured apologetically.

'Oh really,' Georgie said drowsily. 'How tarsome.'

'I left it as long as I dared, sir,' his valet said soothingly. 'Madam started getting ready about fifteen minutes ago.'

'Oh, very well,' Georgie said reluctantly, and rose from his chair.

As they moved through the living room and into the bedroom Francesco seemed a little distracted, as if deciding whether to broach a particular subject of conversation. Finally he came to a decision, and did.

'Beg pardon, sir, but I was wondering if we might have a private conversation at your convenience. There is a matter which I feel we ought to discuss.'

'Why yes, certainly,' Georgie replied, feeling suddenly both uneasy and excited without being sure why. 'We could talk now, if you like.'

Francesco darted a meaningful glance at the door.

'The matter is of a highly personal nature, sir. I was wondering if we might meet in the gardens after dinner?'

'Why yes,' Georgie agreed, slightly breathlessly. 'Let's.'

Chapter 14

Lucia, Georgie and Olga walked, bold as brass, down the driveway of the hotel, having announced loudly to anyone who cared to listen that they were just going for a stroll before dinner, 'and perhaps a quick drink somewhere'. The Wyses and Amelia followed some minutes later, but without any such broadcast, as Mr Wyse was not sure of the propriety of deliberately misleading people as to his intentions. His father had many years earlier, noting this, resigned himself to the fact that his son would be fatally debarred from any career in politics.

The evening was still warm, and so they strolled slowly along the road which ran alongside the lake, leading down to the steamer jetty. One of the last boats of the day was coming in from the northern shores of the lake, and Georgie stopped to cast an expert eye over the docking operations, as befitted a man who owned a yachting cap and had once stayed in a hotel in Folkestone.

Suddenly Lucia gave a little cry of excitement.

'Look!' she cried, indicating the name painted on the bows. 'It's the *Vittoria* – see the name there on the pointy end. That's the one we will be having all to ourselves tomorrow.'

This sudden pride of ownership seemed to make standing there gazing at the steamer a much less dilettante activity. As the steady flow of passengers walking up the landing stage ebbed and then stopped altogether, Lucia strode determinedly in the opposite direction. As she stepped on to the deck, two crew members started gesticulating and shouting at her.

Olga, hurrying to catch up, said 'They're telling you that they've just finished their last voyage of the day, Lucia. They think you want them to take you somewhere.'

'Yes, I know,' said Lucia untruthfully, 'but I just wanted to speak to the dear captain, to say how very much we are all looking forward to our party tomorrow.'

Olga at length managed to make the deckhands understand the grave import of Lucia's wishes, and the captain finally and reluctantly arrived. He listened impassively to Olga's introduction of this prominent lady from English society, but shook hands politely with Lucia, and then, rather quizzically, with Georgie, who essayed a naval salute and nearly dislodged his toupée in the process. He grew more animated when he learned that not only Olga Bracely the opera singer but also the great Gabriele d'Annunzio would be among the guests, and ended up wishing them farewell in a friendly manner. As Lucia insisted on Olga translating her instructions for the following evening in minute detail, his farewells became increasingly enthusiastic.

Finally, Georgie, whose new buckskin boots were pinching him rather dreadfully, said, 'Oh look, here come the Wyses,' at which Lucia reluctantly abandoned her role as supercargo and retraced her steps along the landing stage, pausing every few paces to turn, raise her hand and say '*Arrivederci*' very gravely to the crew.

'Oh, if only I had my paints with me,' Georgie lamented as they strolled towards the restaurant, 'though I'm honestly not sure whether I could do justice to this light. Isn't it wonderful?'

'Truly wonderful, Georgie,' Lucia agreed, imparting a deep, resonant vibrancy to the word 'wonderful' which drew a quick glance of appreciation from Olga as she heard Lucia's voice momentarily connect along its full length.

As indeed was the restaurant, all agreed, with Mr Wyse complimenting, with a bow, naturally, Mr Pillson and Miss Bracely on their splendid choice. They sat outside on a private terrace, the waters of the lake lapping sluggishly just a few feet away.

Mr Wyse seemed on edge, as though feeling a deep need to unburden himself on some distressing topic. After his first glass of prosecco, he felt sufficiently emboldened to do so, prompted largely by dark, meaningful glances of increasing urgency from his sister.

'Dear lady,' he said to Lucia, 'forgive me, but we find ourselves in a situation of some delicacy. May I lay the matter before you and invite your advice?'

'By all means, Mr Wyse,' Lucia replied warmly. After all, giving advice was one of her favourite occupations.

'You see,' he began, his nose wrinkling, a sure sign that the matter was indeed of the utmost delicacy, 'just before we left the hotel we were approached by Mrs Mapp-Flint.'

'Waylaid, more like,' Amelia commented sourly.

Mr Wyse thought it best to ignore this unhelpful interjection and continued serenely as though it had never occurred.

'She intimated that she had decided to hold a party tomorrow evening, and that naturally our presence would be expected.'

'Not "invited", mind,' Amelia stressed, eager that everyone should properly appreciate the situation, 'just "expected" – pah!'

'Amelia, please,' Susan murmured.

'And what did you say?' Lucia asked innocently.

'I must confess that I was in something of a quandary,' he replied awkwardly. 'You see, on the one hand I would normally have explained straightaway, with regrets, naturally, that we already had a prior engagement.'

Lucia made one of her little noises, this time carefully nuanced to convey slight alarm and surprise, all couched in a spirit of further enquiry.

'But, you see, it occurred to me,' Mr Wyse went on, 'that you might not wish the Mapp-Flints to know about your own *soirée* tomorrow.'

'Of course,' he said, becoming increasingly embarrassed and gazing round the table as if hoping that someone would rescue him from his predicament, 'I could not be sure what the true situation was. It was my impression, however, rightly or wrongly, that they had not been invited, hence the difficulty of the situation in which I found myself.'

'And all my fault,' Lucia said at once. 'Dear Mr Wyse, you must forgive me for causing you this embarrassment. How you must have cursed me.'

'Not at all,' Mr Wyse protested gallantly, but Lucia held up an imperious hand.

'It was my fault, and that is an end to the matter. *Mea culpa.*'

'So, what did you say?' asked Georgie, overcome with curiosity.

'I said that we would need to check our diaries and would reply in the morning,' Mr Wyse explained wretchedly, 'but I fear that she saw straight through me.'

'So, I hustled him and Susan away before they could say anything else, or she could ask us about our dinner plans,' Amelia said briskly. 'Best thing for it. Damn woman! Why does she have to make such trouble for everyone?'

'Amelia, dear!' Susan exclaimed, feeling that she ought to be shocked. 'She was only inviting us to a party. That hardly counts as making trouble.'

'And why do you think she is holding a party, at such short notice, mind, at exactly the same time as Lucia?' the Contessa demanded.

'Quite!' Georgie concurred. 'Obviously she has found out about it, from someone at the hotel presumably, and this is her response.'

'How very like Elizabeth,' Olga said sadly. 'How very unhappy she must be.'

'Poor Elizabeth,' Lucia said, trying hard to make it clear that she agreed with Olga's first statement but found the second one somewhat irrelevant. 'How very like her indeed. I would hate to have such a suspicious and vindictive mind.'

The Wyses made little squirming movements indicative of wishing to dissociate themselves from the full force of such sentiments, but any such intentions dissolved rapidly in the face of Amelia's fixed glare.

'And how very much like you, dear Mr Wyse,' Lucia continued, 'to display such charming sensitivity. Elizabeth was of course taking advantage of your kind nature in order to embarrass you, but then of course you know that.'

Any attempt by the Wyses at contradiction, no matter how tentative, were again nipped in the bud by Amelia's stern gaze.

'As it is,' Lucia pressed on, 'you may safely leave matters to me. I will speak to Elizabeth when we return to the hotel.'

'Well,' said Georgie, whose stomach had been rumbling for a few minutes now, hopefully heard by nobody but himself, 'that's all settled then. Why don't we ask for the menus?'

'Yes please,' Olga said with feeling.

Fortunately this did not prove a difficult undertaking, since the waiter had been hovering for some time.

As Lucia put on her *pince-nez* to gaze at the menu, she suddenly remembered something and looked up over its pages at Georgie.

'Georgie,' she said, 'and dear Olga too, since you will remember our days in Riseholme only too well, do you remember that dear little museum we started there? So silly, of course, but it seemed important to us at the time. Do you remember?'

Georgie felt a dreadful premonition and started to say no, but unfortunately Olga said 'Yes' at the same time. Lucia gazed at him rather coldly.

'I am surprised you do not remember, *caro mio*. You were, after all, a member of the committee.'

'Oh, well, now you come to mention it, I think I do remember something of the sort,' Georgie admitted, and then added insouciantly, 'So silly, as you say.'

'I was wondering,' Lucia mused, ignoring his childish sally, 'whether we might not attempt something else in Tilling, but perhaps on an altogether grander scale. Something celebrating the cultural life of our dear Tilling, and its place in the world. Our musical evenings, our new church organ, our splendidly equipped hospital and sporting facilities ...'

'Yes,' Georgie said, pretending to be preoccupied with inspecting the menu, 'that's all very well, Lucia, but don't you think there might be just the teeniest possibility that some people might accuse you of constructing a museum to your own achievements, like that frightful d'Annunzio fellow?'

Lucia decided that now was not the time to launch a frontal assault on Georgie's position, and so gave her silvery little laugh.

'So ridiculous, dear, of course. No, a civic museum, perhaps, a museum of the mayoralty even, celebrating all the famous mayors in Tilling's proud history.'

'Capital idea!' said Mr Wyse, with a little bow to Lucia, 'and as one of our most prominent mayors, dear lady, it would be only right if at least part of a room was indeed dedicated to your own achievements.'

'Oh,' said Lucia, as if greatly surprised, 'well, if you think so, Mr Wyse, then I suppose we must give the idea every due consideration.'

In truth she felt acutely disappointed. She had been envisaging at least two separate rooms of her paintings, together with photographs of her proud record of public patronage. Perhaps there might even be room for a bicycle and a piano? However, part of a room, though sadly demonstrating a paucity of imagination on Mr Wyse's part, was better than nothing. Any subsequent expansion into the rest of the available space could doubtless be arranged on a gradual though natural basis.

'I knew it!' Georgie muttered in exasperation to Olga behind his menu. 'That wretched man!'

'Did you say something, *caro mio*?' Lucia asked sweetly.

'I was just saying that there was wretched ham on the menu again,' Georgie replied. 'Really, it seems quite impossible to get away from it in Italy.'

'Well, my dear,' Lucia replied brightly, 'we are in the land of *prosciutto, non è vero?*'

Suddenly she broke into a little frown and brought her notebook and pencil out of her handbag.

'Do excuse me writing at the dinner table, everybody,' she said, 'but I really must make a note of something while I think of it.'

'Something about tomorrow evening, dear?' Susan asked.

'No, dear,' Lucia answered briskly, 'the Nobel Prize, actually. I find I am most shockingly ignorant about the conditions for eligibility. I really must find out more.'

Major Benjy was once again having to suffer the pangs of hunger as his wife sat squarely and resolutely in the lounge, refusing to go in to dinner, Ramesh installed politely by her side.

'You don't think we might go in, now?' the major suggested for the umpteenth time, gazing at his whisky glass, which seemed somehow to have emptied itself of its contents once again.

His wife fixed him with a stern gaze which mingled reproof and contempt.

'Only a little longer to wait now, Benjy,' she said determinedly. 'I know they've booked for nine, and it's ten to now. I've specially asked for a table for nine people, so there'll be no way they can wriggle out of it this time.'

'Oh well, in that case,' the major said resignedly, and looked around for a waiter to order another chota peg. Elizabeth looked at him forbiddingly, but he managed to avoid her eye.

In fact it was not for another twenty minutes that Elizabeth's quarry entered the lounge. Expressions of delighted surprise volleyed back and forth. Amelia simply grunted and adjusted her monocle.

'Well, now everybody's here,' Elizabeth enthused, 'we can all go in to dinner together. I've asked Giuseppe to give us one big table all together.'

The Wyses shifted uneasily from one foot to another.

'So sorry, dear,' Lucia said sweetly, 'but we've dined already.'

Elizabeth gaped.

'Dined already?' she repeated in disbelief. 'But you can't have. I mean, your reservation is for nine.'

'Oh, what a stupid mistake,' Lucia said with a little laugh. 'Yes, I remember now, we did book a table for nine o'clock, but then we changed our minds. Georgie, dear, how remiss of us, we quite forgot to cancel it. I do hope Giuseppe won't be too cross with us.'

'So, you're not dining, then?' the Major queried. 'Don't quite catch your drift, dear lady. I thought you said you'd eaten already?'

'Yes, in a restaurant in town,' Lucia replied.

'A restaurant?' Elizabeth echoed blankly.

'Yes, just at the end of the road by the steamer jetty,' Georgie proffered helpfully. 'Jolly good, actually. We can recommend it, can't we, Olga?'

'Yes, very good indeed,' she confirmed.

'Perhaps you should try it one night yourselves, dear?' Lucia suggested to Elizabeth. 'It would make such a nice change from hanging around here in the lounge all evening.'

There was a sharp intake of breath from the Wyses. Lucia pressed on.

'Still, I expect you've had plenty of opportunities to dance, eh Major? Which lucky lady was it tonight?'

'Ah,' he replied, 'no, actually, not tonight.'

For some reason Miss Flowers had been whisked straight upstairs after dinner by Frau Zirchner, who perhaps had been suffering from constipation, as she had almost given the impression of scowling across the room at him.

'Perhaps you should try a turn with Olga, Major? I'm sure she'd be happy to oblige,' Lucia said.

'Ah,' came from the Major, this time a rather brighter and more hopeful 'Ah'.

'Sadly we must go in to dinner,' Elizabeth said with glacial calm. 'After all, we have been waiting a long time already.'

'Yes indeed, dear,' Lucia concurred sympathetically, 'you must be absolutely famished. Poor Major Benjy, you look quite faint. Why, you should have positively insisted that Elizabeth gave you something to eat. Poor Ramesh too – not good to go without food at his age surely, Elizabeth dear?'

Mapp managed with difficulty to unlock her jaw, and counter-attacked robustly.

'Dear Mr and Mrs Wyse,' she said with a determined smile, 'and Contessa too, of course. Perhaps you have been able to consult your diaries for tomorrow evening.'

'Tomorrow evening?' Lucia asked, raising her eyebrows.

'Yes, dear, giving a party. You are all invited too, of course.'

The Wyses' unease grew palpable, but Lucia forestalled the need for any response.

'Elizabeth!' she marvelled, drawing our each syllable so that the word almost assumed the proportions of a whole sentence. 'What a wonderful idea! But how unfortunate! Why, I was just about to invite you all to a party of my own tomorrow evening. What a shame you won't be able to come. So sad.'

'But the Wyses?' Elizabeth persisted, her smile more rictus-like than ever.

'Already promised to me, I'm afraid dear,' Lucia said sadly. 'Why, I invited them this morning. Dear Mr Wyse, why all this Italian sunshine must be making you a little forgetful.'

'Indeed it must,' he agreed uncomfortably. 'You see, dear lady,' with a bow to Elizabeth, 'I thought there *was* something but I couldn't quite remember, hence the need to consult my diary.'

'Yes,' Susan assisted him, 'we find that we need to write everything down these days or we quite forget about it.'

'I do hope our presence won't be missed,' Lucia cooed. 'Presumably you have lots of other people coming?'

'Yes,' said Ramesh, 'the whole jolly hotel actually.'

Olga guffawed.

'Really, Ramesh,' she said, 'you are a scream.'

Remembering his appointment, Georgie made his excuses, saying that he wanted a walk in the gardens. Lucia and Olga looked puzzled, but said nothing.

He went through the lobby and out on to the drive. Gravel crunched underfoot as he walked towards the end of the area which was illuminated by electric light. Beyond there seemed to be only darkness, but as he moved into unknown territory his eyes grew accustomed to the moonlight and he realised that he could see quite easily. He moved further into the gardens and looked around uncertainly. Suddenly a figure detached itself from underneath a tree and glided towards him through the undergrowth.

'Francesco?' he said uncertainly.

'Yes,' he answered. 'I'm glad you came. I was afraid you wouldn't.'

'Oh,' Georgie said, unsure how to respond, and then, 'I hope I didn't keep you waiting.'

'Not really,' Francesco replied. 'I was just enjoying the night air. Would you like a cigarette?'

'Oh, yes please.'

There was a pause while Francesco extracted two Turkish cigarettes from his case, put them both in his mouth to light them, and then passed one to Georgie. Somehow this seemed the most effortlessly glamorous thing that Georgie had ever seen.

'I do hope you don't think me too forward to suggest us meeting like this,' Francesco said quietly, 'but there is something we ought to discuss.'

'Oh,' Georgie said again. He was grateful that it was night-time, for somehow he knew that he was blushing.

'Shall we take a little stroll, perhaps?' Francesco suggested.

'Oh yes, let's,' Georgie agreed, grateful for a question he could answer.

They walked in silence towards the pool area.

'I felt we should find somewhere to talk discreetly,' Francesco said after a while, 'because it seems to me that we have become very good friends.'

'Yes, I know what you mean,' Georgie answered uncertainly and then, hardly knowing what he was saying, 'do you know, my life seems to have become much more exciting since I met you.'

Francesco drew his arm through Georgie's and pulled him close. 'It's about to get much more exciting,' he promised.

Lucia, taking a breath of air on the balcony despite her stated aversion to mosquitoes, observed all this from a distance. As they disappeared from view behind a tree, the ends of their cigarettes glowing bright red in the darkness, her mouth set in a thin, straight line.

Chapter 15

The atmosphere at breakfast the next morning was, if possible, even frostier than hitherto. Major Benjy was clearly extremely hungover, presumably the result of a couple of bottles of wine on top of the numerous chota pegs he had imbibed during his long vigil in the lounge. Mr and Mrs Wyse pointedly sat at a table in the exact middle of the room, equidistant between the Mapp-Flint and Pillson parties.

Lucia was reading a note which had been left for her at reception.

'How wonderful,' she beamed. 'Mr Lodge is returning today before departing finally for America. We still have a great deal to talk about concerning our proposed corporate finance transaction.'

'Is that what it's called?' Georgie asked grumpily.

'Indeed it is,' Lucia assured him, 'when there is any question of a control premium. No, I am a humble investor no longer, Georgie, but a financier.'

Georgie grimaced sourly and muttered something inaudible about the poor-house. Truth to tell he was a little hungover too, but had not dared to bring his Kruschen salts downstairs with him after Lucia's comments on the previous occasion he had felt the need to resort to them. Hangover or not, his mind was still in a whirl after his encounter with Francesco the night before, so he was not really in a mood to concentrate on the plans of financiers, whether English or American.

'So does that mean you will be occupied today, Lucia?' Olga asked.

'Probably best to assume so, dear,' Lucia said, the note still in her hand. 'I am sure I can leave you and Georgie to your own devices.'

Giuseppe now came over and addressed some words in Italian to Olga, who said 'No!' in gratifying Tilling style as he slipped away again.

'What is it?' Georgie and Lucia asked in unison.

'Apparently Elizabeth really *has* invited everyone in the hotel to her party,' Olga informed them. 'Giuseppe reckons it's close on two hundred people, and champagne and caviar for everyone.'

'No!' said Lucia and Georgie once again.

'Is she completely mad?' Georgie asked, goggling. 'I mean, what can that possibly be costing?'

'Chalked up on the maharajah's slate, presumably, as Irene would say,' Lucia observed, gazing across the room at Elizabeth.

'But even so ...' protested her husband.

'Giuseppe says it was the only way they would let her take over the lounge at short notice in high season,' Olga informed them. 'They thought she was joking at first, but apparently not.'

'Well!' Georgie said. 'What nerve!'

'So sad,' Lucia lamented with a little shake of the head, 'that she should feel driven to go to such lengths just to trump my little *soirée*. Poor Elizabeth.'

'Poor maharajah, you mean,' Georgie added with feeling. 'After all, he's the one who's going to have to pick up the bill.'

'Oh, and another piece of news,' Olga said. 'There's cholera in Naples now, though nobody's quite sure how it got across from Capri, what with the quarantine and everything.'

They all gazed at the Contessa, who was attacking some toast and black coffee.

'Probably best not to say anything,' Lucia decided.

'Though we should probably abandon any thoughts of heading further south,' she added after a moment's reflection.

Georgie and Olga nodded. Lucia crumpled the note briskly and dropped it in the ashtray.

'And now, dear ones, I must leave you,' she said, and rose from the table. 'Mr Lodge is expecting me at ten. *Au reservoir.*'

With a corporate financial sort of wave she left them. Georgie ordered another pot of tea.

'So, what shall we do with ourselves?' he asked. 'It sounds like we've got all day to ourselves.'

'Well, I don't know if you're game,' Olga said, 'but I have some friends who are staying at the Villa d'Este and they have a couple of professional tango dancers from Argentina giving lessons today. We're invited, if you like.'

'Rather,' Georgie replied. 'How thrilling! I've always wanted to dance the tango.'

'This is the real thing, mind,' Olga cautioned him. 'The Argentinian dance, not the pale imitation of it that the ballroom types trot out. I've seen it done in Buenos Aires. It's terribly naughty. I have to wrap myself round you while you get all masterful with me.'

"Oh," Georgie said, suddenly feeling rather unsure. 'You mean, a bit like a Highland reel?'

'Not exactly, no,' she replied.

She put down her napkin and laughed.

'Don't worry, dear,' she said reassuringly. 'If in doubt, just put your hand on my bottom and push me firmly where you want me to go.'

'Oh,' said Georgie faintly. He decided that he really should take his Kruschen salts after all.

'So, I'm going to some tango lessons with Miss Bracely,' Georgie told Francesco. 'There! What do you think of that?'

'How very exciting,' Francesco commented. 'May I suggest your cherry pink trousers? They are a little tighter than the others, and will show off your figure to advantage.'

He surveyed Georgie's posterior with an expert eye.

'Well, if you think so,' Georgie said. Then, as Francesco was flicking through the clothes hangers in the wardrobe, 'Tell me, is the tango really as shocking as everybody seems to think?'

'It enjoys a risqué reputation, certainly,' Francesco conceded, emerging with an armful of folded pink cotton. 'You know, Kaiser Wilhelm forbade German officers from dancing it while in uniform.'

'Goodness!' Georgie said in surprise. 'That seems a little draconian – to forbid an officer from partnering a lady in the dance of his choice, or her choice come to that.'

'I have always believed his late Majesty was chiefly concerned about his officers dancing it with each other,' Francesco said. 'Various Prussian regiments have some rather strange habits in the mess.'

'Oh, now,' said Georgie rather breathlessly as Francesco unbuttoned him, 'you really can be very naughty, you know.'

'Just trying to relax you, my dear chap,' Francesco said, looking up at him with a smile. 'I can't help feeling that you've been rather tense since our little excursion in the garden last night.'

'Oh, yes, well, perhaps,' Georgie replied uncertainly as Francesco slipped his trousers down his legs. He wondered whether a double dose of Kruschen salts was allowed. He would have to check the label.

The steamer deposited them at Cernobbio and it was but a short walk to the Villa d'Este which was, if anything, even grander than their hotel. Shouts of welcome quickly greeted Olga from her friends, who seemed mostly to be American, and were introduced to Georgie in a bewildering welter of middle initials. This disorientating process over, he was free to observe events as three people came into the room.

Two, a man and a woman, were young and darkly attractive. The third, older, carried a musical instrument like no other Georgie had ever seen. At first glance it resembled a piano accordion, but on closer inspection had no keys, only a baffling battery of buttons. While he was still trying to work out how it operated, the musician started flexing it and suddenly the most amazing music came forth, with swooping, passionate phrases and a pulsing rhythm that set one's feet moving of their own volition in time to it. As the last few guests slipped into the room behind his back, the two dancers demonstrated a few basic steps and, clapping their hands, encouraged everyone to try them for themselves. Georgie half turned as his partner came into his arms and found himself staring from a distance of about two inches at Poppy, Duchess of Sheffield.

He gave an involuntary cry of alarm.

'Don't worry, my dear little man,' she murmured comfortingly, 'I've done this before.'

'But I really don't know what to do,' he replied, panicking.

'It's all a question of getting very close together,' she assured him. 'Like this.'

He felt two strong arms clamp themselves around his ribcage and sweep him onwards and outwards into the room. Poppy gazed intently into his eyes.

'What a dear little beard,' she whispered.

Above the sound of the music he was sure he could hear Olga laughing.

At the end of the dance the *bandoneon*, for such it was, he would later discover, launched straight into another one. This time the rhythm was less insistent and the music had pauses, during each of which it was apparently necessary to Poppy to hold him in a tight clinch and rest her head, and goodness knows what else besides, on his chest while blowing coyly into his beard.

Finally the music came to an end and somebody shouted 'Change partners'. Poppy was separated from him with reluctance, wiggling her fingers in coquettish farewell, and at last the nightmare was over and it was Olga who now nestled in his embrace.

'Poor darling,' she said. 'Are you in shock?'

'Did you know she was going to be here?' he gasped.

'Not for certain,' she said. 'Anyway, it's not my fault you have such power over women.'

'That's not funny,' he said fiercely.

'Sorry, dear,' she said sympathetically. 'Personally I think it's those

173

pink trousers of yours. They're guaranteed to drive anyone wild with desire.'

At this she burst into unconstrained mirth once again, though she would later claim that she had been laughing for pure joy at the combination of him, the dance and the music.

By lunchtime Georgie's nerves could take no more. Since there were only four men and four women at the lesson it meant that he had to dance with Poppy twice out of every eight times, and she was becoming increasingly forward and over-familiar with every occurrence. Worse, the three of them ended up having lunch together.

'Couldn't get into your hotel,' Poppy informed them after she had ordered dressed crab and black coffee, 'so I thought I'd stay here and sort of pop over to see you. But as it was, you saved me the trouble.'

'How wonderful to see you again, anyway, Poppy,' Olga said. 'Now, actually I've got a surprise for you. Lucia's having a party this evening on one of the steamers and you're invited.'

'Are you sure?' asked Georgie. 'I'm not sure there's room.'

'Quite sure,' Olga assured him. 'I've just phoned Lucia at the hotel and she's delighted that Poppy will be joining us. You will, won't you, dear?'

'Lucia?' Poppy queried vacantly.

'Now it's really no good, Poppy,' Olga scolded her. 'You can't go on pretending not to know Lucia like this. Why, you've stayed at her house in Tilling, and she got you dressed crab specially.'

'Ah,' said Poppy with a bare minimum of acknowledgement. 'Paraded me in front of all her friends as I remember it.'

'You can't blame her for that,' Olga replied. 'Why, nobody would believe that you'd been there the last time, and it was the only way the poor woman could prove she wasn't a liar.'

'I dare say,' Poppy said, clearly unconvinced.

'Now you will come, won't you? Georgie will be there, you know.'

'Ah,' Poppy said with much more animation, 'then I will, of course.'

'Oh, goody,' Georgie said, glaring at Olga.

Poppy gazed at him in frank admiration.

'Such a dear little beard,' she repeated, and then, to a waiter who came to serve her coffee, 'he's the mayor of Tilling, you know.'

'And you must stop that as well, Poppy,' Olga said sternly. 'You know very well that Lucia was mayor, not Georgie. It was all a silly misunderstanding, and it was cleared up ages ago.'

Poppy's rather misty eyes were fixed on Georgie.

'You're not the mayor of Tilling?' she asked rather forlornly.

'Certainly not,' he said firmly. 'That was Lucia.'

'My wife,' he added equally firmly, as Poppy's hand strayed on to his knee.

'Such a pity,' she said. 'Such a nice beard.'

'Now you will be nice to Lucia, won't you?' Olga demanded. 'None of this pretending not to know who she is.'

'Wretched woman came to the castle,' Poppy commented. 'When I was ill.'

'That was a misunderstanding too, as I've told you many times,' Olga explained patiently. 'She was expecting to find me and Georgie there. It wasn't her fault we'd changed our plans and hadn't had time to tell her. We didn't tell her you were ill because we thought she would be staying in Tilling.'

To this Poppy made no reply, but began to attack her crab.

After lunch Olga released Georgie from any prospect of further physical contact with Poppy and the two of them made their back to Bellagio by steamer.

'So who exactly is coming, then?' Georgie asked.

'Don't you know?' Olga replied in surprise. 'Surely she's discussed it with you?'

'I'm sure she's mentioned it,' he said airily, 'but you know what she's like when she's organising something. I tend to switch off, rather.'

'Poor Lucia,' Olga said with some asperity. 'Really, Georgie, you're almost as bad as Poppy.'

He shuddered visibly at the mention of her name.

'So, who then?' he repeated grumpily.

'The three of us plus d'Annunzio, who's flying over this afternoon,' she said, ticking people off on her fingers. 'The Wyses, the Contessa and now Poppy. So that's eight, I suppose. A nice number.'

'A lot fewer than Elizabeth will be entertaining,' Georgie said sourly.

'Yes, wasn't that silly?' Olga cried. 'Why, all the woman had to do was wait a bit and Lucia would have invited her to the steamer party. Now instead she's saddled the poor old maharajah with an enormous bill for a totally unnecessary party.'

'Yes,' Georgie concurred. 'Difficult to see what she was trying to achieve. If she was trying to wheedle the Wyses away from us surely there were easier ways to go about it? And anyway, she's failed.'

'She really is a bit cracked, I think,' Olga mused. 'She's genuinely obsessed with going one better than Lucia all the time. And it's such a tragedy because she can't, and she never will. Why can't she just accept that, instead of making herself unhappy?'

They both leaned on the rail and watched the wake streaming away behind the boat.

'I suppose Lucia would have invited her?' Georgie asked thoughtfully. 'What do you think?'

'Oh yes,' Olga said assuredly.

They both watched the wake a bit more.

'But she'd probably have waited to the last possible moment, to make her sweat,' she added.

'Well, really, I'm not sure that she should have done,' Georgie said suddenly. 'I don't mean to sound unkind, but Elizabeth did deliberately try to spoil our holiday by dogging our footsteps, didn't she?'

'Yes, she did,' Olga agreed calmly, 'but if she hadn't invited her then Elizabeth would have seen it as a mortal insult, and the Wyses would have been very upset too, and things would have been quite impossible when everybody got back to Tilling. Lucia knows that, she understands it. Making Elizabeth look silly and petty is one thing, but completely stifling any normal intercourse in Tilling is quite another.'

'I do wonder how it'll turn out,' Georgie said. 'Elizabeth's party, I mean.'

'Hopefully we'll be back in time to go along for the end of it,' Olga ventured. 'I think I'll suggest it to Lucia actually, if she'll listen. If only for the Major and Ramesh, I do think we should at least put in an appearance if we possibly can.'

The wake started to bend away from them as the boat swung to starboard to approach Bellagio.

'You're right of course, Olga,' Georgie said with a sigh. 'As usual.'

The object of their conversation was at that moment drinking tea on her balcony with the Major.

'Poor Mr and Mrs Wyse,' she stated stoutly. 'Acutely embarrassed, poor dears, as well they might be expected to be. Would love to come to our party, but Lady Bountiful won't let them.'

'Maybe she really did ask them first?' the Major proffered unhelpfully. 'After all, Liz-girl, fair's fair, she did organise her party before you arranged yours, you know.'

'I don't believe that for a moment,' she said dismissively.

The Major was not sure exactly which bit of his statement she did not believe for a moment, but wisely decided not to pursue the matter.

'Rum do last night,' he said, changing the subject.

'Mmm?' Elizabeth enquired, showing only the most marginal interest.

'Yes, went for a stroll outside after dinner,' the Major said, sounding dangerously as if he was embarking on one of his Indian stories. 'But discovered I'd left my gaspers up here in the room. Then I saw someone I thought was Pillson up ahead, so decided to go and cadge one from him.'

'Wouldn't have done you much good,' she said curtly. 'He's taken to smoking those frightful Turkish things, and you hate them.'

'Well, that's as may be,' he said gruffly. 'Anyway, thing is, as I get closer I realise he's with someone else, someone I can't make out at all. Thought at first it might be that Bracely woman, but no, it was definitely a man. As he turned side on I could see the outline of an evening dress jacket.'

'Well, what's so remarkable about that?' Elizabeth asked. 'Probably Mr Wyse went out for a smoke with him.'

'No, not at all,' the Major said, warming to his narrative. 'Remembered having seen him in the lounge when I left.'

He stopped to take a pull on a plain, manly Virginia cigarette.

'No,' he said, exhaling. 'Definitely not Mr Wyse. Anyway, next thing I see is the two of them very close together, almost as if they had their arms round each other.'

He had his wife's attention now. She furrowed her brow.

'Are you sure it was Mister Georgie? Perhaps it was two Italian men walking arm in arm. They do that sometimes. I've seen them.'

'Definitely him, Liz. Stake my life on it. Arm in arm? Maybe, but they looked closer than that to me.'

'A mystery, then,' she observed drily.

'Ah!'

He waved his hand from side to side to signify an emphatic negative, scattering cigarette ash over the tea things in the process.

'Suddenly came to me as I was coming back in. They'd vanished by then, incidentally. Damn sure it was that valet of his. Saw him in profile the other evening. Sure it was the same feller.'

'Really?'

Elizabeth was unsure what to make of this nugget of information, but she stored it away all the same.

'I wonder what they were talking about that needed to be so private?' she wondered aloud.

The Major gave a short bark of laughter.

'Discussing embroidery, perhaps? Swapping notes on thimbles, what?'

Finding this highly amusing, he chuckled away to himself for some time. Elizabeth smiled indulgently and pretended to be studying a crossword puzzle. She was, however, turning this new intelligence over and over in her mind trying to think how it might be deployed to best advantage. Nothing occurred to her for now, but surely an answer would present itself to her in time.

Below them hotel workers were beginning to carry baskets along the road, slowly, for it was a hot day, in the direction of the steamer jetty. Elizabeth gave a little snort of derision when she realised this must be for dear Lulu's party. Within the hotel, two floors below, much lengthier and grander preparations had been going on since dawn for her own far more august gathering. She was confident that for once she would comprehensively outshine her rival. It was maddening, though, that due to Lucia's selfishness, nobody at all from Tilling would be there to witness the ice sculptures, the champagne, the liveried flunkies, the caviar and the hundreds of guests. How fortunate that she had thought to hire a photographer to record the event. At least she would have some evidence of the grandeur of the occasion. Perhaps she might be able to persuade the *Tilling Gazette* to print some of them on her return? Yes, there was no reason why not.

A low buzzing noise heralded the arrival of d'Annunzio's seaplane, which circled slowly, losing height, and then touched down, leaving a plume of white spray behind it as it taxied towards the hotel.

'That's that friend of the Bracely woman, I think,' the Major observed. 'Coming for Lucia's party, I'll be bound.'

'Who is he?' Mapp asked savagely. 'The King of Italy, perhaps, or the Pope? Or maybe just a Rothschild or a Rockefeller?'

'Damned if I know,' the Major replied, ignoring his wife's heavy sarcasm. 'I think one of the waiters said he was some sort of prince.'

Elizabeth swallowed hard.

'So Lulu's having a prince to her party, is she?'

She started breathing noisily and went rather red in the face. It was perhaps as well for her blood pressure that she did not know that Lucia was also now expecting a duchess.

Chapter 16

Olga had of course been one out in her calculations since she had forgotten completely about Brabazon Lodge, with the result that they were nine for dinner, not eight.

They walked in procession down the road from the hotel two by two, Mr Lodge accompanying the Contessa, and d'Annunzio escorting Olga. Poppy was late, as usual.

The *Vittoria* ('What an appropriate name,' d'Annunzio said) had been transformed since her last appearance. She was decked out in bunting from stem to stern and the main deck had become a terrace for a drinks party, while the saloon was now a dining room, boasting a single table with a gleaming white cloth laid for nine people. The rather surly deckhands of the night before were now dressed in crisp, clean white sailor tops which Georgie found most fetching. Stewards in white mess jackets held trays of canapés and glasses.

'Oh, Lucia,' Georgie marvelled as they approached, 'how marvellous everything looks. Aren't you clever?'

'Thank you dear,' she said. 'Actually the hotel did most of the work.'

'Yes, but it was you who had the idea,' Georgie replied, 'and what a brilliant idea it was. Fancy! Dinner on a steamer in the middle of Lake Como.'

As they walked along the landing stage a crowd began to gather and some desultory applause broke out. Lucia knew that this was really directed at d'Annunzio, but contrived to look gracious anyway. There were some shouts, though they sounded good-natured.

'What are they saying?' Lucia asked Olga. 'I find I have problems with this strange dialect they use up here in the lakes.'

'They're complaining that they didn't know d'Annunzio would be here, so they couldn't prepare a proper welcome for him,' Olga explained. 'He's sympathising with them.'

Lucia considered.

'Well, if we tell them we'll be back at ten o'clock, they can be all ready and waiting.'

'Don't worry,' Olga assured her, 'he already has.'

'Oh,' murmured Georgie, rather thrilled. 'Just fancy that! Perhaps they'll get the town band out.'

'They will,' Olga said. 'He's just suggested it.'

'Who is this guy, anyway?' Brabazon Lodge demanded loudly of nobody in particular. 'He sure thinks he's the cat's whiskers, doesn't he? How much is he worth?'

Just for a moment Mr Wyse looked as though he had just caught a particularly nauseating waft of bad drains on a hot day.

'It's complicated, dear Mr Lodge,' Lucia replied. 'He seems to be all sorts of things. A writer, of course ...'

She looked to Georgie and Olga for help.

'But he's also by way of being a war hero,' Georgie explained.

'On land, at sea and in the air,' Olga added.

'And a politician, and a journalist, and a poet, and a novelist, and a speech-maker,' Georgie rattled off, counting them on his fingers.

'And he's building a museum to himself,' Olga volleyed across the net.

'The nation demands it,' came Georgie's forehand return.

At this the two of them collapsed in giggles, and Lucia looked very disapproving.

'Really, you two are like children sometimes,' she said reprovingly.

'Well, he just looks like a little guy with big ideas to me,' Mr Lodge said, pitching his cigar butt rather savagely into the lake.

He glared at d'Annunzio. Lucia smiled apprehensively.

'Oh, I rather thought you liked having big ideas in America?' Georgie asked innocently.

Lucia sighed. Just possibly this might prove a rather difficult evening.

Since they were forced to wait for Poppy, the steamer remained tied up while they congregated on deck and drank champagne. As they did so, more and more townsfolk began congregating good-naturedly at the end of the landing stage. Many of the women had shawls over their heads and babies in their arms, or children holding on to their skirts.

'My God, it's a scene straight out of an opera,' Georgie said.

'Strange you should say that,' Olga replied. 'I could have sworn I just heard a tuning pipe.'

Somebody, presumably the local organist, choirmaster or both, stepped out to the front of the crowd, and a ragged note was hummed in unison and then died away. Clearly the crowd was about to indulge in a spontaneous display of patriotic fervour.

As the crowd struck up '*Va, pensiero*', d'Annunzio strode to the prow of the vessel, put a clenched fist on each hip, and gazed sternly into the distance. Georgie closed his eyes so as not to spoil the moment, and felt tears beginning to run down his cheeks as they always did when he heard this piece. There was at least one genuine tenor in the crowd, and the top notes bounced back off the surrounding mountains, blending with the lapping of the water.

As the music died away, d'Annunzio dismissed the crowd with a lordly wave of the hand and they silently dispersed, looking once more for all the world like an opera chorus moving quietly offstage.

'Say, what was that?' Mr Lodge asked. 'Their national anthem?'

'No,' Georgie told him, 'though they all think it should be.'

'They sang it at Caruso's funeral,' Olga said quietly.

'Too bad it wasn't written by anyone famous,' Mr Lodge said. 'I guess that's what gets something chosen as a national anthem – like that Beethoven guy for Germany.'

Everyone looked startled. Only Amelia, characteristically and loudly, said 'I think you mean Haydn,' in a tone of some contempt.

Lucia sighed again. Fortunately, just as Amelia drew breath to begin enlightening their American guest on the qualities of the composer of *Nabucco*, Lucia was able to say, 'Oh look, there's Poppy! Dear Poppy – the Duchess of Sheffield you know.'

Mr Wyse rose loyally to the occasion, fussing to the rail to say how well he remembered Her Grace and attempting with great courage, for he could guess only too well at the possible consequences, to stand on his sister's foot.

It was not Her Grace's custom to apologise for tardiness, nor, with the very marked exception only of members of the royal family and men with beards, to acknowledge the presence of other people in anything other than the most cursory manner. His Majesty the King, who suffered the grave misfortune of falling into both categories, had attempted at one stage to ban the Duchess from court owing to the effusiveness of her approaches.

Her greeting to Lucia, who of course fell into neither category, consisted of, 'Yes, well, here we are again,' to which Lucia naturally replied very loudly, 'Dearest Poppy, how nice to see you again. How well I remember the last time you visited me in Tilling.'

Brushing aside Lucia's attempted introductions, she waved a hand at the assembled company and said, 'Charmed, I'm sure,' thus getting all the social niceties over in one job lot. Then, as an expectant silence fell she glanced around, said, 'Yes, well, I thought I'd just pop over,' accepted a glass of champagne from a steward, and then made a beeline for Georgie, who was attempting unsuccessfully to hide behind a deckhand, and seized him firmly by the arm.

'Dear little man,' she said, smiling happily. 'Dear little beard.'

Back at the hotel, the Mapp-Flint party could hardly be counted a great success. Back in the old Riseholme days many people had tried painstakingly to recreate the elements of a wonderful romp which Olga had managed spontaneously to create, only for the evening to fall flat, for it was the very spontaneity of her romps, and the random set of ingredients this spontaneity threw together, which made them what they were. Having one or two chairs too few for a romp took on the most amusing quality, whereas deliberately removing one or two chairs from a dinner table before one's guests arrived simply led to confusion, indigestion and lasting ill-feeling.

On this occasion Elizabeth had carefully contrived all the ingredients necessary for a successful party. But, unlike a fruitcake, one could not simply mix all the ingredients in their recommended proportions, bake them for the specified time, and be confident of removing a perfectly finished product from the oven at the end of the process. Mapp, perhaps ironically since she had been known to stoop to turning a rival's oven up surreptitiously in a bid for victory in a baking contest, found herself in the sad position of having carefully measured out ingredients, mixed and baked them, only to be left with a rather sorry mess.

For one thing, very few people at the hotel knew each other. While they might have muttered the odd greeting when passing in the breakfast room (and usually deliberately in the wrong language) they had very sensibly never been tempted to push matters any further, since one never knew to what nameless social terrors careless casual conversation might lead.

For another, those few hardy souls who had recklessly pressed beyond the level of 'Good morning', perhaps to touch daringly upon the weather, had generally only done so with their own countrymen. It seemed sensible to treat the period since 1918 as a sort of extended Christmas Day truce, and, while the occasional game of football in no-man's-land might be tolerated, such episodes of social intercourse were probably generally bad for morale overall. The German contingent, in particular, seemed to be taking a most unsporting view of the Versailles Treaty and contemplating the possibility of a rematch if only somebody would let them have their ball back.

Finally, almost nobody in the hotel knew her, and those few people who had met her, even briefly, had tended not to like what they saw. To be fair to Mapp, this happened also to chime with her own traditional view that a stranger was just an enemy she had never met. Throughout her life, which had been somewhat longer than she was prepared officially to admit, she had worked on the principle that disliking someone on sight was likely to prevent all sort of tiresome problems later. While this was a principle which had served her loyally and effectively over the years, it was not a quality normally to be found, or at least not openly displayed, in natural society hostesses, and the reader should therefore exercise some measure of compassion and understanding on learning that this was not a role in which she naturally excelled.

In brief, many people never turned up at all, taking the opportunity to leave the hotel for the evening and eat out in the town. Others put their heads into the room, looked round uncertainly and, on seeing Elizabeth essay what she fondly imagined to be a warm, welcoming smile in their direction, recoiled in horror. The third category stood in small groups resolutely speaking their own language very loudly, consumed a great deal of food and champagne as quickly as possible, and then left with a passing nod to their hostess. Ramesh attempted to rescue the situation, moving suavely between the groups and switching effortlessly between French, English and German, but by nine o'clock, with the room deserted, the band playing to an empty room, and vast quantities of food left uneaten, even Elizabeth was forced to admit defeat. The party had been an unmitigated disaster.

The Major had taken solace in the large amounts of alcohol on offer and had to be helped upstairs by Ramesh who, his obligations now fully discharged, changed out of his evening dress and went into town in search of unmarried Italian girls of a warm and giving disposition, a completely pointless yet occasionally enjoyable pursuit which has diverted many men over the ages, though frequently separating them from large amounts of money in the process.

As for Elizabeth, by nine-thirty she was unable to survey the wreckage of her evening with equanimity for any longer and went upstairs, intending to throw herself on the bed and weep for her shattered dreams. Sadly she found that position already occupied by her husband, whose tie, collar and shoes had been removed by the dutiful Ramesh and who was now snoring loudly, pitched diagonally across the bed. She glared at him balefully and retreated to the living room. However, she soon found that it was most unsatisfactory trying to have a really good emotional interlude in a non-horizontal attitude, and, more importantly, in total solitude with nobody available to witness her grief, sympathise, and perhaps seek to intervene or even participate, so in due course she gave it up as a bad job and wandered morosely into town.

Downstairs, the waiters gathered uncertainly in the deserted lounge. They looked to Giuseppe for guidance, who shrugged and gestured for them to begin clearing away. The staff would eat well tonight.

Lucia had also experienced a taxing evening, though her problems had been of a different nature and she had in general discharged them successfully. Brabazon Lodge, d'Annunzio and Amelia were a highly volatile mix, and several matches had been struck only to be deftly blown out before some explosion might ensue, these safety operations being largely conducted by Lucia, though ably assisted by Olga and Mr Wyse. Poppy at least said little and really was no trouble at all, so long as she could be seated next to Georgie (which, to his horror, she was), hold his hand under the table (which he had by now decided to be the lesser of two evils – at least this way he knew where the damned woman's hand actually *was*), and be assured of a constant supply of black coffee and dressed crab.

Brabazon Lodge had wanted to speak of nothing other than money, usually in the context of large and impressive deals which he had successfully brought to a triumphant, and highly profitable, conclusion. His only fall-back position seemed to be to quiz people interminably and in intimate detail about their investments.

D'Annunzio of course wanted to talk about nothing other than d'Annunzio, though he did interrupt people impatiently to ask if they knew anybody on the Nobel Prize committee, or to denounce instantly and with derision any poet or novelist other than himself.

Amelia had no time for any of this and was prone to interject 'Pah!' or 'Balderdash!' into other people's statements, and she seemed to have quite decided views on Italian politics which, while Lucia knew nothing of such matters, were clearly at variance with d'Annunzio's. She was pro-Mussolini because he had made the trains run on time. D'Annunzio was anti-Mussolini because Mussolini had tried to kill him by throwing him out of a window. When this fact had been made clear, the party gathered around the dinner table in the saloon had fallen silent, clearly weighing the pros and cons of each position, and most siding mentally with Mussolini on the grounds of justifiable homicide.

It will thus be appreciated that Lucia's task had been one of such complexity that most hostesses would have been inadequate to the challenge. Unlike Mapp, however, Lucia was a consummate hostess, and had passed the test with flying colours.

As the meal drew to a close, she caught Poppy's eye. Her Grace was, however, reluctant to relinquish the trophy which she was clutching doggedly under the table, Georgie's face having by this time acquired a fixed, glassy, white, mask-like quality.

Poppy struggled to remember Lucia's name but failed dismally.

'Yes, well,' she said, 'I don't know about everybody else, but why don't we all go on deck, instead of just the ladies retirin'?'

This was met by a general murmur of approval, as suggestions from duchesses normally are. Everybody dropped their napkins on the table and the ladies were gallantly shepherded out of the cabin, d'Annunzio and Mr Wyse rivalling each other magnificently in the exquisiteness of their bowing.

Arriving on deck they found they were already back in clear sight of the steamer quay, though chugging very slowly through the water. It was clear, even from this distance, that extensive preparations had been made to welcome them back. At least three times as many people as before had gathered (some had actually come from as far away as

Como) and the electric lights of the bars and restaurants glinted on the instruments of a brass band. Even the saint from the church had put in an appearance, stoutly held aloft on a sort of decorated stretcher by various choirboys in surplices.

As the stewards served coffee and liqueurs, cigars and cigarettes were lit and a mood approaching a companionable calm finally settled upon the company. Lucia breathed a sigh of relief. Finally, she could relax.

'It was so wonderful, wasn't it, to hear that wonderful singing earlier?' Lucia enquired generally. 'How magnificent to hear people express such a real pride in their country.'

D'Annunzio shrugged modestly.

'We are a great people,' he said. 'Perhaps the greatest of all. We trace our origins back to the Romans and, through their conquests and empire, to the Greeks, the Assyrians and the Egyptians.'

'Today's what counts, though, buddy,' Mr Lodge said unhelpfully. 'In case you haven't noticed, it's the United States that dominates the world today, not the Romans.'

'America is a very powerful country,' d'Annunzio acknowledged, 'though of course culturally deficient. Where are your novelists, your poets, your composers, your painters?'

'You never heard of Mark Twain?' Mr Lodge asked incredulously.

'No,' d'Annunzio replied simply.

'America and Italy were allies in the war, of course, gentlemen,' Mr Wyse interjected, looking keenly at each of them in turn.

'Yeah, I dare say,' Mr Lodge said dubiously.

He and d'Annunzio gazed at each other and evidently decided to call it quits, much to everyone's relief. However, the latter was not a man to let anyone have the last word.

'Italy's age of true greatness is yet to come,' he declaimed, with the air of a prophetic announcement. 'In the meantime, we will continue to claim our place on the world stage. We will be the major Mediterranean power. We will work through the League of Nations.

We will claim colonies overseas. We will even work with our former enemies where this is possible.'

'Bravo!' cried Mr Wyse.

'Bravo indeed,' Lucia agreed warmly. 'Why, it is so wonderful to hear that *la bella Italia* will act responsibly in world affairs. Long may she continue to be an ally of Great Britain – oh, and America too, of course, dear Mr Lodge.'

Strangely, this ringing endorsement did not bring forth the gracious response from d'Annunzio which Lucia had confidently been expecting.

'And why, pray,' he asked coldly, 'might you think that Italy would *not* act responsibly?'

'Oh, I'm sure Lucia didn't mean that,' Susan said hurriedly.

Lucia, however, was quite capable of clarifying her own statements.

'Thank you, Susan dear, but I did,' she said, smiling quizzically. 'I intended it as a compliment.'

'After all,' she continued, her voice filling as if a sail catching a wind, 'it was not always so. Just look at all those reckless fools who seized Fiume. They hardly had Italy's best interest at heart, did they? Why, didn't Italy end up declaring war on them? Quite right too! Hardly compatible with acting responsibly in world affairs, was it? Trying to tear up the Versailles Treaty that nice President Wilson worked so hard to put together.'

'And Mr Lloyd George too, of course,' she added reluctantly, for she was of course a Conservative.

As she looked around to make quite sure that her meaning had now been properly understood, she had the feeling that something was not quite right. Olga and Georgie were gazing at her with their mouths open. Mr and Mrs Wyse looked as though they were about to burst into tears. Amelia was smiling wickedly. D'Annunzio looked as though he was struggling to speak. Lucia wondered if he had a history of heart trouble.

For a very long few seconds nobody said anything at all. Then d'Annunzio turned on his heel, put his glass down, and walked very stiffly below decks.

'Lucia!' Georgie cried in aguish.

'Oh, Lucia,' Olga said sadly. 'If only I'd realised that you didn't know.'

'What, pray?' Lucia asked, the horrible realisation beginning to dawn that she had committed some fatal *faux pas*.

'D'Annunzio led the expedition to Fiume,' Amelia informed her with relish. 'It was all his idea. And it wasn't Italy that declared war on him, but the other way round.'

'A perfectly understandable mistake to make,' Mr Wyse ventured wretchedly. 'Perhaps I could go and talk to him?'

'Probably best if I do,' Olga said, and slipped away.

'I shall of course apologise, dear,' Lucia called after her magnanimously.

By now they were getting dangerously close to the jetty. The band struck up a jaunty little tune which Amelia and the Wyses recognised as '*Giovinezza*'. As the tune progressed Olga completed her mission below decks.

'No go, I'm afraid,' she reported glumly. 'He won't come up. He doesn't even want to speak to anybody.'

The band fell silent. On the quayside, Mapp had completed her slow, sad, progress from the hotel and was dully watching the approaching steamer as it drifted expertly towards its mooring position.

Then the cheering started. It was full-throated Italian cheering, and the noise was immense.

Suddenly, Lucia knew that the Elizabethan pageant in Riseholme, the *tableaux vivants* in Tilling, all the mayoral engagements, had been but mere preparation for this moment. She knew an instant of glittering clarity. This was her destiny, and she seized it with both hands. Calmly, serenely, and with Elizabeth Mapp-Flint watching, unseen, in horrified disbelief, Lucia stepped forward, raised her hands, and started acknowledging, gracefully but sincerely, the cheers of the assembled multitude, cheers which rang again and again around the lake, cheers for her, for her, for her.

Olga bravely volunteered to stay behind and, together with the crew, gradually coax d'Annunzio first out of the foetal position, and then out of the saloon. She spoke quickly to the captain, who explained to the intrigued townsfolk that the English lady was a great friend of Italy, whom d'Annunzio had wished them to honour in his place. Hearing this, they pursued Lucia and her party to the very gates of the hotel, cheering them all the way, Lucia turning every few steps to wave anew and beg them, ineffectually thank goodness, to desist.

They really did look in on Mapp's party, but of course they found only an empty room, the band departed, and only the ice carvings remaining, now largely melted and dripping forlornly. It was if a great civilisation had once lived here, but long since vanished.

With that, they dispersed. Georgie went in search of Francesco and a Negroni, his nerves completely gone to pieces after his experience with Poppy, to say nothing of the dramatic denouement of the party.

Lucia went in search of her maid, removed her make-up, applied her night cream and went to bed, but sleep, unsurprisingly, eluded her.

She switched on the light and reached for her book from the bedside cabinet, only to realise that she had left it on the table in the living room. She put on her dressing gown and crept out to retrieve it. A strip of light showed underneath Georgie's door, and as she picked up her book she clearly heard Francesco's voice.

'Dear Georgie,' he was saying, 'you have been so very kind to me, that I hope you will allow me to show you my appreciation in return.'

'Well, that's very kind of you,' came Georgie's rather muffled voice, 'but just being with you is reward enough – privilege enough, really, I should say.'

'You are a shameless flatterer,' Francesco said playfully, 'but it's no good. My mind is quite made up. I am going to do something very special for you.'

'Shall I like it?' Georgie asked dubiously.

'Oh, yes,' Francesco assured him. 'Trust me.'

'Very well then,' Georgie said nervously. 'If you're sure.'

Lucia froze, and then tiptoed back into her bedroom.

Chapter 17

'I was most surprised to find that man still ministering to you, Georgie, after I have taken so many occasions to convey my views to you,' Lucia said severely. 'I am sorry to have to broach the subject so directly, my dear, but you seem suddenly impervious to subtler methods.'

'Not at all, Lucia,' Georgie replied, trying to sound unperturbed. 'I do understand your feelings on this matter, but I wish to exercise my own judgement. Surely that is not too much to ask?'

'Judgement?' Lucia's voce rose perceptibly both in pitch and volume. 'I am sorry to say, Georgie, that you appear to have exercised no judgement at all on this matter. You have allowed him to become altogether too familiar, to try to turn you into a drug addict, to encourage you in the most lascivious of painting styles, and generally to exercise a very malevolent influence over you.'

'Nonetheless, Lucia, he is my valet, not yours,' came the firm reply, 'and I must ask that you allow me to decide what is best.'

'May I remind you, *caro mio*, that *I* am in charge of all domestic matters, including disposing of the servants?' Lucia riposted. 'Really, I thought that was well understood, Georgie. After all, it is what happens in any normal household.'

'Yes, but this isn't the household, is it?' Georgie challenged her, feeling that he was being quite clever. 'We're away on holiday.'

'Don't quibble, dear,' Lucia admonished him. 'Anyway, it won't do any good. My mind is quite made up on the subject.'

'Then you can just unmake it again,' Georgie flashed back.

There was no response to this, Lucia simply gazing at him implacably. He decided that a different approach was needed.

'Look, my dear,' he said more amenably, 'there are aspects of this situation of which you are unaware. Let me assure you that if you *did* know them then you would exercise a little more understanding and compassion.'

'What sort of "aspects", pray?'

'Well, that's really rather difficult to explain without giving everything away,' Georgie said awkwardly. 'You see, Francesco and I have a secret which I have promised to respect.'

'Surely you can at least hint?' Lucia asked icily. 'After all, I am your wife, Georgie. I always thought that we were not supposed to have secrets from each other.'

'Oh, this is so difficult,' said Georgie wretchedly.

Lucia continued to stare at him quizzically.

'Well,' he ventured at length, 'let's just say that our relationship, Francesco's and mine that is, is not exactly as it might appear on the surface. There, now can we please leave it at that? This really is all most tarsome.'

Flustered, he produced his handkerchief and mopped his brow.

'I think I understand all too well, my dear,' Lucia said kindly. 'How little you know of the ways of the world. Why, you forget that I have spent some considerable time in London society. Come and sit by me and let me explain.'

Georgie settled himself next to her on the sofa, and she almost went so far as to take his hand.

'You see, my dear, Francesco is not unique. On the contrary, the quality holiday destinations of Europe are filled with Francescos. They are all men of a certain sort, good-looking, charming, who prey upon the weaknesses of travellers to worm their way into their affections in the hope of financial gain. Perhaps some valuable gifts, perhaps even an offer of permanent employment as a personal servant. In the case of some vulnerable ladies even marriage may be suggested.'

'Weaknesses?' Georgie asked in some confusion. 'What weaknesses?'

'In your case, my dear, let's just say an over-generous nature and leave it at that, shall we?' Lucia said briskly. 'You were seen, you know, wandering arm in arm with him. That's hardly ... appropriate, is it?'

'Oh, Lucia, you just don't understand,' Georgie maintained. 'Now please just leave it alone, or you'll spoil everything. Francesco needs me, and I have promised to help him.'

'Ah-hah!' Lucia exclaimed triumphantly.

'There's no "ah-hah" about it,' he retorted impatiently. 'Just leave it, that's all. You promised to obey me when we got married, Lucia, and I've never asked you to do it before, but I ask you now. Leave it. Be pleasant to Francesco, for my sake at least.'

Lucia gave a twisted little smile.

'As it happens, Georgie, I am unable to obey you,' she said sweetly, and then, her voice becoming decidedly Elizabethan, 'though I think it most ill that you should seek to employ such a crude attempt to impose your will upon me.'

'What do you mean, "unable"?'

'Because Francesco is no longer in your employ, Georgie,' she answered with a little toss of her head.

'I don't understand,' he said foolishly.

'That man is no longer in your employ, my dear, because I fired him about an hour ago. It gave me great pleasure to tell him exactly what I thought of him, as well. I made it very clear to him that I was astute enough to know when a perfumed, brilliantined Lothario was trying to worm his way into a gentleman's affections.'

'What?' gasped Georgie in horror.

'Let me tell you what your precious Francesco said then, Georgie,' Lucia pressed on, well aware that she was twisting the knife in the wound. 'He just smiled and asked me if I was jealous.'

Georgie was beyond speech. He just gaped. He felt a hot flush on his face.

'At which point,' said Lucia with satisfaction, 'I slapped his face, very hard I may add, and told him to leave at once. Without a reference, naturally.'

She stood up.

'Now then, *caro mio*, let us forget this whole unpleasant episode ever happened and go back to enjoying ourselves. You will though, I trust, remember what a narrow escape you have had.'

She gazed at him evenly and then turned to leave the room.

'You might even,' came her parting shot, 'consider apologising for having doubted my suspicions.'

At this Georgie could stand no more.

'You stupid woman!' he positively shouted.

Shocked, she spun on her heel. Hot with rage, he seized her arm and threw her back on to the sofa. She opened her mouth, but no words would come out. Quivering with anger for the first and only time in his life, he knelt down and thrust his contorted face very close to hers.

'That man,' he hissed furiously, 'is King Zog of Albania.'

Miss Flowers had slipped away from Frau Zirchner while she was having her afternoon nap and was sitting with Major Benjy in a fairly remote corner of the gardens, screened from the hotel by a hedge and some beds of rhododendrons. She was smoking a cigarette and sitting on a low wall, her legs crossed.

'So you managed to escape from the old girl?' the Major commented, taking a drag on his own cigarette. 'Sorry she gave you a hard time yesterday.'

'No worse than the one your wife gave you, by all accounts,' she replied. 'I could hear her shouting from the other side of the hotel. Apparently the staff were worried that someone was being murdered.'

'Ah,' said the Major uncomfortably. 'No, not quite.'

There was a pause which he felt obliged to fill.

'But, it has to be said,' he continued reflectively, 'that she is a woman of most decided opinions.'

'Dear Major,' Miss Flowers cooed, 'it does you great credit that you continue to take her with you as you travel around the world. Why, many men would simply leave her at home while they go off with more enjoyable company.'

'Do you know,' he said wonderingly, 'I never thought of that.'

'Really? I am surprised. Why, there was a charming gentleman I met with Frau Zirchner while we were in Monte Carlo who claimed never to see his wife from one Christmas to the next.'

'By Jove!' the Major exclaimed, suddenly seized by an intriguing possibility. 'What a lark!'

'Not sure I'd get away with it, though,' he went on after a pause for thought. 'She can be a bit difficult about a chap going off to have fun on his own, you know.'

Miss Flowers raised her eyebrows.

'Really? How very unreasonable.'

'Yes,' he said, as if struck by the realisation for the first time. 'It *is* jolly well unreasonable, isn't it?'

As they both drew on their cigarettes, a light breeze blew at the hem of her dress, tugging it upwards. The Major derived new eloquence from the sight.

'Fact is,' he confided, 'I think the old girl's a bit touched, what? Not right in the head, I mean. Always likely to fly off the handle about nothing at all. Apparently her mother was the same. Hit her husband with a teapot once, they say. Runs in the family, I suppose.'

'Poor Major!' Miss Flowers said, clearly deeply touched. 'Do you mean that you bring this woman to live at your splendid house at Tilling, spend huge amounts of money taking her around the world with you, and this is how she repays you, with scorn and derision?'

The Major contrived to look both unfortunate and noble at the same time. Miss Flowers reached out and patted his hand sympathetically.

'Do tell me more about your house, Major. How very nice Tilling sounds.'

'Well,' he said, trying to choose the right words, 'it's not actually my house at all, strictly speaking.'

'I do understand,' she said soothingly. 'Doubtless you have it owned by a family trust to keep it out of the hands of your wife, should the unthinkable happen and you have to confine the poor woman in a mental hospital. Permanently, I mean. I'm sure she's in and out of them all the time, from what you say.'

'Good God, yes. Damned expensive it is too. Spend a fortune on flowers and grapes whenever I have to go to visit.'

The Major caught a glimpse of an alternative future, and fell in love with it instantly. He wondered just how a chap went about having his wife committed. He dimly remembered that it needed the signature of two doctors. There was old Smithers at the golf club, for one. Surely he would do a favour for an old friend? Then there was that old fool who had put 'drowning' as the cause of death on Captain Puffin's death certificate just because he had fallen forward into a plate of soup after suffering a heart attack. Yes, surely something might be done ...

Miss Flowers leant forward, her earnest blue eyes making a deep impression.

'Of course, it would be as well to check the terms of the trust just to make absolutely sure,' she said.

'Oh, quite,' he agreed instantly. 'Jolly sensible, what?'

'Perhaps,' she proffered, 'we might meet in London one weekend and go through the trust deed together. Naturally, it would entail staying in a hotel.'

'Naturally,' he agreed enthusiastically.

'And to avoid any possible embarrassment,' she went on smoothly, 'it might be best if you stayed at your club. We could meet for lunch somewhere on Sunday, and you could bring the trust deed with you.'

'Ah,' he said, brought up short by this idea. 'I don't actually have a club.'

Again her eyes widened.

'I *did* have, of course,' he assured her hurriedly. 'The Empire Club in Calcutta. Used to go there quite a bit for a while, until there was a spot of unpleasantness.'

'Unpleasantness? What sort of unpleasantness?'

'Oh,' he waved his hand dismissively, 'some damn fool of a tea planter said I'd upset his wife or something. Threatened to horsewhip me on the front steps, if you please.'

'Oh, my word!'

She covered her mouth with her hand, the picture of concern.

'Nothing to worry about,' he said soothingly. 'I think Benjamin Flint knows how to take care of a tea planter.'

In fact he had taken care of the planter by arranging himself an urgent posting to Ranaghat, but his mien convincingly suggested a more heroic outcome.

'Thing is, though,' he said, conscious that this conversation was in danger of running rapidly out of control, 'there is no trust, actually.'

'No trust? Then who owns the house?'

'Well, stupid I know,' replied the Major, looking sheepish, 'but I put it in the wife's name when we got married. Seemed the thing to do, somehow.'

'Oh dear,' Miss Flowers said sharply and then, softening, 'but what a warm, generous spirit it shows, Major.'

'Yes, indeed,' he concurred. 'Over-generous, perhaps, do you think?'

'Definitely over-generous,' she said decidedly. 'But at least you have your capital, Major. That at least is beyond her reach.'

'Ah, yes, of course,' he said, though come to think of it, he wasn't too sure. His post office savings book was behind the clock in the living room.

'And you certainly know how to spend it,' she said coyly, clasping her hands around her knee and (surely inadvertently) lifting it higher in the process. 'Why, just look at that magnificent car.'

198

'Ah,' he said uncomfortably, 'not mine actually, just borrowing it from a friend.'

'A very generous friend, surely, Major? My, you must move in exalted circles.'

'A maharajah, actually,' he confided proudly. 'Saved the chap's father out in India, don't you know.'

He eagerly embarked on the most heavily embellished version of his tiger story, but Miss Flowers' attention seemed unequal to the task.

'Very interesting,' she cut in as he paused for breath just at the dramatic moment when three ravenous tigers were gazing hungrily at the old maharajah while Major Flint stood between them armed only with his swagger stick and a fountain pen, 'but I do hope, Major, that you are looking after your capital sensibly?'

'Eh?' he said, still wondering exactly how he was going to extricate himself from his predicament with the tigers.

'Though of course there must be a great deal of it,' she went on, reassured. 'Do pardon me, Major, I don't wish to pry and of course it's none of my business, but after all, this is not a cheap hotel, and you are occupying one of the best suites ...'

He thought rapidly about whether this topic had come up in conversation before, perhaps while his attention had been temporarily distracted in the car. Tricky blighters, women, it was just the sort of thing they might pull, to try to catch a chap out.

'Oh, I thought we'd been through that,' he said airily. 'Matter of fact the maharajah's paying. Sort of present, you might say. Sort of belated thank-you, I dare say, for saving his father's life. Now, that reminds me ...'

He brought his tiger story to a triumphant, though highly unconvincing, conclusion, and became aware that somewhere along the way Miss Flowers had uncrossed her legs and was now sitting with her hands in her lap gazing into the distance in a somewhat distracted fashion.

'Tell me,' she said when it became apparent that he had finished making tiger noises and flourishing a twig which was doing duty for his trusty fountain pen. 'This maharajah of yours. I suppose he is fabulously wealthy?'

'Oh yes, rich as Croesus,' he assured her. 'One of the richest men in the world, I hear tell.'

'I see,' she said thoughtfully. 'Thank you, Major, but I fear I must go in now. A sudden breeze seems to have sprung up.'

As she stood up he cast around desperately for a new approach.

'Of course, if my wife were to die,' he said, 'then there'd be no problem, would there? I mean, the house would come to me, yes, and everything else too.'

She paused and looked back.

'Is that likely?' she asked. 'She strikes me as a very robust woman, physically at least. Certainly there is nothing wrong with her lungs. Has she been in poor health?'

'No,' he said regretfully and then, his mind running rapidly over the contents of the garden shed at Glebe, 'but anything's possible, what?'

Lucia was still ashen-faced with shock and disbelief.

'You see,' Georgie was explaining, 'his life was in danger from the Greeks, or the Serbs, or the Croats, or somebody, I can't quite remember which, the Italian government told him so.'

'And how did they know?' asked Lucia, more for the sake of something to say than anything else.

'Oh, intercepted letters, spies, that sort of thing, you know,' he replied airily, as one who was newly *au fait* with the ways of the world's intelligence agencies.

'Anyhow, he asked them for their protection, but they said they couldn't guarantee keeping him safe in Albania just at the moment, but suggested he hide *incognito* in Italy for a bit while things calmed down back at home.'

'But why a valet? And why here?'

Georgie shrugged.

'Why not? Actually, I think it was simply brilliant. Who would possibly think of a valet as a king in disguise? And anyway, Bellagio's hardly Rome or Milan. He thought it was unlikely he would see anyone who might recognise him, but he was jolly careful anyway. That's why he made some flimsy excuse not to risk being seen by d'Annunzio. The two of them fell out over Fiume, and d'Annunzio was bound to remember him.'

'But why on earth, Georgie,' Lucia asked, some of her customary asperity returning, 'didn't you tell me about all this? Really, I can only assume that you didn't trust me.'

'Of course I trust you,' he replied firmly, 'but he expressly asked me not to tell a living soul, including you. As a matter of fact, I didn't know myself until quite recently. He only told me a couple of days ago.'

Lucia was silent.

'Just think,' Georgie marvelled, 'me being waited on by a king! And how exciting to think of assassins lurking in the bushes – do you know he has a revolver with him, just in case?'

'It will make a fine story, certainly,' Lucia conceded. 'It certainly trumps the Mapp-Flints' maharajah.'

'Yes, doesn't it?' Georgie said happily. 'Actually, we've become very good friends. I've invited him to come to Mallards next summer. Of course, that might be a little difficult now that you've slapped his face and accused him of being a *gigolo*.'

'Yes, thank you, Georgie,' Lucia answered sharply. 'I am well aware of the dreadful situation in which you have placed me.'

'I?' he queried, some of his hot blood returning. 'I have done nothing, Lucia. If only you had trusted me to know what I was doing then none of this would have happened, and the King and I could still be friends.'

'The fact remains, Georgie,' she said calmly, trying to be reasonable, 'that if *you* had trusted *me* then the whole unfortunate scene could have been avoided in the first place.'

'Oh, don't be so silly,' he exclaimed in exasperation. 'I've already explained all that. Why can't you just admit for once that you've been wrong?'

'Georgie!' Lucia flinched and gasped as though she had just had *her* face slapped.

She waited for him to say something, but nothing more was forthcoming. She came to a decision, stood up, and moved over to the door to her room.

'I find, Georgie dear, that my financial affairs compel me to return to London to consult with dear Mr Mammoncash,' she said tightly. 'Perhaps you would be so kind as to ring for my maid to help me pack?'

Georgie felt hot, peppery breath in his throat and, resisting a strong urge to say 'Oh, don't be so silly' again, said 'Sartenly' as calmly as he could, and pressed the bell push.

'Thank you, dear,' she said calmly.

'Naturally you won't require me to accompany you?' he enquired. 'After all, my financial affairs are less complex and rather more exiguous than your own.'

She made one of those little noises intended to express extreme disappointment masked by polite resignation. 'Naturally,' she echoed.

At the door she turned.

'You might perhaps do me one small favour, Georgie. I shall be drafting a telegram to Mammoncash before I leave, instructing him to sell all my holdings so that I can avail myself of Mr Lodge's kind proposal. Perhaps you will be kind enough to see that it is sent after I leave.'

'You know my views on that,' Georgie said stiffly.

'Yes, Georgie, I do,' she replied, equally stiffly, 'but surely you will trust me to know what I am doing.'

With this Parthian shot she left the room, and Georgie, feeling just for once like Major Benjy, went in search of Olga and a Negroni, though not necessarily in that order.

In the lounge, the Mapp-Flints had parked themselves on a sofa next to the Wyses' party, so that the latter could not easily leave the scene without appearing rude. Actually, Amelia would have had no great problem with such an appearance, as Mr Wyse well knew. He darted a hopeful meaningful glance at her, but his influence over his sister, never strong, had been completely punctured forever by the unforgiving touch of fire tongs on twelve year-old flesh.

'Excellent party, Elizabeth,' Susan was saying. 'Everyone is talking about it.'

'Indeed!' Mr Wyse concurred, with a little bow. 'Why, it must rank as the grandest affair the hotel has ever seen. Delightful! Charming!'

Amelia grunted and Susan, sensing that her sister-in-law might say something less than gracious, cut in to explain that they had decided to leave in the morning to return to Tilling.

'But why?' Elizabeth cried in dismay.

'The cholera,' My Wyse answered blandly. 'There is talk of it now in both Tuscany and the Romagna. It is clearly moving north, and we feel that one cannot be too careful.'

'Quinine,' the Major suddenly interjected. 'Quinine and lots of gin. That's the stuff. Keep you right as rain as long as you take it regularly.'

'Capital advice, Major,' acknowledged Mr Wyse with a bow. 'For myself I would be quite prepared to take it and stay, but I do have responsibility for both these ladies.'

Amelia grunted again and shifted her monocle.

'Some damn fool fisherman,' she growled.

'Well, we shall stay,' Elizabeth announced decidedly.

'Absolutely,' the Major concurred, catching sight of Miss Flowers coming into the lounge with Frau Zirchner. 'Having such a wonderful time, what?'

'Anyway,' Elizabeth said, beaming determinedly to make it clear that she had not noticed Miss Flowers and that even if she had it was *tout égout* to her, 'we have an obligation to stay. We promised His Highness we would remain here with Ramesh until he arrives to join us.'

'Absolutely,' the Major said again, shifting in his seat so as to present what he fondly believed was his best profile to Miss Flowers should she happen to glance in his direction, 'and that's not likely to be for weeks yet.'

He smiled contentedly, looking forward to an unlimited bar tab, and discreet discussions with Miss Flowers about their future living arrangements, stretching uninterrupted into the future.

At this point Ramesh arrived and politely made his bow to the assembled company. So touched was Mr Wyse by such delicacy of manners that he rose to return it, murmuring, 'Delighted.'

'What's that you've got there, old boy?' asked the Major, indicating a brown envelope in Ramesh's hand.

'It's a telegram from the pater,' Ramesh explained.

'And how is the maharajah?' Elizabeth asked, smiling broadly.

'You will soon have a chance to ask him that yourself, dear madam,' Ramesh replied. 'It says here that he's arriving tomorrow morning.'

Chapter 18

The maharajah, accompanied by Ramesh, was gazing unhappily at what had once been a very fine motor car.

'There is the Major now, I fancy, Pater,' son murmured to father.

'Ah,' the Major said as he approached them, 'Good morning, sir. Rather earlier than we anticipated. We didn't expect you for a week or two yet. Nothing wrong, I trust?'

He was acutely aware that his royal master seemed to be paying altogether more attention than was surely necessary to the mangled coachwork of the Royale.

'There was talk of cholera,' the maharajah said distractedly, 'so I thought it best to leave Rome. Apparently some idiotic fisherman brought it over from Capri and it has been spreading like wildfire on the mainland ever since. In any event, I was tiring of Rome's – ah, attractions. But pray tell, Major, what have you done to the old jalopy here?'

'Italian drivers,' the Major said bluffly. 'You know how it is, sir. Damned fools, the lot of them. Drive too fast – don't give a chap a chance to get out the way, what?'

There was a silence.

'And on the wrong side of the road,' he added.

There was a further silence. The maharajah gazed, perhaps significantly, at his own gleaming car, which he had clearly just driven from Rome entirely without mishap. The Major began to feel uneasy.

'French drivers too, of course,' he proffered, finding fresh inspiration. 'Worse than the Italians, some of them.'

Encountering only further silence, he fixed what he hoped was a convincingly expert eye on the Bugatti.

'Bit of panel beating required, eh? That's all. Right as rain after that, I dare say.'

Ramesh gazed inscrutably at his father and then at the Major.

'Most unfortunate,' the maharajah said finally. 'Why, here comes your dear lady wife, I believe.'

'Ah yes, the *memsahib*,' Major Benjy commented gratefully as Elizabeth beetled across the gravel, wearing the widest smile her face could possibly accommodate without risking permanent muscle damage.

'Why, this is a pleasant surprise, sir,' she greeted him. 'We were not expecting you for some weeks yet.'

She essayed a curtsey, but cautiously in view of the mixed results which earlier attempts had produced.

'I was just telling the Major,' the maharajah explained courteously, 'that there was talk of cholera arriving in Rome, so I thought it prudent to cut short my stay.'

This was in fact being somewhat economical with the truth, since it was not only cholera that had been threatening to return to Rome unexpectedly, but also a certain lady's husband.

'What a pity you could not have been here a few days earlier, sir,' Ramesh said innocently. 'You missed a wonderful party.'

Lucia stood beside a Pullman carriage on Milan station as a porter stowed her luggage. He finished at length, for Lucia did not believe in travelling light, climbed down on to the platform, and tugged the peak of his cap expectantly. She handed him some money. Clearly it was at least adequate, for he opened the door for her and invited her to mount the steps.

'No, *grazie*,' she said, waving her hand, and gestured wanly to the magazine stand, as if to convey that she knew the Italian to explain that she needed to buy some reading matter, but was much too tired to trot it out just now. Smiling, he tugged his cap again and was gone.

She was unsettled, undecided and out of sorts, none of which were feelings with which she was either familiar or comfortable.

That wretched misunderstanding with the King had affected her badly, though she believed she had carried it off well. It would have been intolerable to remain at Bellagio under his gently reproachful gaze. Though the more she thought about it, the more convinced she became that it was a misunderstanding which could hardly be laid at her door. Georgie was the true culprit. If only he had taken her into his confidence in the first place. Come to think of it, if only he had not lured her to Bellagio under false pretences in the first place ...

She found herself turning over magazines on the stand in a desultory sort of way, the aged female proprietor hovering toothlessly. There were almost all in Italian, apart from some dreadful American publication with photographs of film stars. A pity. She had been hoping for either the *Financial Times* or the *Wall Street Journal*. As it was, there were no English newspapers at all. She toyed with taking an Italian newspaper home to leave nonchalantly in the living room the next time people came to tea, having first carefully looked up all the words in the dictionary, but even this amusing idea failed to rouse her from her melancholy.

She sighed and turned away. Clearly she was going to have to make a start on the second chapter of *I promessi sposi* after all.

Her relationship with Georgie had always been one of magnanimous sovereign and loyal, adoring subject. Not for nothing had she been known as Queen Lucia back in the old days in Riseholme when Pepino had still been alive, and Georgie was Riseholme's dashing young man, Francis Drake to her Elizabeth. Yet it was based on both parties knowing their place, and there were undeniably times when Georgie exhibited a rebellious streak. It was also undeniable, she mused, that the likelihood of such unfortunate episodes tended to increase when Olga was in close proximity. There had been various regrettable occasions when Lucia's authority had been challenged in Riseholme, and all of them after Olga had moved into New Place, just a stone's throw from Georgie's house.

Now her departure from Bellagio, necessary and entirely justified though it had been, had left them together, and she wondered just when Georgie would return. When he had been to stay with Olga in the past, for example at Le Touquet, he had stayed away so long that tongues had started to wag, not that much time was required to elapse in Tilling for such a phenomenon to be observed. The ritual greeting 'Any news?' more or less cried out for something to be extemporised, even if no solid factual basis for it in fact existed.

Though Lucia would never admit it, least of all to herself, she was afraid of loneliness. She needed to feel people around her, to feed off their esteem, to be at the centre of things. Most of all, she needed Georgie. Their relationship was one of being together every day, except when she was engaged on civic duties of course, of a hundred and one private jokes and asides during the course of the day, and of piano duets as the evening drew in, and after dinner of him sitting doing his needlepoint while she stuck her press clippings into their appropriate scrapbooks. She realised at once that she would miss him dreadfully until his return, was in fact missing him dreadfully already.

As she distractedly scanned the station surroundings, her eyes alighted on a telegraph office. Suddenly she realised something else: that Georgie, or at least Georgie while in the presence and under the influence of Olga, would never send that telegram. She checked her watch and, calculating that she still had over twenty minutes before her train was due to depart, set off across the platform with a determined tread, already feeling inside her handbag for a pencil.

The maharajah was used to people bowing, and discreetly handing him pieces of paper. Usually they were communications from the Viceroy, or invitations to the next Durbar. Occasionally, while travelling overseas, they could even be *billets-doux* from ladies whose eye he had caught at dinner the night before. On this occasion, however, the document which the duty manager was attempting, with quiet determination, to bring to his attention was the Mapp-Flints' bill to date. Major Benjy realised this belatedly and tried to snatch at it himself, but by some *legerdemain* presumably passed on from one generation of hotel managers to the next, it still somehow ended up in royal, rather than military, hands.

Just for a moment the maharajah visibly flinched. Then he raised his eyebrows at the manager, who shrugged apologetically in reply. The Major had the bright idea of asking the little woman to proffer an explanation, but when he looked round it was only to find that she had slipped away into the gardens.

The maharajah sat down at a convenient marble-topped table with a crossing of legs which would have made Georgie weep with envy, and, with that natural elegance that characterised all his movements, gracefully extracted a cheque book and a fountain pen, both very splendid, from his inside jacket pocket. Expressionlessly, he wrote down a very large figure and appended the royal signature. The manager seized the Hoare & Co. cheque gratefully with a deep bow.

'My dear Major,' the maharajah said casually, 'I will ask the hotel to pack your bags. There is no need for you or your dear wife to trouble yourself about any of the arrangements. The concierge will provide a taxi to take you to the station. If I am not mistaken you will be just in time for the midday train to Milan.'

'But ...' essayed the Major, his world crumbling about him.

The maharajah smiled thinly.

'No thanks are necessary, old chap,' he said blandly. 'On the contrary, it is I who must thank you for looking after Ramesh so very expertly.'

Ramesh, who was hovering deferentially as befitted a royal son and heir, bowed to the Major and added his Etonian murmured thanks to those of his father.

'Ah,' said the Major, who had until a few seconds previously been looking forward to a chota peg or two before lunch.

'Do give my very best regards to your wife, my dear fellow,' the maharajah said urbanely. 'It has been so very good to see you again.'

This last phrase was delivered slightly over the shoulder, as the royal pair were already in motion, on their way out of the hotel.

'Ah,' said the Major sadly.

Lucia's lady's maid was making a last sweep through her former mistress's room to make quite sure that nothing had been overlooked during the somewhat hastily conducted packing exercise of the previous day, when suddenly she came across what was clearly intended as a telegram lying on the dressing table.

Dutifully, she took the paper downstairs to the office and directed its occupant rather haughtily, given the superior status which a lady's maid enjoys over a mere clerk, to send the telegram and then leave the draft on the *signor*'s desk to signify that it had been despatched. This mission safely accomplished, she adjusted her hat in the mirror and headed for the steamer stage, feeling most virtuous. After all, the *signora* had not only paid her to the end of the summer, but had also left her a generous tip, so she was happy to have been able to render her this final service.

The royal pair were once more regarding the battered Royale.

'What shall we do with it, Pater?' Ramesh enquired at length.

'Whatever you like,' his father replied curtly. 'It displeases me. Pray dispose of it, old man,'

'Yes, sir,' his son replied dutifully.

Como is not one of the more obviously attractive Italian towns, but, being Italian, it is inevitably possessed of a certain elegance, upon which Georgie and Olga were reflecting as they sat at a café close to the cathedral, looking for all the world as though they might be Italian themselves, with little cups of *espresso* set before them together with a bottle of *naturale*.

'You're going to have to do it, you know,' Olga said abruptly. 'After all, it is her money.'

'Oh, I know,' Georgie said miserably, 'but suppose just for once she is wrong about this? Suppose that by deliberately not sending the telegram I can save her from losing all of it?'

'Do you really believe that?' she asked quietly.

'No, of course not,' he admitted. 'The truth is I really don't know one way or the other, but it all just feels horribly wrong, somehow.'

'I know what you mean,' Olga admitted, pouring herself some more *naturale*. 'I feel a huge uneasiness about it all, and I'm used to trusting my instincts. Of course, part of it may just be that I don't much like that Lodge character, which I freely admit.'

Georgie's face brightened for a moment.

'I say, you don't think he might be some sort of international fraudster, do you, like that Horatio Bottomley? Perhaps he's trying to steal Lucia's money, and we'd really be doing her the most enormous service by thwarting his evil designs ...?'

He looked at her without much hope, which was just as well, for she promptly dashed whatever little might have remained.

'No, I'm afraid that horse won't run, my dear. If you must know, I've sent some discreet telegrams to check him out, and it seems he's the genuine article all right. My pal Bruno at Rothschild's says he's OK.'

She gazed at him fondly.

'So what it comes down to, then,' Georgie said slowly, 'is a straightforward question of judgement.'

'Yes,' she agreed simply. 'Are you prepared to back your financial judgement over Lucia's?'

'Well, no, of course not,' came the sharp rejoinder, 'and even if I was, I wouldn't, because it's her money, not mine.'

He tossed some coins on to the table and stood up.

'Come on,' he said resignedly. 'There's a telegraph office over on the other side of the square. Let's go and send the damn thing and be done with it.'

'I thought you left it at the hotel,' she observed, as she quickly checked her reflection in her powder compact.

'Yes, I did,' he concurred, 'but I can remember exactly what it says.'

So saying, he put his panama on his head with a most determined air, quite forgetting in the stress of the moment to position it at its usual rakish angle, and offered Olga his arm.

Back at the hotel the maharajah leaned on his motor-car bonnet and watched with a certain morose detachment as a squad of hotel workers, under the languid direction of Ramesh, slowly rolled the Royale to the end of the steamer pier and pushed it into the water. There was hardly a splash as it disappeared from sight. Being an Eton man, Ramesh could have told anybody who cared to ask that Lake Como was one of the deepest lakes in the world, but nobody did, perhaps because they were all from Como anyway and thus already possessed of this tantalising titbit of information.

The maharajah pitched his cigarette away rather savagely but paused with his foot poised in mid-air to grind it out as Miss Flowers suddenly came out of the front door. She was wearing a tennis dress which if anything seemed to end further above the knee than the last one, and which positively gleamed in the bright Italian sunlight. Once again, she could only be described, if it were not already an over-used and absurdly mawkish phrase, as a vision of loveliness.

'Hello there,' she said to him as he raised his hat, gazing at her with frank admiration. 'I say, what a gorgeous car! Is it another Bugatti?'

He sighed, and then remembered that women could not be expected to understand cars.

'No, my dear,' he replied, and then, enunciating the words with all the gravity they demanded, 'it is a Hispano-Suiza.'

He was gratified to observe that Miss Flowers was clearly properly impressed by this news.

'Gosh!' she exclaimed. 'It looks frightfully expensive. God knows what it must have cost. Oh, I forgot – I *am* a fool. Of course, if you're a maharajah you're simply frightfully rich, aren't you?'

'Fair to middling,' he confessed. 'I say, are you off to play tennis?'

'Yes,' she said, looking around for a startled hotel employee to whom to hand off her racquet and, failing to find one, tossing it nonchalantly into the back of the Hispano-Suiza, 'but I don't particularly like tennis. Why don't we go for a drive instead?'

Somehow this seemed to the maharajah the best idea anyone had ever had. He immediately opened the passenger door and she clambered in, displaying rather more leg than before and rather less fleetingly, for she was quite getting the hang now of how to display herself to advantage while climbing into a car. Her new-found companion felt a sudden flush of warmth coursing through his veins that had nothing at all to do with the Italian sun.

'Where to?' he asked, as he walked around the car and vaulted rather thrillingly into the driver's seat, without bothering to undo the door. He breathed a silent sigh of relief. The last time he had attempted this manoeuvre he had ripped his trousers, gone sprawling on the *Promenade des Anglais* in Nice, and been left feeling undeniably foolish. He pressed the self-starter and the engine, still warm, responded at once.

'Lunch somewhere?' she suggested.

'Why not?' he concurred, sliding into first gear.

Obligingly, she moved her knees closer to the gearstick.

Francesco passed quietly through the suite, his suitcase standing outside on the landing. To his chagrin, it was empty. He had been hoping to say his final goodbye to Georgie. He sat down at the desk and carefully wrote a short note of farewell. As he was sealing it inside one of the hotel's envelopes, he suddenly spotted a piece of paper lying face down, picked it up, and turned it over. It was clearly intended as a telegram, and was both urgent and important. He tucked it into his inside pocket and went downstairs, carrying his briefcase.

On his way through the lobby he looked in on the office. It was empty. He pulled the piece of paper out of his pocket and frowned. Then his face cleared as he realised that he could easily send it from the station *en route* to Venice. Picking up his bag anew, *incognito* for only a few hours more now, His Majesty stepped out of the hotel and into the pages of history.

By this juncture the Mapp-Flints had already been waiting at Como station surrounded by their luggage for what seemed like a very long time. On arrival they had discovered that the maharajah's grasp of the railway timetable had definitely been at fault. In fact the next train to Milan was not due for nearly seven hours. The Major had by now heard his wife bemoan this fact many times. Many, many times.

Chapter 19

'Telegram for you, if you please, mum,' Grosvenor announced, proffering the silver tray as Lucia ate breakfast.

'Thank you, Grosvenor,' Lucia replied, taking it and then resolutely, seeing it was from Italy, 'No answer'. Grosvenor gave a bob and departed.

She reached for her letter knife, which was always to hand, and opened the little brown envelope. In truth she was in some inner turmoil. She realised that she might have overplayed her hand in leaving Bellagio so abruptly. It was one thing to expect Georgie to follow tamely after her, but quite another whether he would actually do so. The telegram, she found, gave no clue to his intentions.

WELL WHAT DO YOU THINK STOP MAPP FLINTS SENT PACKING BY MAHARAJAH TAILS BETWEEN LEGS STOP MISS FLOWERS ELOPED WITH MAHARAJAH STOP STORMY PARTING WITH FRAU Z STOP ANGRY WORDS STOP FLOOZY AND LITTLE TRAMP PLUS SOME IN GERMAN WHICH OLGA SAID VERY UNLADYLIKE STOP ALL TOO THRILLING STOP WISH YOU WERE STILL HERE STOP LOVE GEORGIE

She glanced up at the clock and went upstairs to prepare herself for her journey. Precisely one hour later Cadman drove her to the station, and carried her bags on to the train for her. On arriving in

London she took a taxi to the Ritz, checked into her room, drank a little mineral water, and then took a taxi into the City for her meeting with Mr Mammoncash. The streets were busy with hurrying people as she alighted outside his building and stepped into his waiting room at the appointed time.

The Mr Mammoncash who greeted her seemed a sadly distracted Mr Mammoncash, not the calm, urbane stockbroker of her recollection.

'Ah, Mrs Lucas – I beg your pardon, Mrs Pillson, of course.'

Lucia waved a hand, and said '*Niente*' in a vague sort of way as she sat down.

'Mrs Pillson,' Mammoncash said, 'I have to ask you the meaning of this.'

He laid her telegram in front of her. She gazed at it coldly and then at him, equally coldly.

'The instructions which it contains seem quite clear,' she responded tightly. 'I trust that you have carried them out?'

Without saying anything in reply, he laid three additional telegrams on the desk in front of her. All were identical to the first. She gazed at them dumbly, uncomprehending.

'We carried out *all* your instructions, madam,' he said grimly, after a pause. 'I regret that the orders were executed by various different clerks and so were not brought to my attention until too late.'

'Too late for what?' cried Lucia, beginning to realise that something had gone horribly wrong. In a flash she knew that she liked being rich very much indeed, and would hate being poor even more. She would be no good at it; she would not even know where to begin. She had always been rich, thanks to dear Pepino. She began to panic.

'Too late for me to countermand them, of course,' Mammoncash answered sternly, a Dickensian authority figure bending over her in a black frock coat. He suddenly seemed very tall indeed as Lucia shrank into her chair.

'To think that a client of this firm would short the market!' he fulminated. 'Have you no consideration, madam, for our professional reputation? I had the Stock Exchange on the telephone twice yesterday demanding an explanation, which, naturally, I was unable to give.'

Lucia gulped, but could make no answer.

'Are you aware of what you have done?' Mammoncash went on, glaring at her. 'Some of the stocks you held have very restricted free floats – you remember I warned you about investing in such high-risk companies – and your multiple sell orders have forced at least one of them to seek a suspension of trading. Why, you may even have helped cause the crash.'

'The crash?' Lucia asked in a small voice. 'What crash? I don't understand.'

Mammoncash went across to a glass dome in the corner of his office, from which issued forth spools of white ticker tape. He looked at it, gasped, walked slowly back across his office, and at last sat down opposite her. His face was white and drawn.

'Wall Street crashed yesterday,' he said quietly. 'Several important banks have failed. Depositors were queuing up in the streets to withdraw their money. In many towns they rioted when they realised there was no money left in the banks, and the police had to disperse them. It is disaster. It is the end of the world as we have known it.'

He picked up a pencil with trembling hands and absently snapped it.

'New York has just opened today and is heavily down again. London followed it, made worse certainly by your sell orders the previous day, and is doing so again. If we are lucky it may close down only about thirty per cent from two days ago.'

'If we are lucky,' he repeated. He seemed close to tears. 'Probably it will be more like forty. Most of my clients will be ruined by Monday lunchtime. Many of them are friends. What will they do? My God, what will any of us do?'

There was a long silence. Then Lucia found her voice.

'You said "the previous day" ...?'

'Yes.'

'Then may I dare to hope ...?'

'Oh yes,' Mammoncash said heavily, 'never fear, madam, your money is safe. In fact, depending on what happens on Monday and when you go back into the market to buy before the end of the account, I calculate that you will have at least doubled your money. But I must warn you that there may be an enquiry. You may have created a false market.'

'The remaining three telegrams were sent by mistake,' Lucia said promptly and serenely. 'I have no idea who sent them or how they came to be sent, though I suspect my husband may have sent one of them – in error, naturally.'

Her interlocutor seemed unconvinced, and certainly uncomforted.

'The president of the Stock Exchange is in my lodge,' he said dully, 'I expect something can be worked out.'

'Now,' he went on, 'if you will excuse me, I have a great many telephone calls to make.'

Lucia stood up to go, but was then struck by another thought.

'You said that one of my portfolio companies had been suspended, I think?'

'That is so.'

'At what price?'

Mammoncash shrugged.

'It hardly matters. Even if they are restored to the Exchange they will be effectively worthless. Perhaps a penny ...'

'Then perhaps you would make enquiries as to whether it might be possible to buy the company, the whole company I mean, and, if so, at what price?'

Mammoncash gazed at her in silence and, it seemed to Lucia, rather stupidly. Clearly further elucidation was in order.

'It's all about the control premium, you see,' she went on brightly. 'Why, I met the most charming man on holiday who explained it all to me. Yes, my dealings through you may be a little different in future, dear Mr Mammoncash. Let us think no more of shares but of companies, well, of controlling interests anyway. I hope you will be equal to the challenge?'

She gazed at him coyly. Still he said nothing. Then he stood up, walked around her, and held open the door.

'My firm will probably no longer be in business on Monday, madam,' he said simply. 'My partners and I all have most of our capital invested in the market. Good afternoon.'

'Oh, I do hope not,' Lucia said as she exited. 'That really would be most inconvenient.'

'For *all* concerned,' she added darkly, looking back over her shoulder.

'Poor Georgie,' Olga said tenderly, laying her hand on his arm. 'Are you very unhappy?'

'Unsettled rather than unhappy,' he said after a pause for reflection. 'And angry too, if you must know, at Lucia for having caused all this upset.'

'She is what she is,' Olga replied. 'She really is a most marvellous person, you know, but it's like one of those Shakespeare tragedies. Big people have big faults. If you really love her, as we all do in our different ways, you just have to put up with them.'

'Yes, I suppose so,' said Georgie miserably.

'Just think what life would be like if there was no Lucia,' she went on. 'Think of all the joy she has given you over the years: the music, the plots, the companionship. What would Riseholme have been like without Lucia? And as for Tilling, why, you would never even have gone there if it had not been for her.'

'Yes, yes, you're right of course,' Georgie said wretchedly.

'So, what are you going to do?' asked Olga. 'You know the Wyses are going back to Tilling with Amelia? They say they're worried about the cholera. Apparently it's in Rome now. So we could have a wonderful few days here all by ourselves, if you want.'

'Of course I want,' he burst out. 'That's all I've ever really wanted since I met you, Olga. You know that.'

'Yes, my poor lamb, I do know that,' she said quietly, 'and I think I will always feel horribly guilty for it. You see, when we first met I never quite realised just how close you and Lucia really were. After all, most of the time in Riseholme it was you and me plotting against her and that poisonous London society bunch.'

'But I *should* have realised,' she continued, 'and I didn't. Sorry.'

'Oh, never mind,' he said fondly, stroking her hand. 'It's always so lovely being with you, you know.'

He took a gulp of his pre-lunch Negroni.

'It all seems so unnecessary anyway,' he complained. 'I'm sure Francesco, or the King or whatever one is supposed to call him, would have forgiven her remarks. In fact I know he would, because he took it as a compliment. He told me it all meant he'd been playing his part very successfully.'

'So, when is he leaving?' Olga asked.

'He's left already,' Georgie said mournfully. 'Went yesterday afternoon. Left me his address to write to him and said he'd send me some of those cigarettes of his. Oh yes, and he's given me an Albanian knighthood, the Order of Skanderbeg or something. Fancy, me an Albanian knight!'

'Well!' Olga exclaimed. 'That'll be one in the eye for Susan Wyse. You'll have to wear it with your evening dress, Georgie, and very dashing you'll look too.'

'Oh, I expect he'll forget all about me when he's back in his palace with all sorts of important things to do,' Georgie said sadly. 'Anyway, is one even allowed to wear a foreign order? Doesn't one have to get the King's permission or something like that?'

'I think that's only if you're in the forces,' Olga said dubiously, 'but I know a dear little general at the War Office I can ask.'

Georgie took another sip of his Negroni, which seemed to be having rather a melancholic effect on him today.

'So that's it, then,' he concluded. 'Everyone's leaving. It's just you and me left now.'

'But that's good isn't it?' Olga asked. 'I don't have to be anywhere at all until I have to go to New York in a couple of weeks' time, so we can have a whole two weeks together, either here or anywhere you like. That was the deal, wasn't it? And it wasn't you who decided to cut the holiday short, but Lucia.'

'Oh, I know,' he said wretchedly, 'but she's spoilt it all somehow. Wherever we go I know that she'll be sitting in Tilling brooding and waiting for me to come home.'

'Don't decide now, anyway' she encouraged him, 'not while you're feeling blue. Wait until this evening at least.'

'Oh yes, all right then,' he agreed. 'I'm sorry that I'm such bad company today.'

Olga nodded sympathetically.

'I think I know what will cheer you up,' she said gently. 'How about a table for lunch on the terrace? I know there's *risotto ai frutti di mare* today, and you know that's one of your favourites.'

'Oh yes,' he said more happily. 'That would be lovely.'

'And then this afternoon if you like I could ask the staff to move my bags into Lucia's room,' she suggested casually. 'I'm sure you don't really want to be in that big suite all by yourself, do you?'

'Bless you, Olga,' he said, more happily still, 'no, of course I don't. You think of everything.'

As they stood to go into lunch she took his arm and drew him close. They walked slowly yet contentedly together like a pair of newly-weds exploring the sensation of being no longer alone, and as they disappeared from view anybody sitting in the lounge with particularly acute hearing might have made out her saying to him, 'And you know there is this simply wonderful little place I know on Lake Trasimeno ...'.

Lucia was some time in finding a taxi, which really was most vexing.

The City seemed to have lost its senses. Young men, obviously clerks, were scurrying about urgently like worker ants. By Bank underground station she passed a middle-aged man crying openly in the street, tears running unchecked down his cheeks as he walked slowly along. She tutted in dismay and despair at this unseemly show of emotion, and continued on her way.

By a different entrance to the station another middle-aged man sat on a bench staring straight ahead of himself, unblinking and unmoving. Two other men, friends or colleagues obviously, stopped and tried to talk to him but, receiving no answer, shook their heads sadly and moved on.

She briefly considered heading down into the station but quickly decided against it. She had never travelled on the Underground in her life and would have no idea even how to go about purchasing a ticket, let alone finding her way on to the right train and navigating herself across London. She thought of the potential for unwanted physical contact on a crowded train or platform, and was overcome by a spasm of nausea.

Swallowing bile, she spied at long last a taxi, and waved her umbrella at it in an imperious manner. Recognising an umbrella possessed of a natural air of command, the driver stopped and she got in, stating the Ritz Hotel as her destination, to give herself time to think.

There was an errand that she needed to run near the British Museum, but she had a mind also to see some of her old London friends. She wondered whether it was now socially acceptable to be seen with Babs Shyton. The divorce case had indeed been scandalous, though much of it had passed over Lucia's head as she sat in the public gallery avidly watching proceedings. The reference to a headless man in a photograph had left her particularly bemused. Surely it could not have been that nice Lord Middlesex, the one Babs called Woof-Dog? And why should anyone have taken a photo which showed Bab's head but not her companion's? She shook her head afresh at this enduring puzzle.

Of course, much water had passed under the bridge since then, but perhaps it was safest to ask some of the old crowd first about whether people in polite society were receiving Babs yet. Perhaps dear Adele

Brixton would know, certainly she would know, and so too would dear Tony Limpsfield.

She pulled out her diary and scanned the address section. Adele was still at her old address in Belgravia but Tony had moved very dashingly to Hampstead which, while very dashing, was also very inconvenient, since it meant that Lucia had to choose between spurring her taxi in one of two totally different directions.

While she was turning over these geographical complexities in her mind, Lucia became aware that any spurring might for the time being prove merely hypothetical, since her taxi had come to a halt in a long queue of traffic at the end of Throgmorton Avenue and did not seem to be showing any interest in proceeding further. However, since it was now raining quite hard, there was clearly no question of alighting to seek either an alternative form of transport or the explanation for the long delay. She had read many times of how slowly traffic moved in the City; clearly everything she had read in that regard was true. How very annoying.

As she sat in the cab, the windows of which were now misting up, she realised that she had yet another decision to make.

She was intending to visit one of her favourite milliners in Mayfair, and was as yet undecided between the rival merits of two different new hats. A dark blue cloche, with peacock feathers, would set off her Old Imari print dress to perfection. Yet she was also tempted by a purple pillbox hat with a racy little half-veil which she knew would draw attention to her eyes, which she had always considered to be one of her finer features.

Not just her, either, now she came to think of it; two successive husbands, Stephen Merriall (Hermione of the *Evening Gazette* to the *cognoscenti*), and countless dozens of her subjects in her kingdoms of Riseholme and Tilling, had concurred repeatedly and enthusiastically on the very fine quality of her eyes. Yes, the pillbox certainly had a lot to commend it, but the annual civic service at the church was fast approaching, and as a former mayor she felt it important that she should grace it with her presence, and that her presence should in turn be graced by her Old Imari. So many decisions! If only Georgie and Elizabeth and the others realised how many important matters she had for which to take responsibility while they were wandering around Tilling with their shopping baskets, or making cakes, or embroidering doilies.

She became dimly aware that the driver had clambered out and disappeared, presumably, she hoped, to ascertain the reason for the delay rather than to answer an urgent call of nature, but then you never quite knew with the lower classes.

He reappeared after some time, only to be noisily and disgustingly sick in the road next to the taxi. She put an immaculately gloved hand to her face in disbelief. Presumably the fellow had been drinking. She made a note of his number in her notebook so that she could write later to Scotland Yard and report him.

'Sorry, lady,' he said unnecessarily as he got back into the cab.

She made no reply and so a lengthy pause ensued, since the traffic still showed no signs of moving on. Another tuppence halfpenny clicking up on the meter was the sole event of any note. Finally, the driver looked back over his shoulder to speak to her. She recoiled back into her seat as far as she could.

'Looks like we may be here some time,' he announced bleakly. 'There's the police up ahead.'

She made a little noise that blended regret and irritation, and hoped that he would not attempt to engage her in discussion again. She was to be disappointed.

'Some poor gentleman's topped himself up there,' came the new conversational gambit. 'Thrown isself outter a winder, 'e as. Spread all over the road. Very nasty.'

'Probably an investor or a stockbroker,' she found herself saying. 'He should have shorted the market like I did, poor man.'

'Copper up there says it's his third today,' the driver intoned, shaking his head and sucking his teeth mournfully.

She made no reply, nor did she need to, for she had just been struck by a sudden realisation. She was now a very wealthy woman indeed, and had no need to trouble over such trifles as which hat to buy. She could buy them both. Indeed, she could buy every single hat in the shop if she chose to.

She settled contentedly back in her seat and started jotting down the list of things she planned to do.

'Museum Street please, cabbie, as soon as you can move,' she said briskly.

Gabriele d'Annunzio: a remarkable man

Gabriele d'Annunzio was lauded in the period leading up to the First World War as both Italy's finest poet and finest novelist. He was also by that time an established journalist, politician (espousing the cause of irredentism, the occupation by Italy of all territories with substantial Italian-speaking communities), playwright, and theatrical producer.

His extravagant lifestyle landed him with massive debts which forced him to flee Italy for France in 1910, but the war party paid off his debts and brought him back after the war began to whip the Italian people, originally distinctly isolationist, into a patriotic fervour. A hugely successful mob orator, d'Annunzio performed as expected, and Italy came into the war on the side of the Allies in 1915, having signed the Treaty of London with the Triple Entente (Britain, France and Russia) which promised Italy most of the territorial gains she craved, conditional on a successful outcome of the war. This treaty was later to prove highly controversial since it meant that Italy alone of the Allies was seen, particularly by the Americans, as waging an offensive war of conquest as opposed to resisting foreign aggression.

During the war d'Annunzio, despite already being in his fifties, joined first the army, then the navy and finally the air force, losing the sight of one eye in a flying accident. While his personal pursuit of glory was conspicuous in each arm of the military, his record as an army officer was controversial, since many claimed that he regularly sacrificed his men's lives in spectacular but futile frontal assaults. However he was undeniably prominent as a naval officer in charge of a flotilla of torpedo boats and as an aviator, leading a historic long distance leaflet raid on Vienna, at that time one of the longest flights ever attempted. He was an avid collector of medals, his quest finally being frustrated only when an exasperated Italian government imposed a maximum quota which could be awarded to any one individual.

At the end of the war the surviving Allies found themselves in a difficult situation as President Wilson had unilaterally published his "Fourteen Points", the principles which he claimed formed the only basis for a just and lasting peace, and proceeded to impose these on the Europeans – ignoring the fact that they had never even discussed them, let alone approved them. These principles were inconsistent with the Treaty of London, and Britain and France promptly abandoned Italy, who had been fighting alongside them enthusiastically since 1915, in favour of the Americans, who had joined the war only very reluctantly in 1917 and had refused to fight as part of Allied formations.

This betrayal was keenly felt, and a group of patriots led by d'Annunzio occupied Fiume, one of the disputed towns, and proclaimed it part of Italy. During this period d'Annunzio arguably set up the first fascist state, coining the title Duce for himself, and dressing his supporters in black shirts. Mussolini cannily promised to support him but then failed to do so, leaving d'Annunzio exposed and alone. Under pressure from the Allies, Italy renounced his actions, whereupon d'Annunzio, in a final act of characteristic bravado, declared war on his own country. After an Italian warship lobbed a few shells into Fiume, d'Annunzio's Ruritanian regime was brought to an abrupt and rather pathetic end.

He was nonetheless treated as a hero, rather than a traitor, on his return home, and once Mussolini came to power he supported d'Annunzio with public funds as he bought a villa on Lake Garda and began transforming it into a museum to himself, presumably in return for a tacit understanding that the latter would stay out of politics. After all, there was only room for one Duce. To reinforce this understanding Mussolini sent a couple of heavies to throw d'Annunzio out of a window (a murder attempt which he somehow survived) when d'Annunzio briefly considered joining the March on Rome.

D'Annunzio was a passionate believer in free love, and pursued women throughout his life with a verve and dedication that makes Major Flint's enthusiastic efforts seem paltry by comparison. He was romantically linked at different times with many of the celebrated beauties of Europe, living for many years with the famous actress Eleonora Duse, a relationship that ended abruptly and acrimoniously when he gave the starring role in his new play to Sarah Bernhardt. In his later years on Lake Garda he pursued a punishing schedule, frequently making love to two different women in an evening, and taking copious amounts of cocaine to improve his sexual stamina. Had Olga Bracely accepted his invitation to stay it is likely that even she would have been deeply shocked at what she encountered. Finally an evening with a Tyrolean blonde called Emy Heufler, almost certainly a German secret agent sent to kill him, perhaps at Mussolini's request, proved a tryst too far; the one-eyed poet died suddenly and mysteriously in March 1938. Emy left Italy immediately, and was next seen working in the private office of von Ribbentrop, Hitler's foreign minister.

D'Annunzio's poetry remains some of the finest ever composed in Italian, and much of it was immortalised in the songs of Tosti, who is now sadly out of fashion. His novels, on the other hand, are almost unreadable by a modern audience, and are a comforting example of what ultimately happens to novelists whose sales are driven largely by media hype. They are simply not in the same class as those of Manzoni, for example.

While his verse alone would secure his greatness, the variety, scope and sheer chutzpah of his life make him one of the most vivid figures of modern history. When the idea occurred of introducing Lucia to someone even more self-obsessed than herself, there really could only ever be one candidate. It remains to be seen whether enough of his greatness has brushed off on her for her to succeed in her plans for building a museum to herself during her own lifetime, and whether she will be awarded the Nobel Prize for Economics for having brilliantly and presciently shorted the market just before the Wall Street Crash.